Kat & mouse™

2 tripped

Story by Alex de Campi
Art by Federica Manfredi

HAMBURG // LONDON // LOS ANGELES // TOKYO

Kat & Mouse Vol. 2
Written by Alex de Campi
Illustrated by Federica Manfredi

Tones - Christine Schilling
Lettering - Lucas Rivera
Cover Design - Jose Macasocol, Jr. & Federica Manfredi

Editors - Tim Beedle & Carol Fox
Digital Imaging Manager - Chris Buford
Pre-Production Supervisor - Erika Terriquez
Art Director - Anne Marie Horne
Managing Editor - Vy Nguyen
Production Manager - Elisabeth Brizzi
VP of Production - Ron Klamert
Editor-in-Chief - Rob Tokar
Publisher - Mike Kiley
President and C.O.O. - John Parker
C.E.O. and Chief Creative Officer - Stuart Levy

A  Manga

TOKYOPOP Inc.
5900 Wilshire Blvd. Suite 2000
Los Angeles, CA 90036

E-mail: info@TOKYOPOP.com
Come visit us online at www.TOKYOPOP.com

ISBN: 978-1-59816-549-4

First TOKYOPOP printing: January 2007
10 9 8 7 6 5 4 3 2 1
Printed in the USA

Cat & mouse

TABLE OF CONTENTS

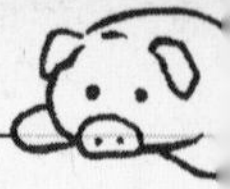

PREVIOUSLY...

Kat Foster would have been happy finishing off he seventh grade year in her hometown in Iowa. But whe her father accepts a new job teaching science at prestigious private school in New Hampshire, she has n choice but to pack up her things and move with her fami to Dover—a wealthy community where they don't exactly f in. Kat stands out at her new school, and quickly falls t the bottom of the social ladder, but she does make on new friend: Mee-Seen Huang. Mee-Seen—or "Mouse" a she prefers to be known—is a punky skateboarder wh also has trouble fitting in at Dover Academy...and that' just the way she likes it.

Together, Kat and Mouse face many challenges, most o which are caused by The Artful Dodger—a mysterious thie who has been stealing valuables at their school. Kat an Mouse have vowed to bring the thief to justice. However despite their best efforts, the identity of The Artf Dodger remains a mystery.

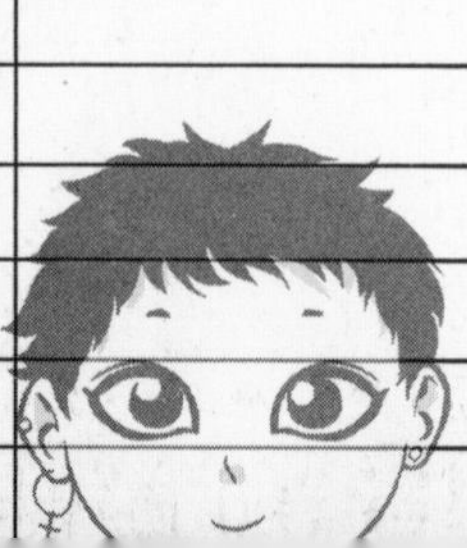

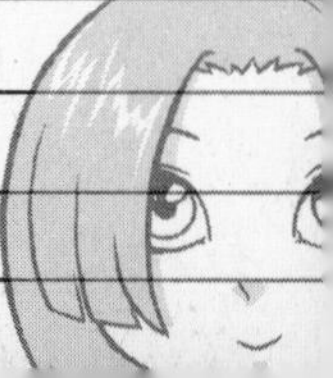

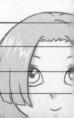

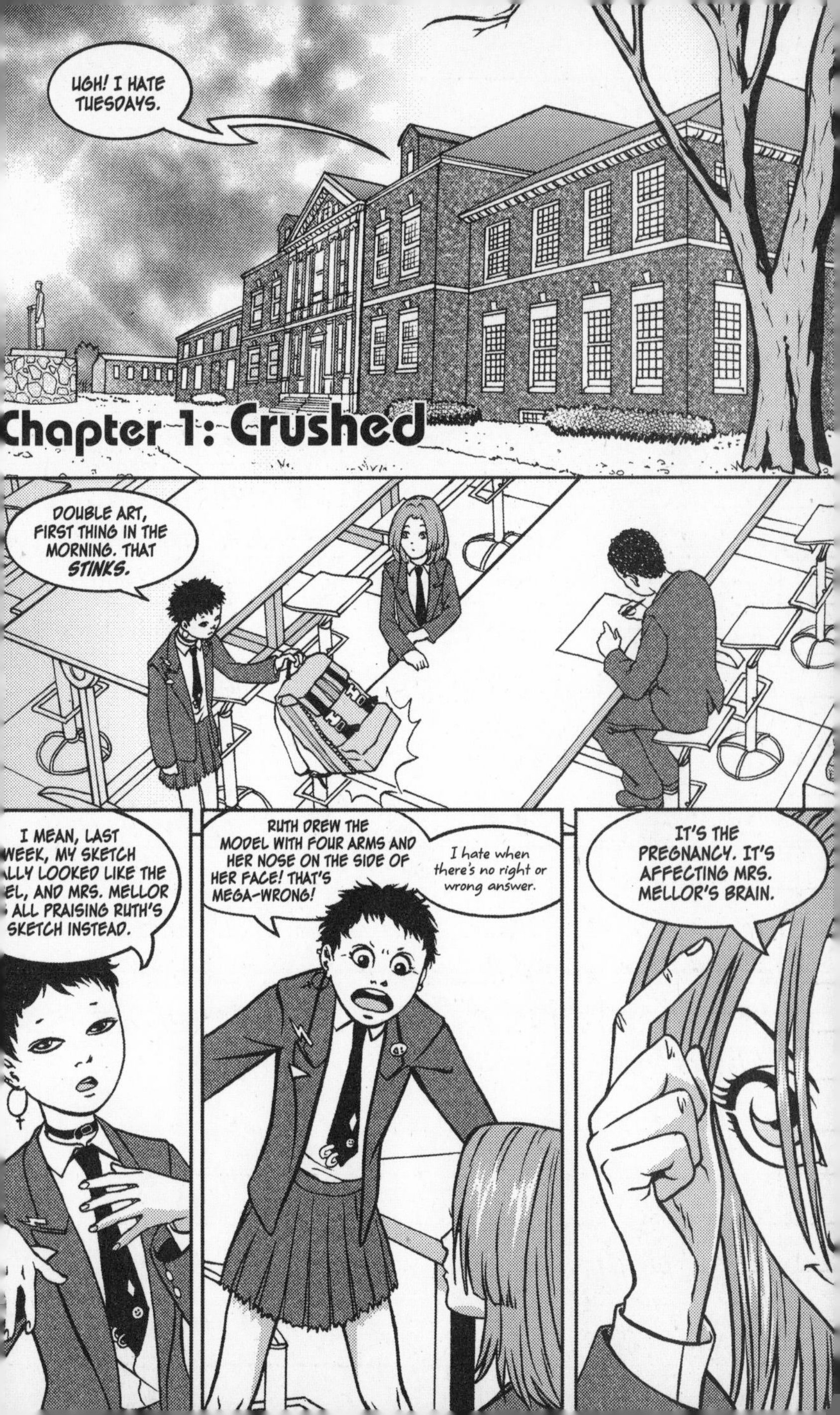
UGH! I HATE TUESDAYS.
Chapter 1: Crushed
DOUBLE ART, FIRST THING IN THE MORNING. THAT *STINKS.*
I MEAN, LAST WEEK, MY SKETCH ALLY LOOKED LIKE THE EL, AND MRS. MELLOR ALL PRAISING RUTH'S SKETCH INSTEAD.
RUTH DREW THE MODEL WITH FOUR ARMS AND HER NOSE ON THE SIDE OF HER FACE! THAT'S MEGA-WRONG!
I hate when there's no right or wrong answer.
IT'S THE PREGNANCY. IT'S AFFECTING MRS. MELLOR'S BRAIN.

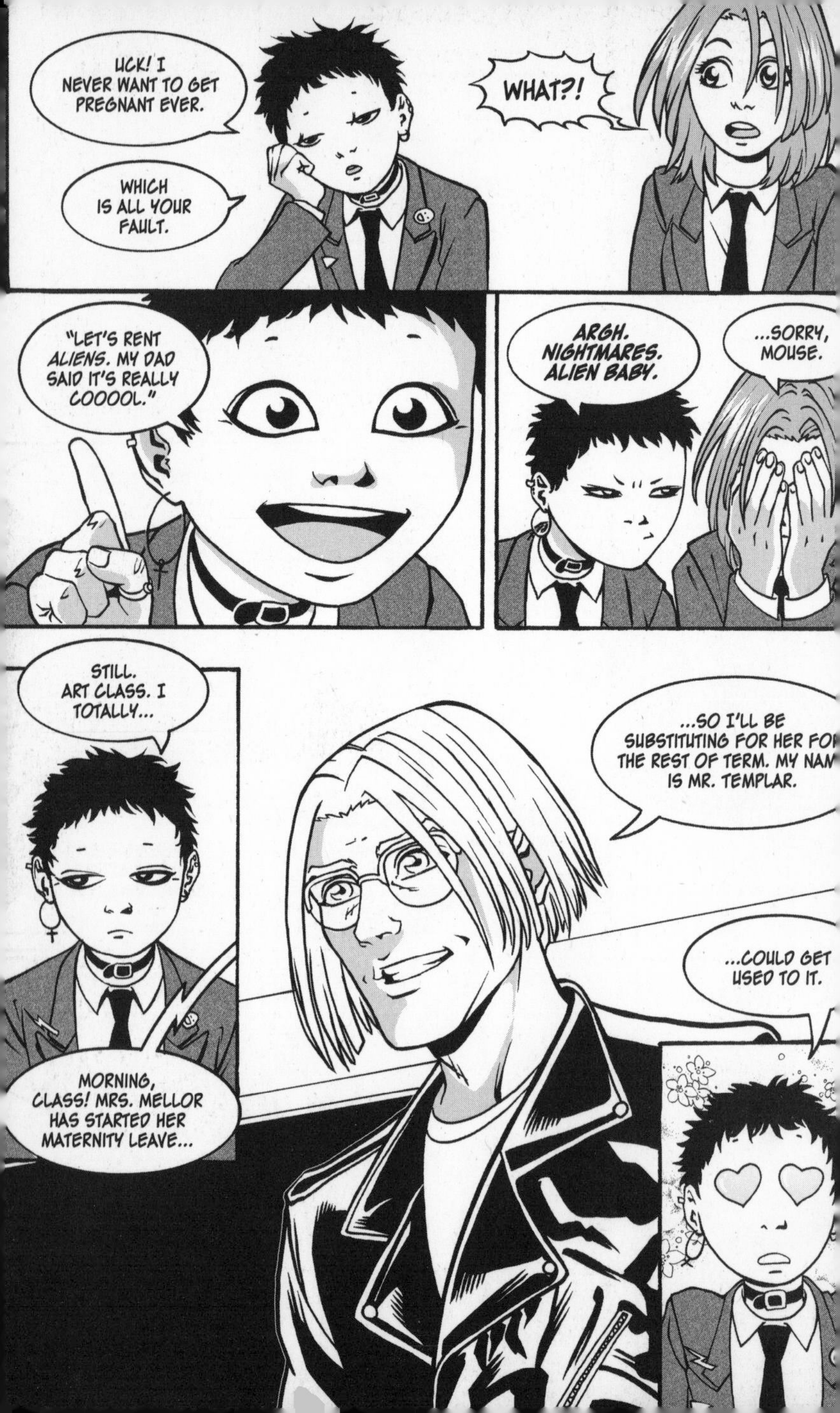
UCK! I NEVER WANT TO GET PREGNANT EVER.
WHICH IS ALL YOUR FAULT.
WHAT?!
"LET'S RENT ALIENS. MY DAD SAID IT'S REALLY COOOOL."
ARGH. NIGHTMARES. ALIEN BABY.
...SORRY, MOUSE.
STILL. ART CLASS. I TOTALLY...
MORNING, CLASS! MRS. MELLOR HAS STARTED HER MATERNITY LEAVE...
...SO I'LL BE SUBSTITUTING FOR HER FOR THE REST OF TERM. MY NAME IS MR. TEMPLAR.
...COULD GET USED TO IT.

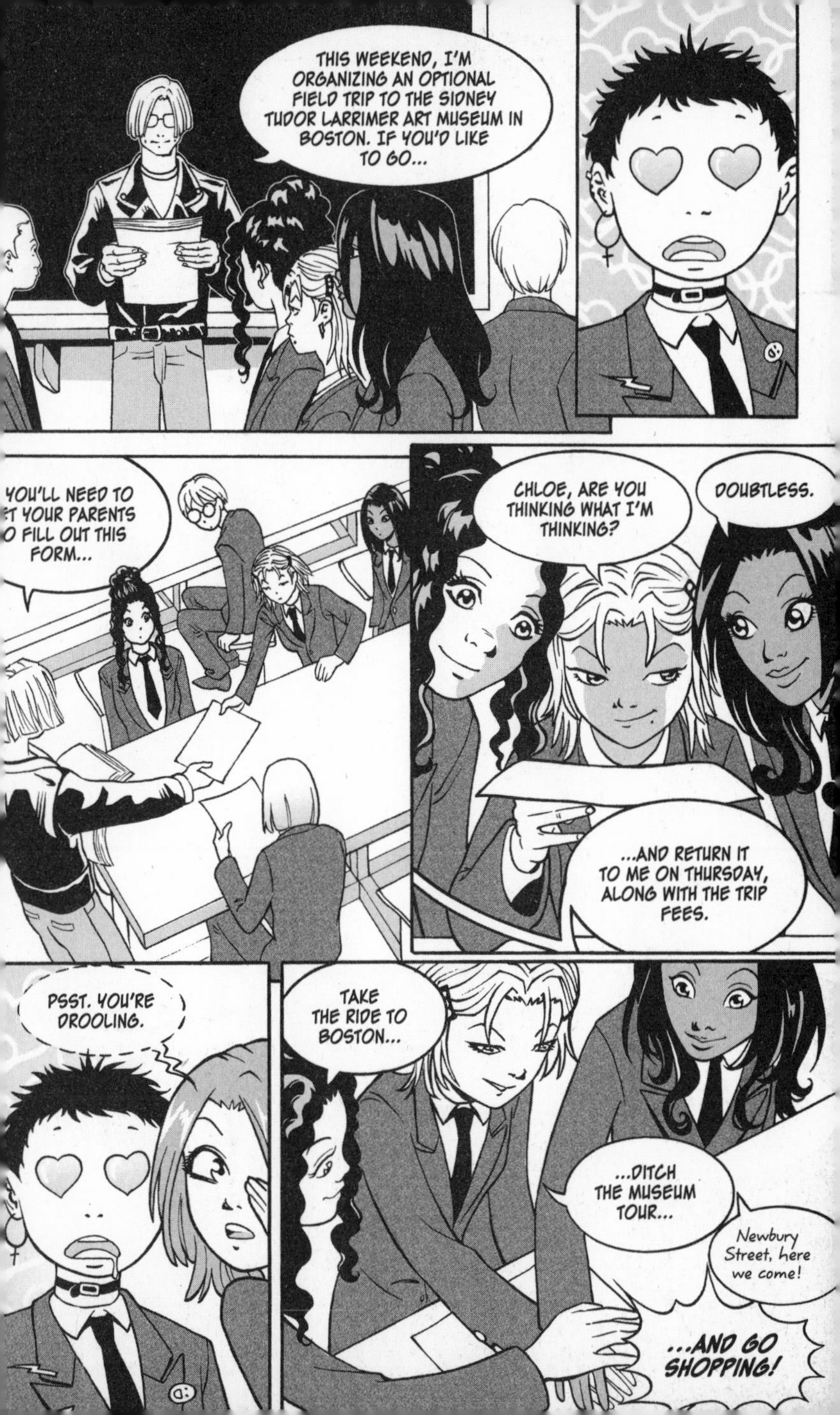
THIS WEEKEND, I'M ORGANIZING AN OPTIONAL FIELD TRIP TO THE SIDNEY TUDOR LARRIMER ART MUSEUM IN BOSTON. IF YOU'D LIKE TO GO...
YOU'LL NEED TO GET YOUR PARENTS TO FILL OUT THIS FORM...
CHLOE, ARE YOU THINKING WHAT I'M THINKING?
DOUBTLESS.
...AND RETURN IT TO ME ON THURSDAY, ALONG WITH THE TRIP FEES.
PSST. YOU'RE DROOLING.
TAKE THE RIDE TO BOSTON...
...DITCH THE MUSEUM TOUR...
Newbury Street, here we come!
...AND GO SHOPPING!

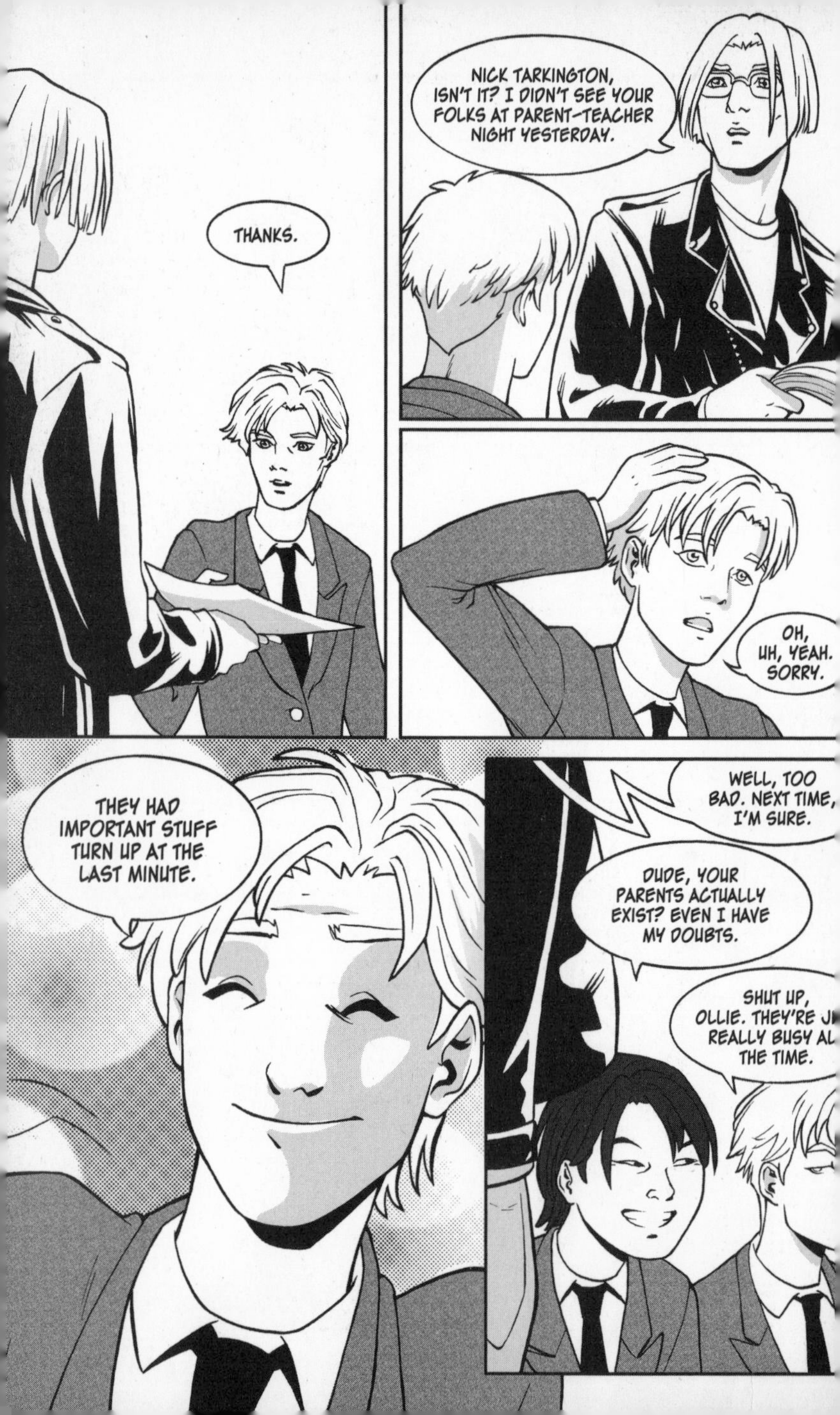
THANKS.
NICK TARKINGTON, ISN'T IT? I DIDN'T SEE YOUR FOLKS AT PARENT-TEACHER NIGHT YESTERDAY.
OH, UH, YEAH. SORRY.
THEY HAD IMPORTANT STUFF TURN UP AT THE LAST MINUTE.
WELL, TOO BAD. NEXT TIME, I'M SURE.
DUDE, YOUR PARENTS ACTUALLY EXIST? EVEN I HAVE MY DOUBTS.
SHUT UP, OLLIE. THEY'RE JU REALLY BUSY AL THE TIME.

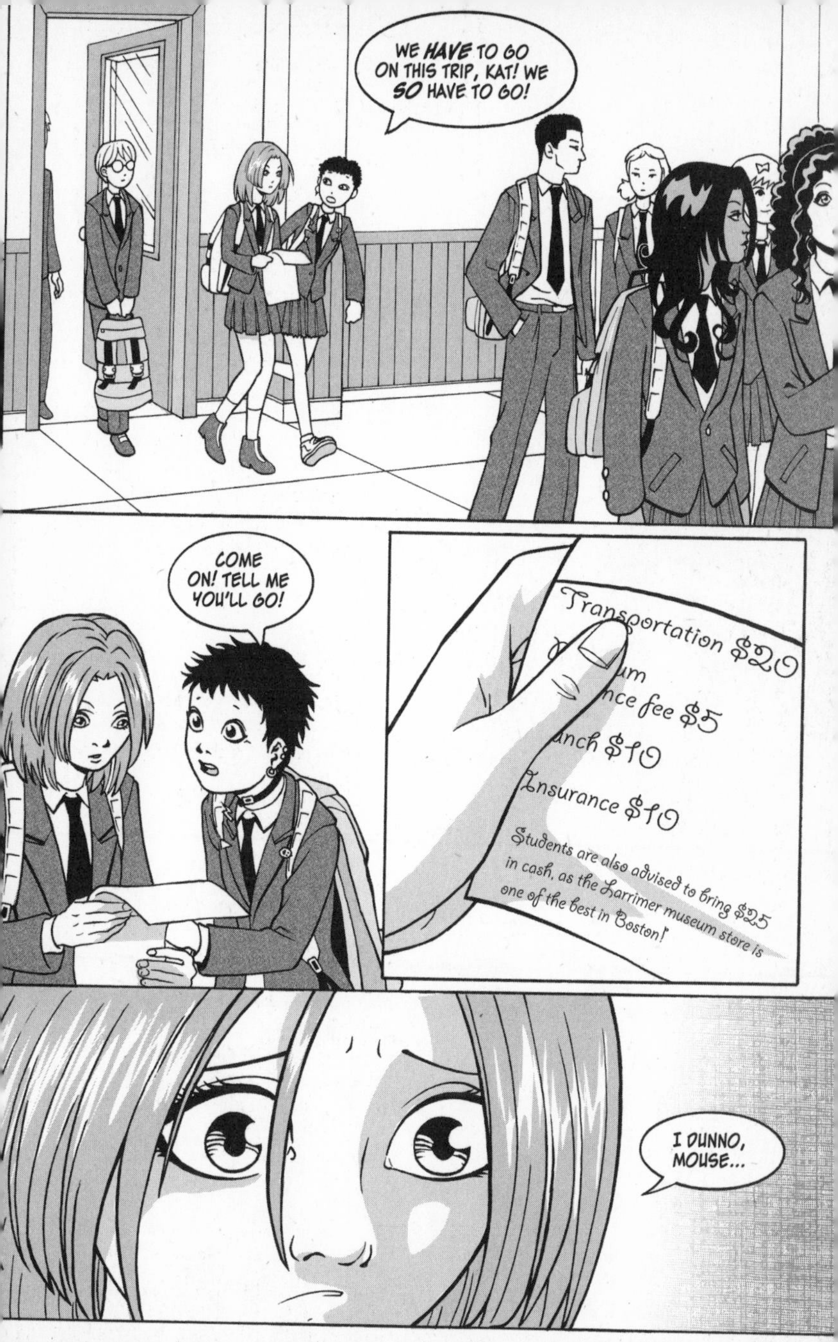
WE *HAVE* TO GO ON THIS TRIP, KAT! WE *SO* HAVE TO GO!
COME ON! TELL ME YOU'LL GO!
Transportation $20
um
nce fee $5
unch $10
Insurance $10
Students are also advised to bring $25 in cash, as the Larrimer museum store is one of the best in Boston!
I DUNNO, MOUSE...

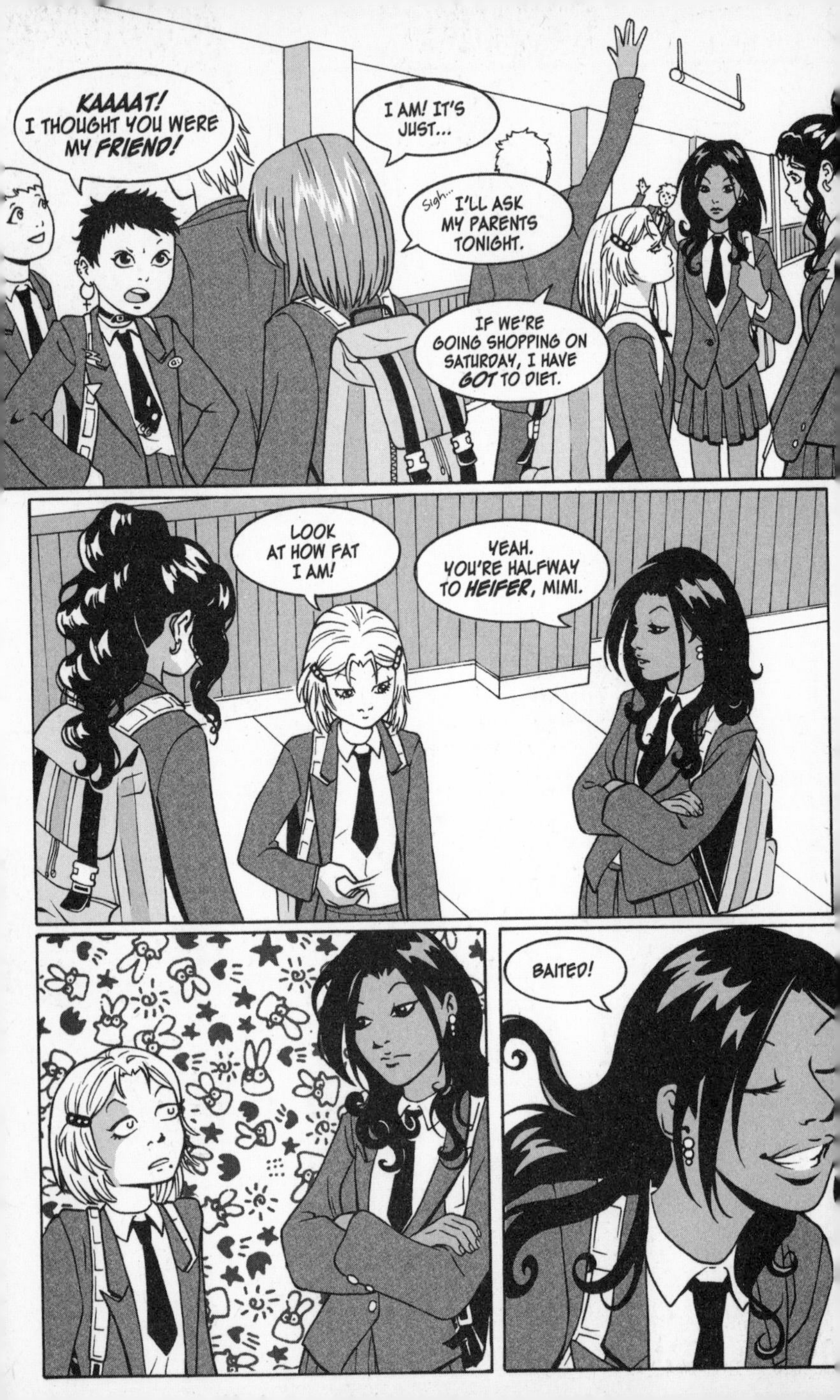

KAAAAT! I THOUGHT YOU WERE MY *FRIEND!*
I AM! IT'S JUST...
Sigh... I'LL ASK MY PARENTS TONIGHT.
IF WE'RE GOING SHOPPING ON SATURDAY, I HAVE *GOT* TO DIET.
LOOK AT HOW FAT I AM!
YEAH. YOU'RE HALFWAY TO *HEIFER*, MIMI.
BAITED!

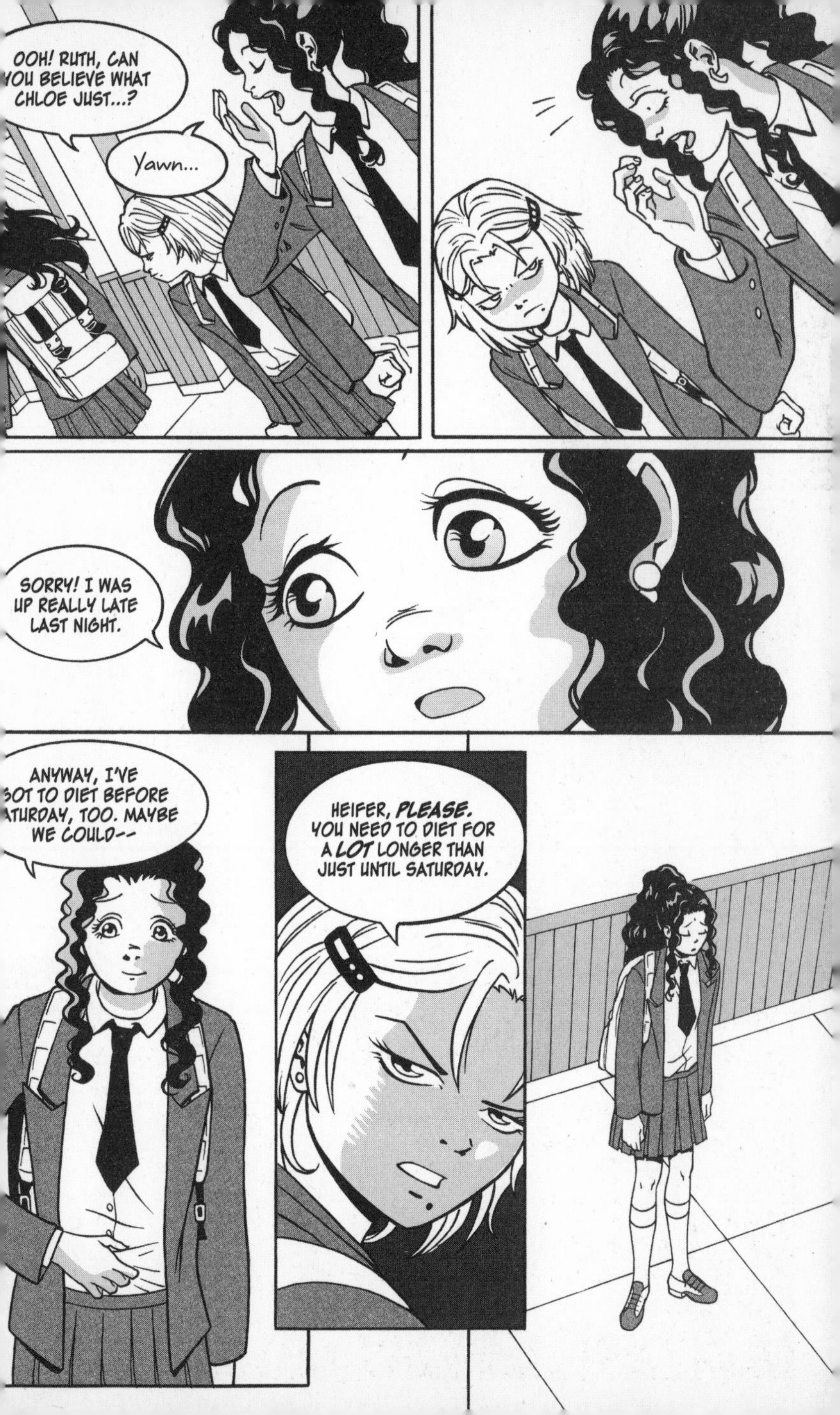

OOH! RUTH, CAN YOU BELIEVE WHAT CHLOE JUST...?
Yawn...
SORRY! I WAS UP REALLY LATE LAST NIGHT.
ANYWAY, I'VE GOT TO DIET BEFORE SATURDAY, TOO. MAYBE WE COULD--
HEIFER, **PLEASE.** YOU NEED TO DIET FOR A ***LOT*** LONGER THAN JUST UNTIL SATURDAY.

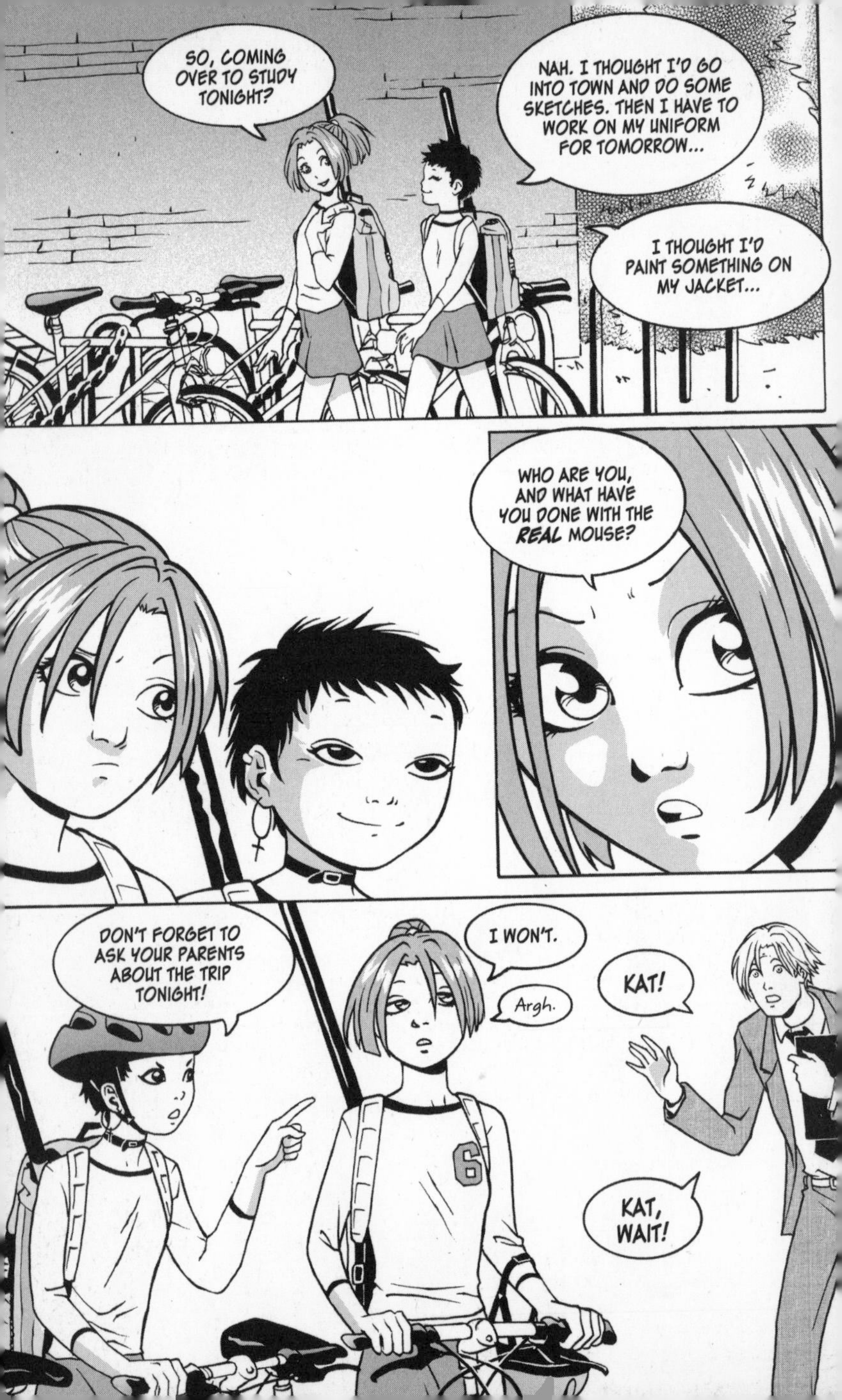
SO, COMING OVER TO STUDY TONIGHT?
NAH. I THOUGHT I'D GO INTO TOWN AND DO SOME SKETCHES. THEN I HAVE TO WORK ON MY UNIFORM FOR TOMORROW...
I THOUGHT I'D PAINT SOMETHING ON MY JACKET...
WHO ARE YOU, AND WHAT HAVE YOU DONE WITH THE REAL MOUSE?
DON'T FORGET TO ASK YOUR PARENTS ABOUT THE TRIP TONIGHT!
I WON'T.
Argh.
KAT!
KAT, WAIT!
6

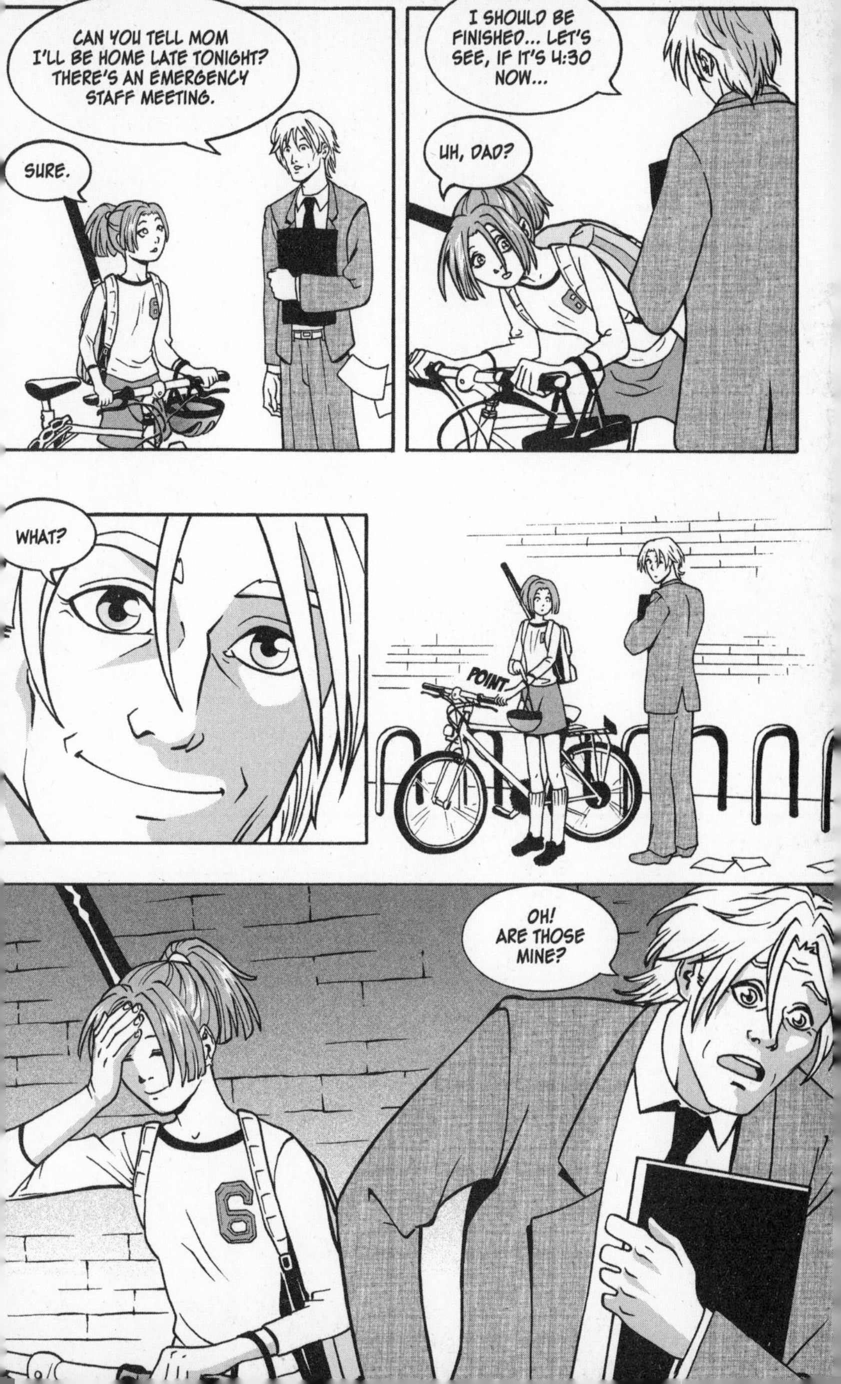
CAN YOU TELL MOM I'LL BE HOME LATE TONIGHT? THERE'S AN EMERGENCY STAFF MEETING.
SURE.
I SHOULD BE FINISHED... LET'S SEE, IF IT'S 4:30 NOW...
UH, DAD?
WHAT?
POINT
OH! ARE THOSE MINE?

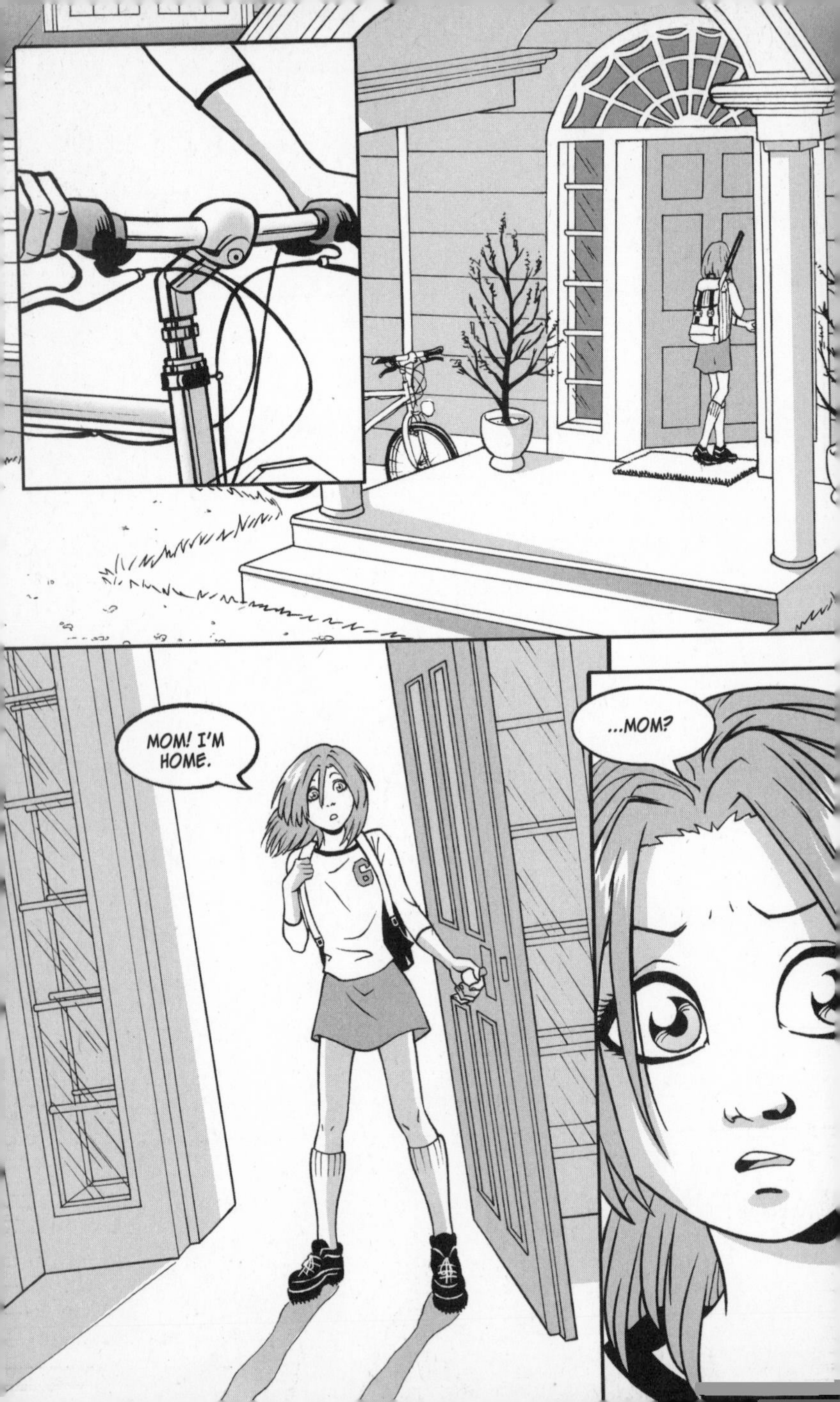
MOM! I'M HOME.
...MOM?

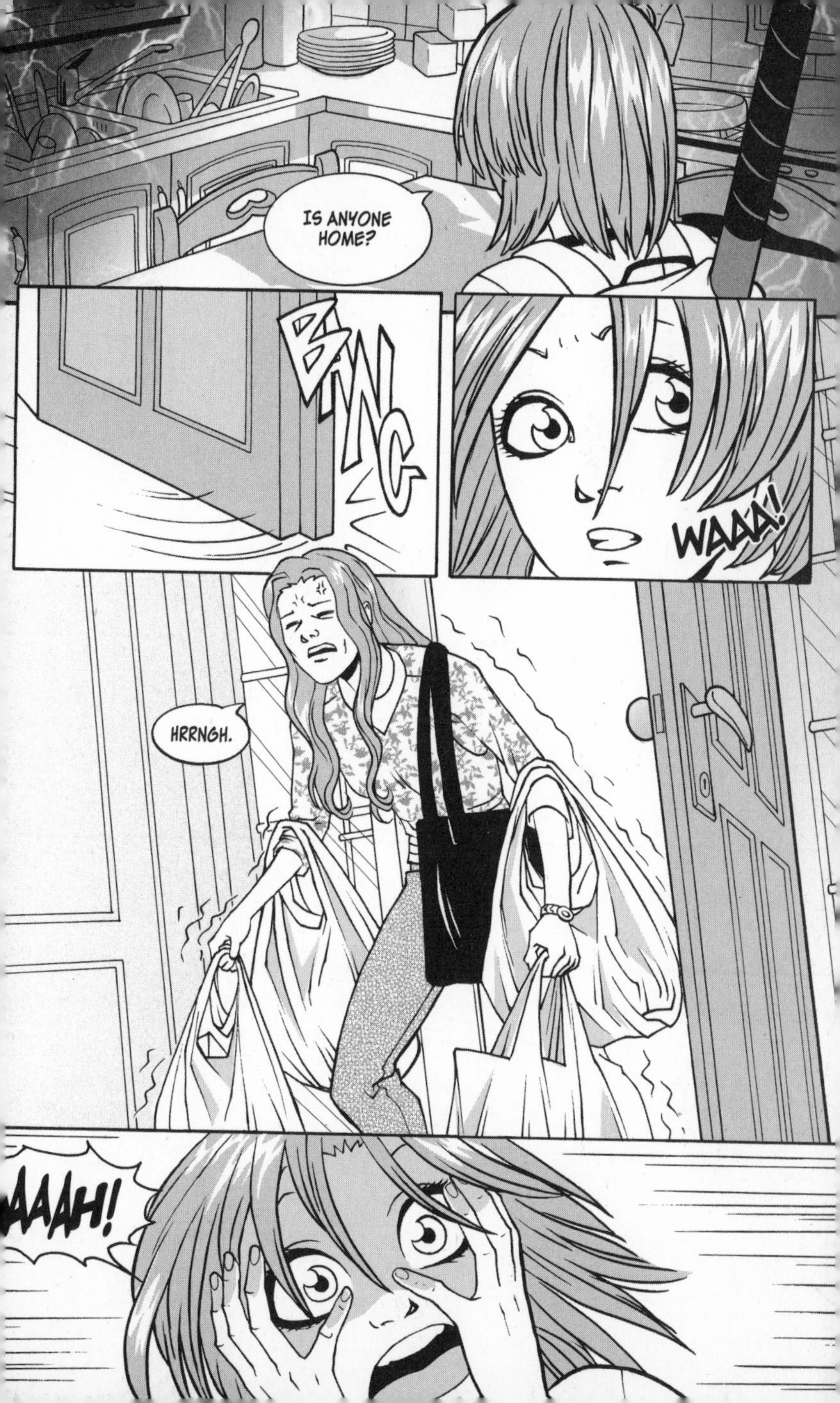
IS ANYONE HOME?
BANG
WAAA!
HRRNGH.
AAAH!

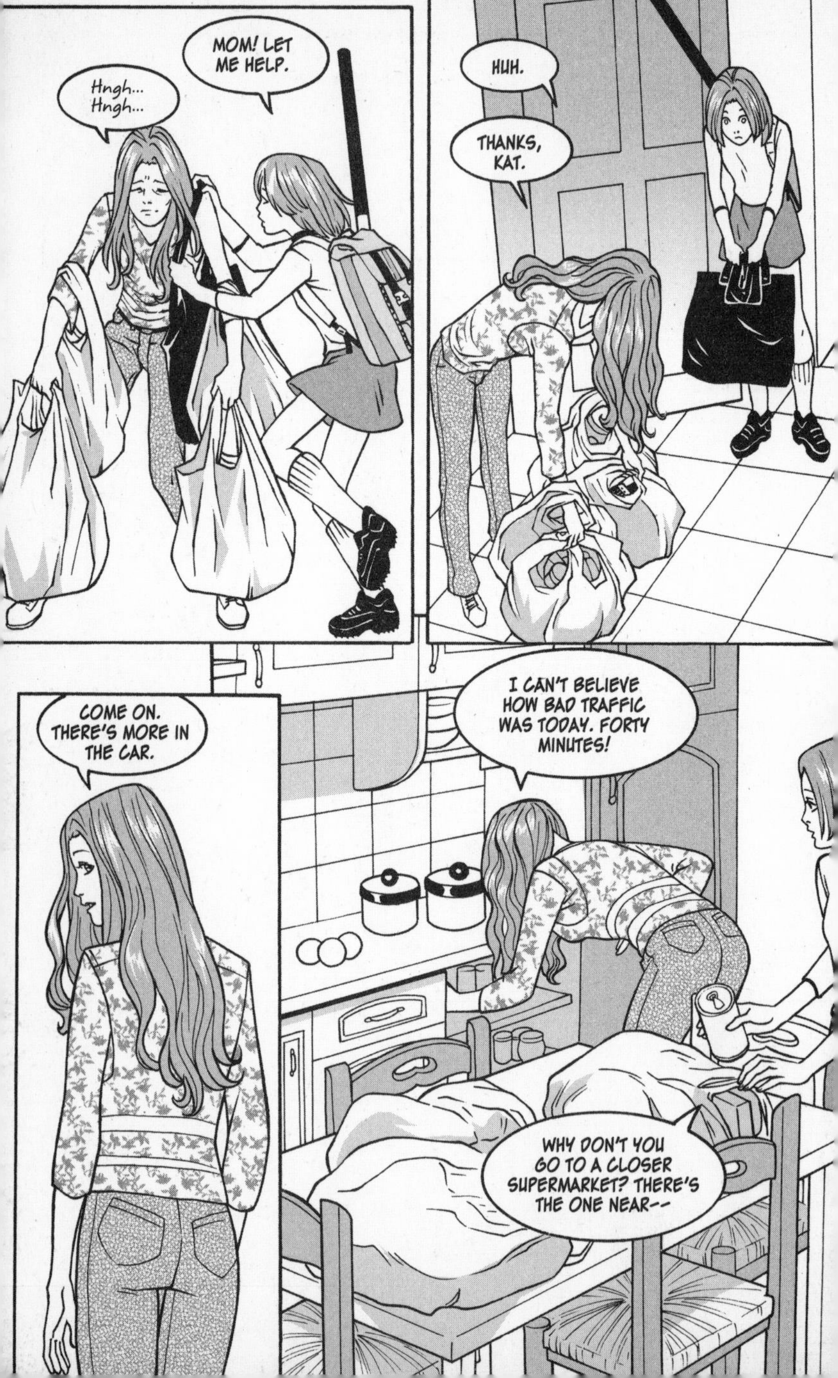
Hngh... Hngh...
MOM! LET ME HELP.
HUH.
THANKS, KAT.
COME ON. THERE'S MORE IN THE CAR.
I CAN'T BELIEVE HOW BAD TRAFFIC WAS TODAY. FORTY MINUTES!
WHY DON'T YOU GO TO A CLOSER SUPERMARKET? THERE'S THE ONE NEAR--

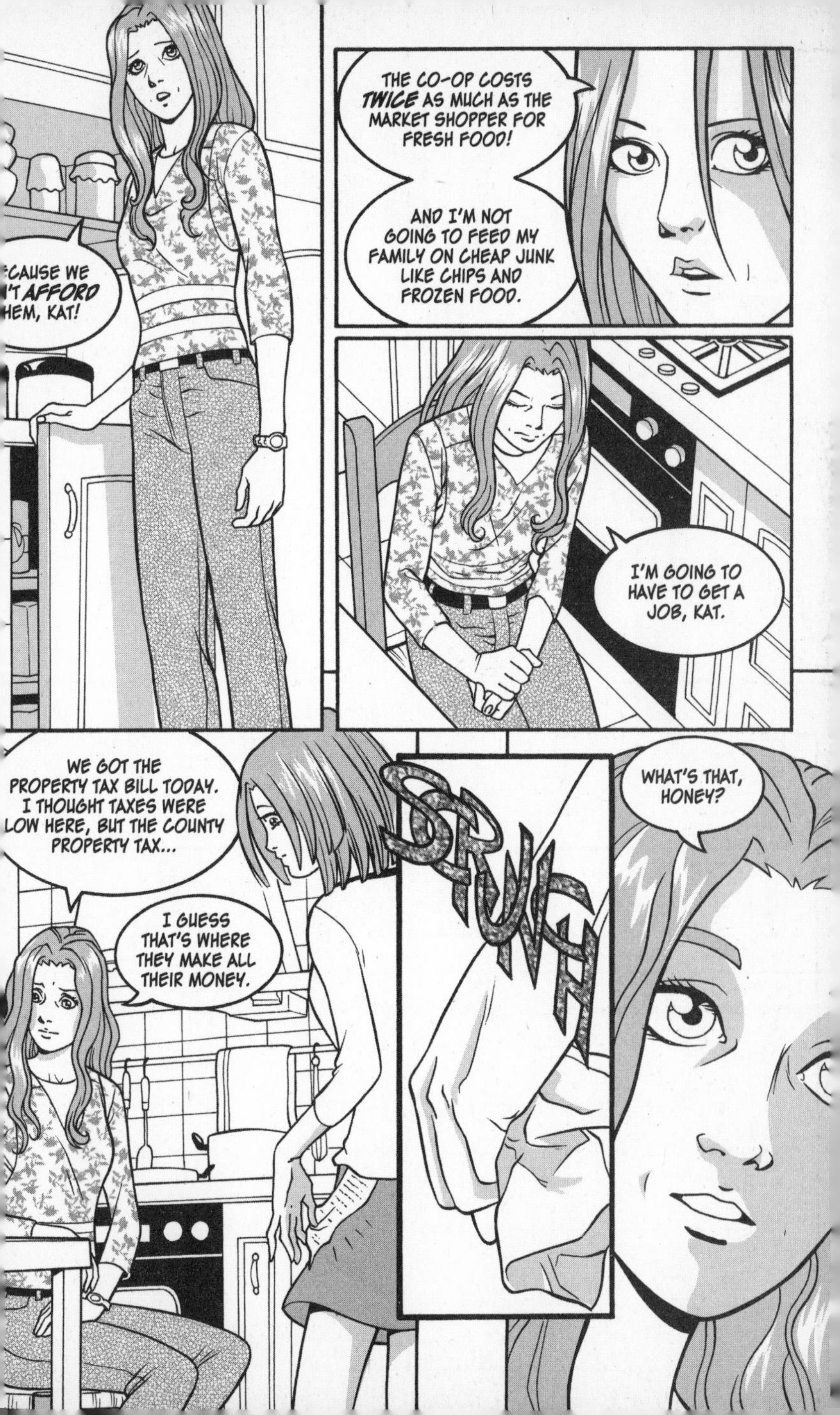

ECAUSE WE
'T **AFFORD**
HEM, KAT!
THE CO-OP COSTS **TWICE** AS MUCH AS THE MARKET SHOPPER FOR FRESH FOOD!
AND I'M NOT GOING TO FEED MY FAMILY ON CHEAP JUNK LIKE CHIPS AND FROZEN FOOD.
I'M GOING TO HAVE TO GET A JOB, KAT.
WE GOT THE PROPERTY TAX BILL TODAY. I THOUGHT TAXES WERE LOW HERE, BUT THE COUNTY PROPERTY TAX...
I GUESS THAT'S WHERE THEY MAKE ALL THEIR MONEY.
SCRUNCH
WHAT'S THAT, HONEY?

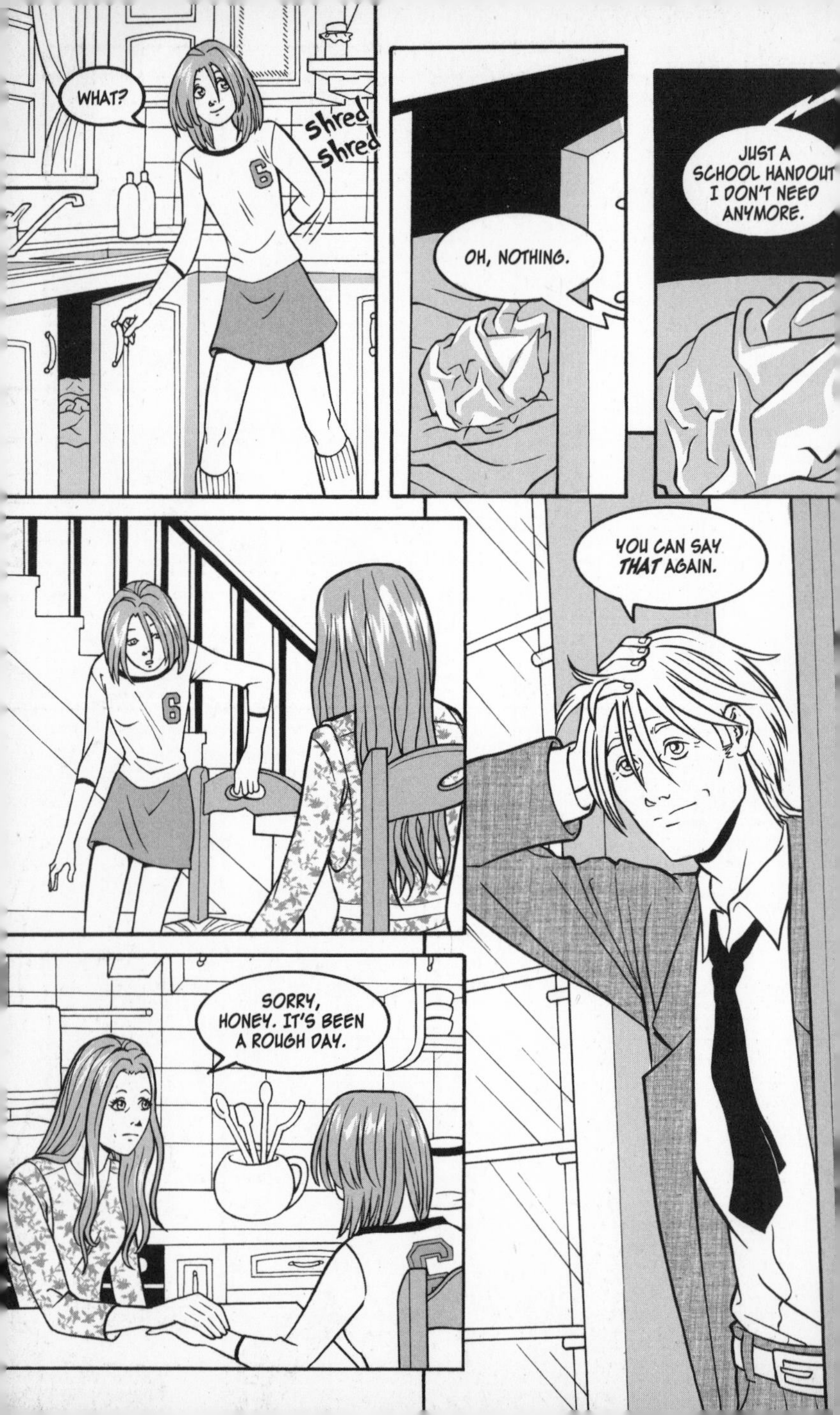
WHAT?
Shred Shred
OH, NOTHING.
JUST A SCHOOL HANDOUT I DON'T NEED ANYMORE.
YOU CAN SAY *THAT* AGAIN.
SORRY, HONEY. IT'S BEEN A ROUGH DAY.

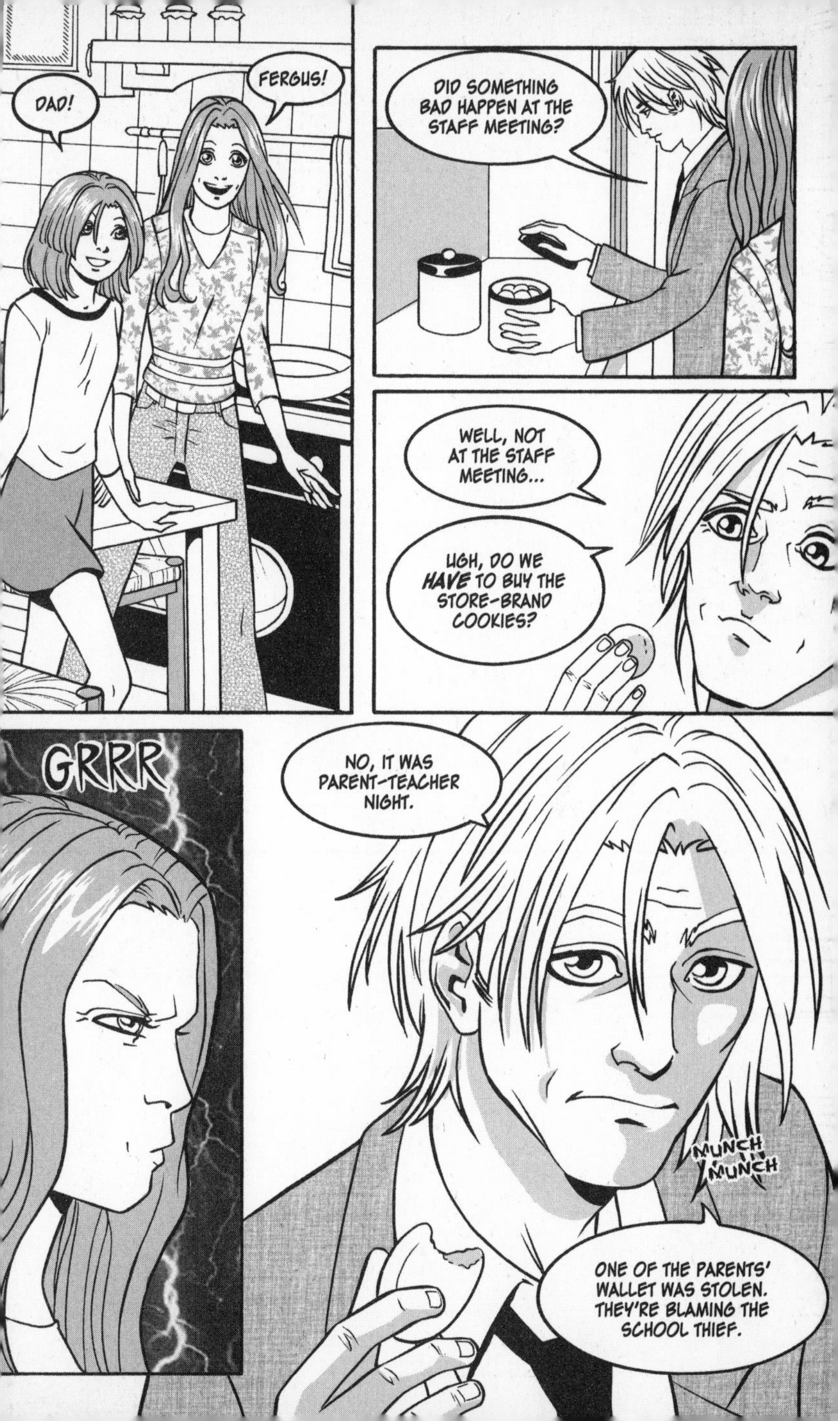

DAD!
FERGUS!
DID SOMETHING BAD HAPPEN AT THE STAFF MEETING?
WELL, NOT AT THE STAFF MEETING...
UGH, DO WE *HAVE* TO BUY THE STORE-BRAND COOKIES?
GRRR
NO, IT WAS PARENT-TEACHER NIGHT.
MUNCH MUNCH
ONE OF THE PARENTS' WALLET WAS STOLEN. THEY'RE BLAMING THE SCHOOL THIEF.

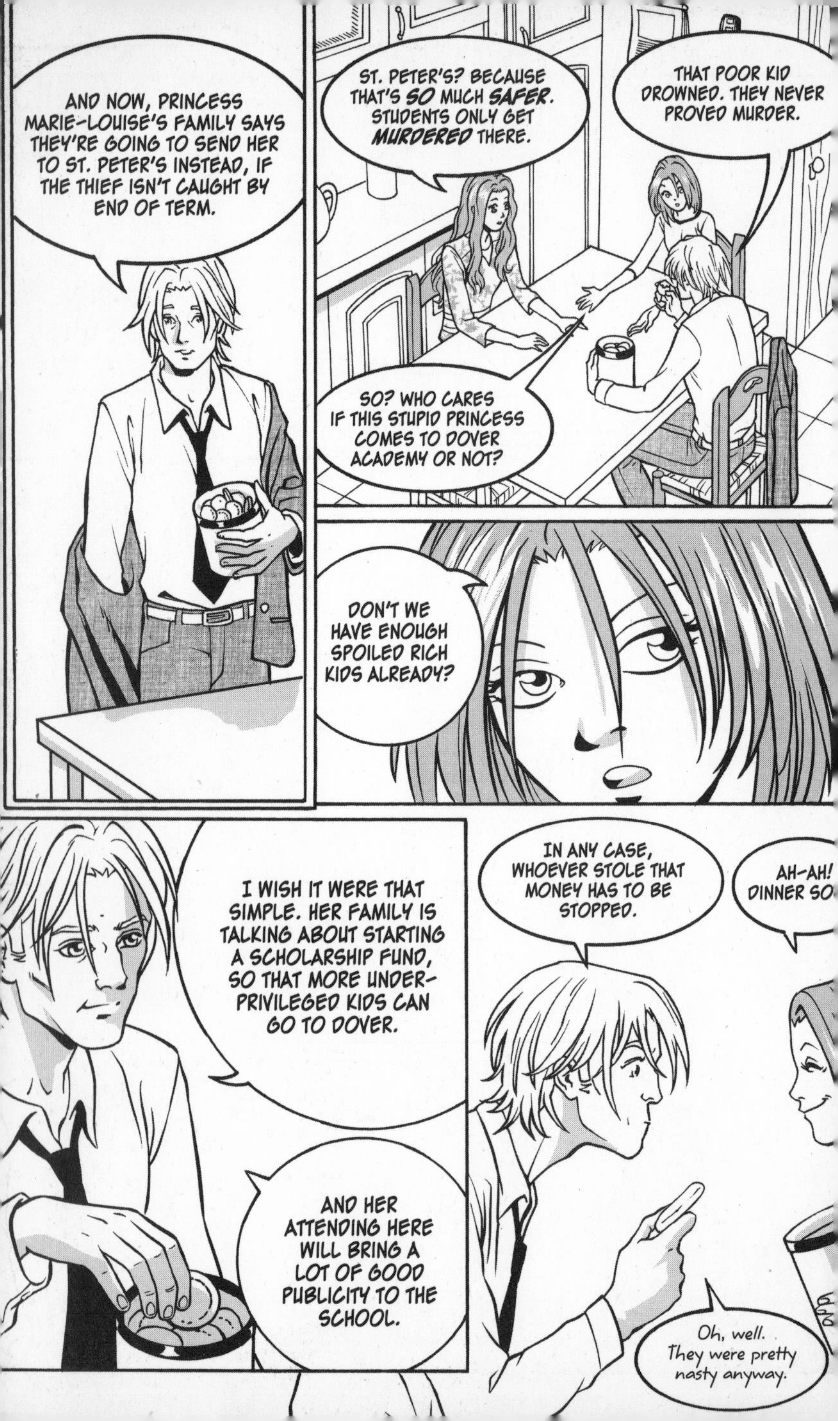
AND NOW, PRINCESS MARIE-LOUISE'S FAMILY SAYS THEY'RE GOING TO SEND HER TO ST. PETER'S INSTEAD, IF THE THIEF ISN'T CAUGHT BY END OF TERM.
ST. PETER'S? BECAUSE THAT'S **SO** MUCH **SAFER**. STUDENTS ONLY GET **MURDERED** THERE.
THAT POOR KID DROWNED. THEY NEVER PROVED MURDER.
SO? WHO CARES IF THIS STUPID PRINCESS COMES TO DOVER ACADEMY OR NOT?
DON'T WE HAVE ENOUGH SPOILED RICH KIDS ALREADY?
I WISH IT WERE THAT SIMPLE. HER FAMILY IS TALKING ABOUT STARTING A SCHOLARSHIP FUND, SO THAT MORE UNDER-PRIVILEGED KIDS CAN GO TO DOVER.
AND HER ATTENDING HERE WILL BRING A LOT OF GOOD PUBLICITY TO THE SCHOOL.
IN ANY CASE, WHOEVER STOLE THAT MONEY HAS TO BE STOPPED.
AH-AH! DINNER SO
Oh, well. They were pretty nasty anyway.

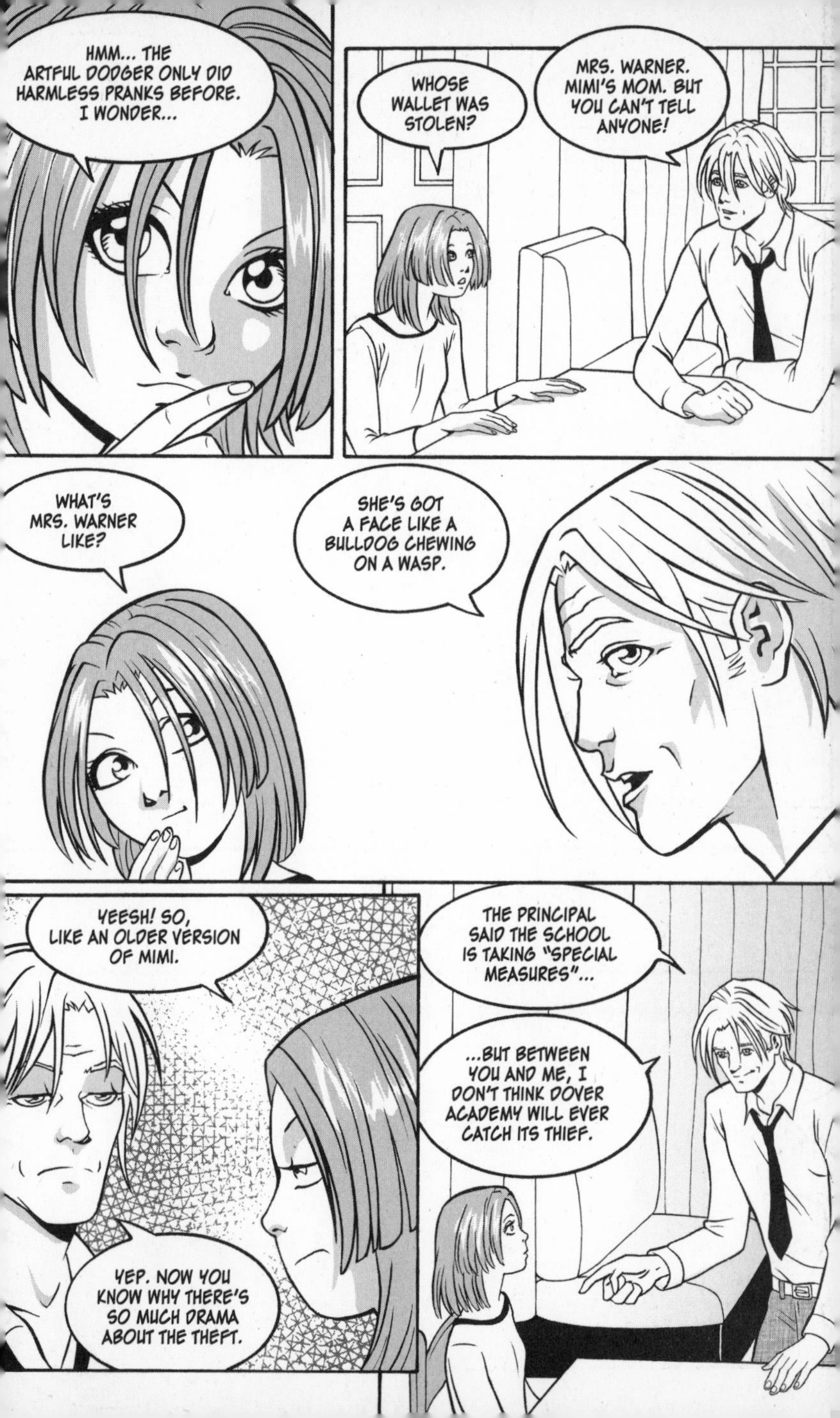
HMM... THE ARTFUL DODGER ONLY DID HARMLESS PRANKS BEFORE. I WONDER...
WHOSE WALLET WAS STOLEN?
MRS. WARNER. MIMI'S MOM. BUT YOU CAN'T TELL ANYONE!
WHAT'S MRS. WARNER LIKE?
SHE'S GOT A FACE LIKE A BULLDOG CHEWING ON A WASP.
YEESH! SO, LIKE AN OLDER VERSION OF MIMI.
YEP. NOW YOU KNOW WHY THERE'S SO MUCH DRAMA ABOUT THE THEFT.
THE PRINCIPAL SAID THE SCHOOL IS TAKING "SPECIAL MEASURES"...
...BUT BETWEEN YOU AND ME, I DON'T THINK DOVER ACADEMY WILL EVER CATCH ITS THIEF.

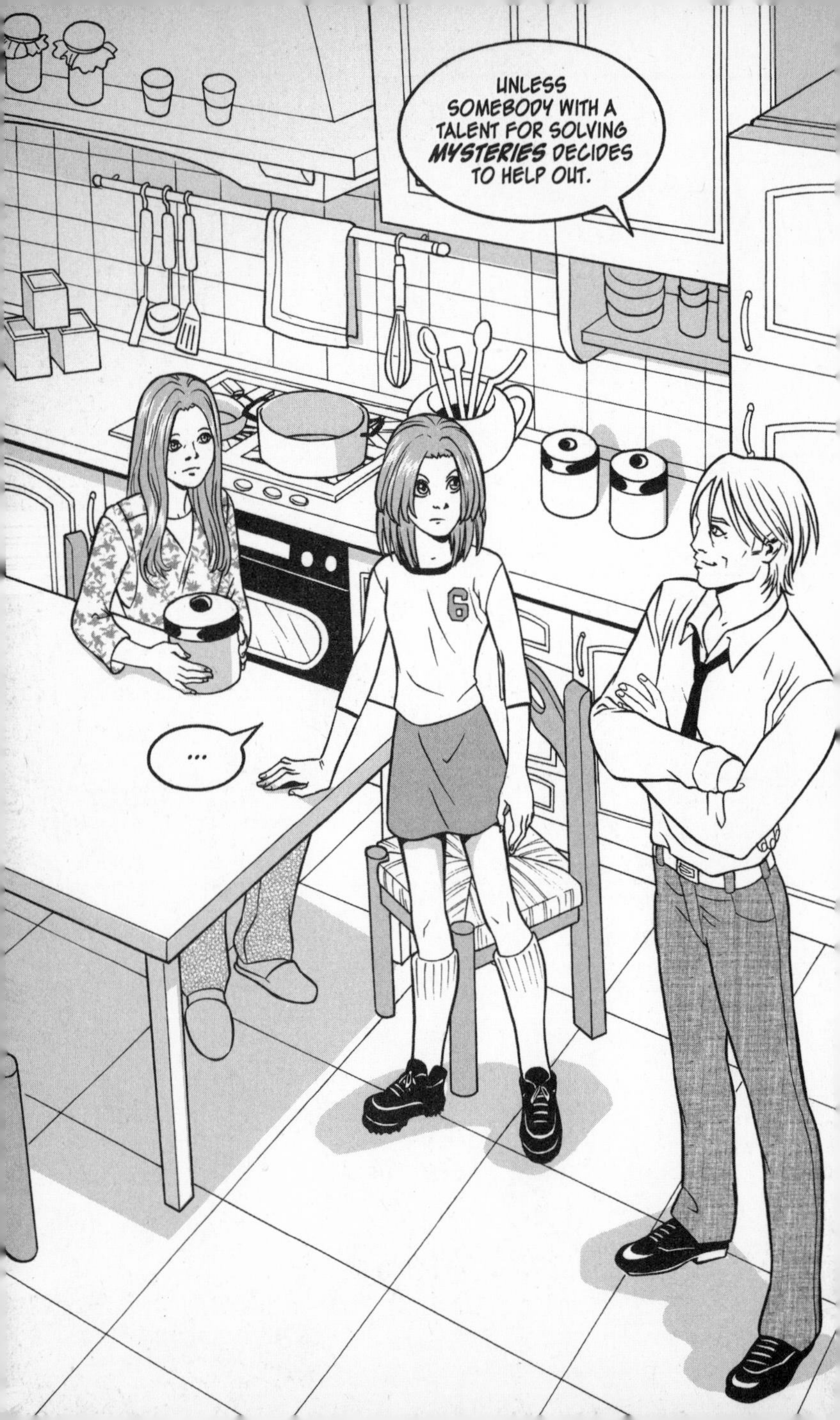
UNLESS SOMEBODY WITH A TALENT FOR SOLVING MYSTERIES DECIDES TO HELP OUT.
...

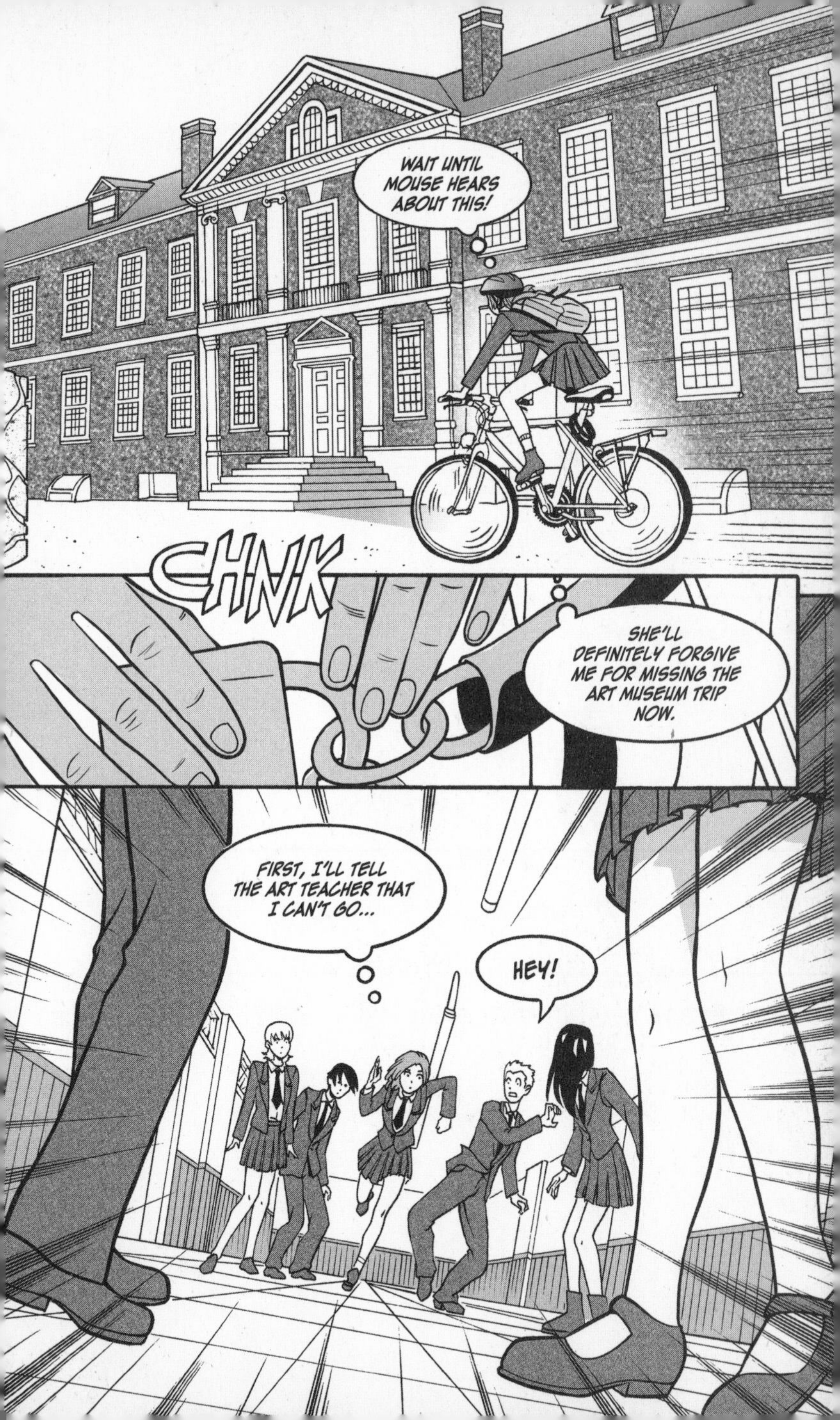
WAIT UNTIL MOUSE HEARS ABOUT THIS!
CHNK
SHE'LL DEFINITELY FORGIVE ME FOR MISSING THE ART MUSEUM TRIP NOW.
FIRST, I'LL TELL THE ART TEACHER THAT I CAN'T GO...
HEY!

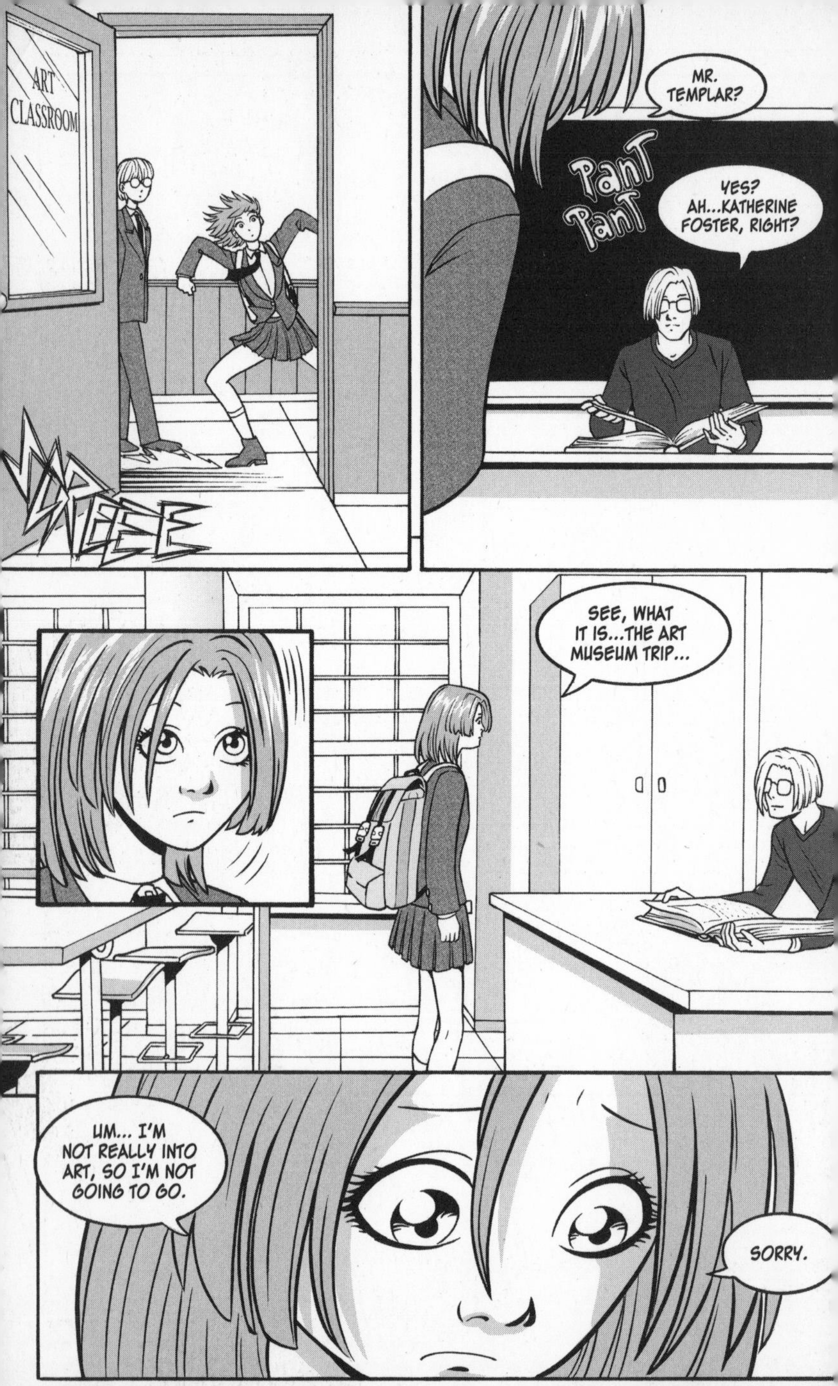
ART CLASSROOM
SKREEE
MR. TEMPLAR?
PANT PANT
YES? AH...KATHERINE FOSTER, RIGHT?
SEE, WHAT IT IS...THE ART MUSEUM TRIP...
UM... I'M NOT REALLY INTO ART, SO I'M NOT GOING TO GO.
SORRY.

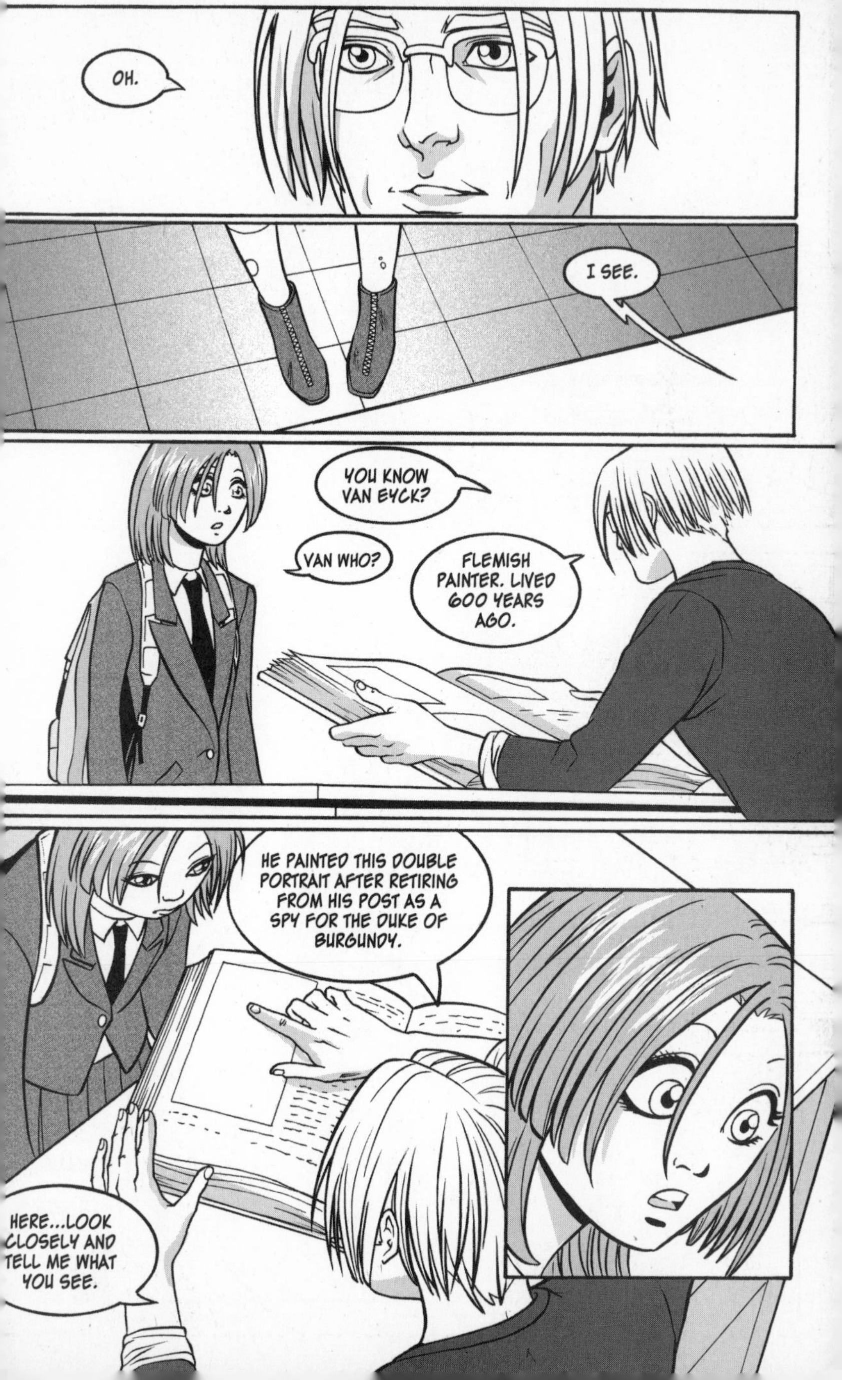
OH.
I SEE.
YOU KNOW VAN EYCK?
VAN WHO?
FLEMISH PAINTER. LIVED 600 YEARS AGO.
HE PAINTED THIS DOUBLE PORTRAIT AFTER RETIRING FROM HIS POST AS A SPY FOR THE DUKE OF BURGUNDY.
HERE...LOOK CLOSELY AND TELL ME WHAT YOU SEE.

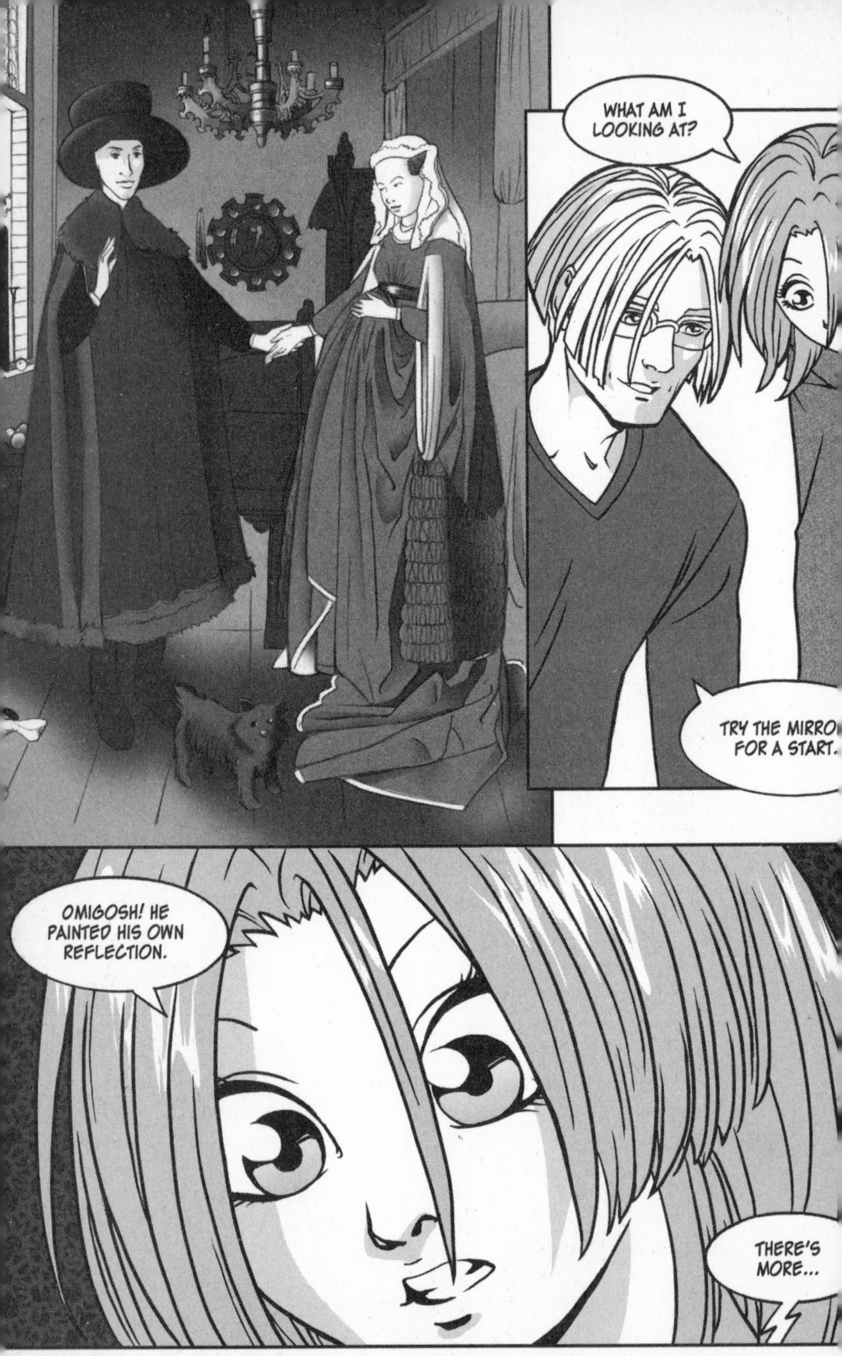
WHAT AM I LOOKING AT?
TRY THE MIRRO FOR A START.
OMIGOSH! HE PAINTED HIS OWN REFLECTION.
THERE'S MORE...

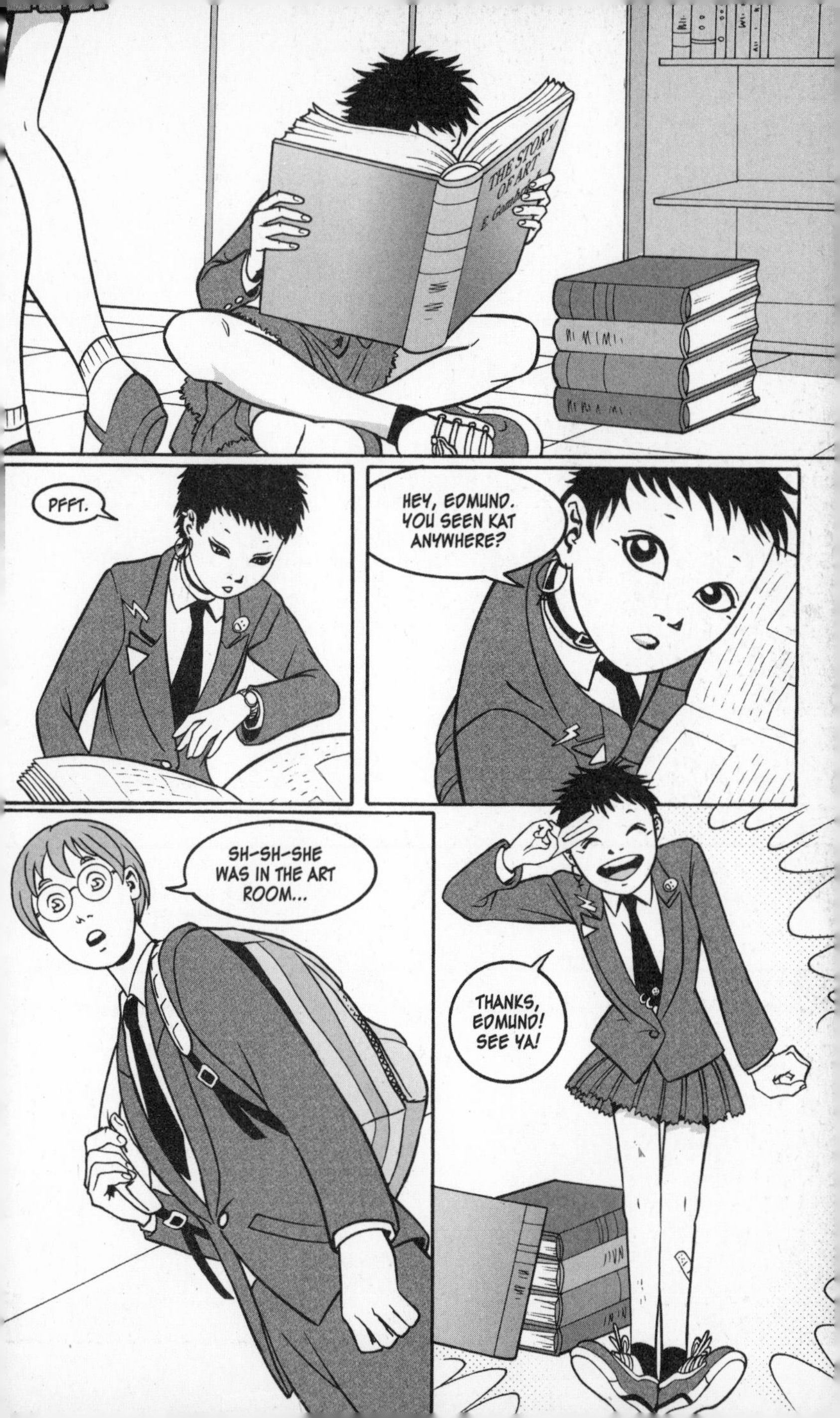
THE STORY OF ART
E. Gombrich
PFFT.
HEY, EDMUND. YOU SEEN KAT ANYWHERE?
SH-SH-SHE WAS IN THE ART ROOM...
THANKS, EDMUND! SEE YA!

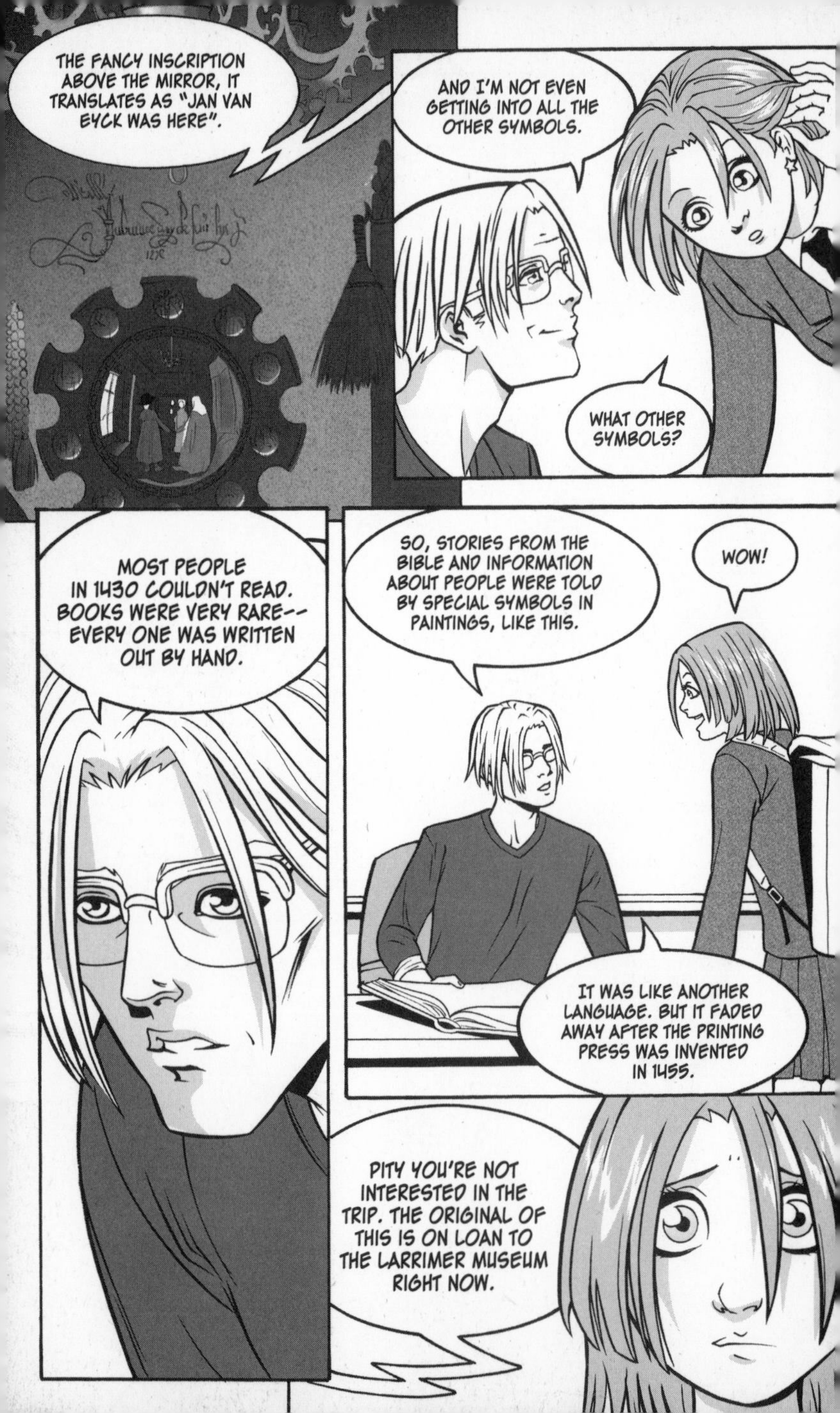
THE FANCY INSCRIPTION ABOVE THE MIRROR, IT TRANSLATES AS "JAN VAN EYCK WAS HERE".
AND I'M NOT EVEN GETTING INTO ALL THE OTHER SYMBOLS.
WHAT OTHER SYMBOLS?
MOST PEOPLE IN 1430 COULDN'T READ. BOOKS WERE VERY RARE--EVERY ONE WAS WRITTEN OUT BY HAND.
SO, STORIES FROM THE BIBLE AND INFORMATION ABOUT PEOPLE WERE TOLD BY SPECIAL SYMBOLS IN PAINTINGS, LIKE THIS.
WOW!
IT WAS LIKE ANOTHER LANGUAGE. BUT IT FADED AWAY AFTER THE PRINTING PRESS WAS INVENTED IN 1455.
PITY YOU'RE NOT INTERESTED IN THE TRIP. THE ORIGINAL OF THIS IS ON LOAN TO THE LARRIMER MUSEUM RIGHT NOW.

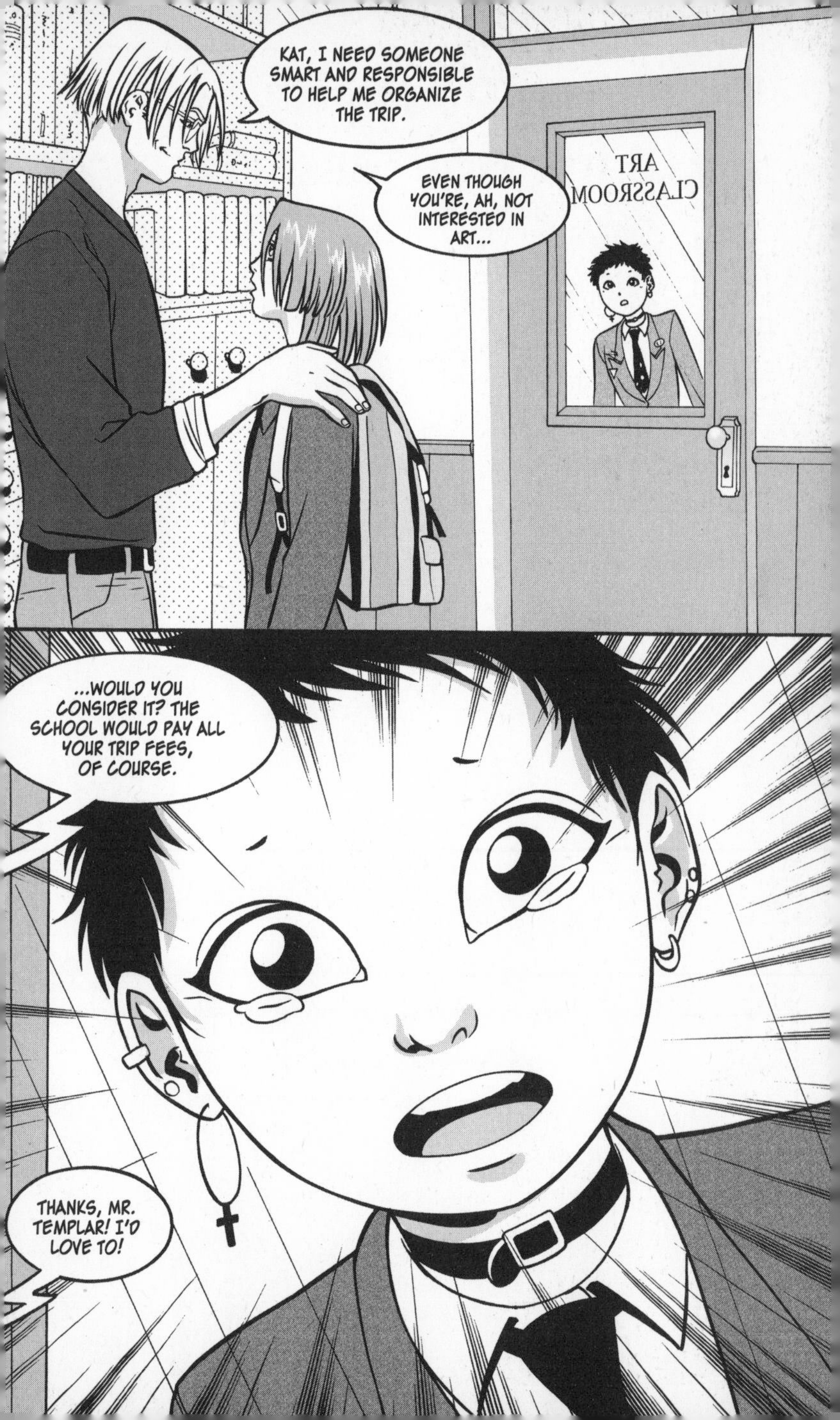
KAT, I NEED SOMEONE SMART AND RESPONSIBLE TO HELP ME ORGANIZE THE TRIP.
EVEN THOUGH YOU'RE, AH, NOT INTERESTED IN ART...
ART CLASSROOM
...WOULD YOU CONSIDER IT? THE SCHOOL WOULD PAY ALL YOUR TRIP FEES, OF COURSE.
THANKS, MR. TEMPLAR! I'D LOVE TO!

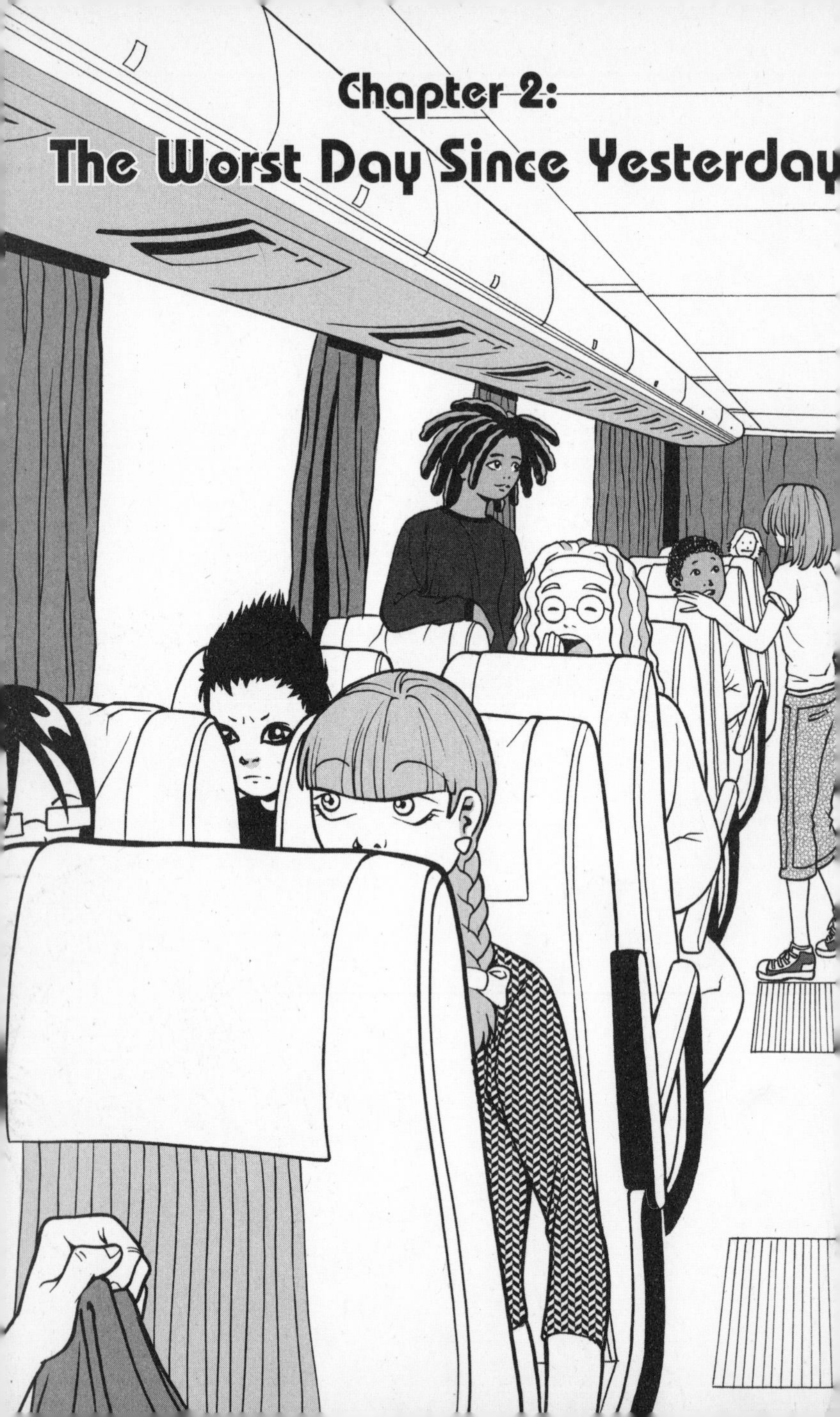
Chapter 2:
The Worst Day Since Yesterday

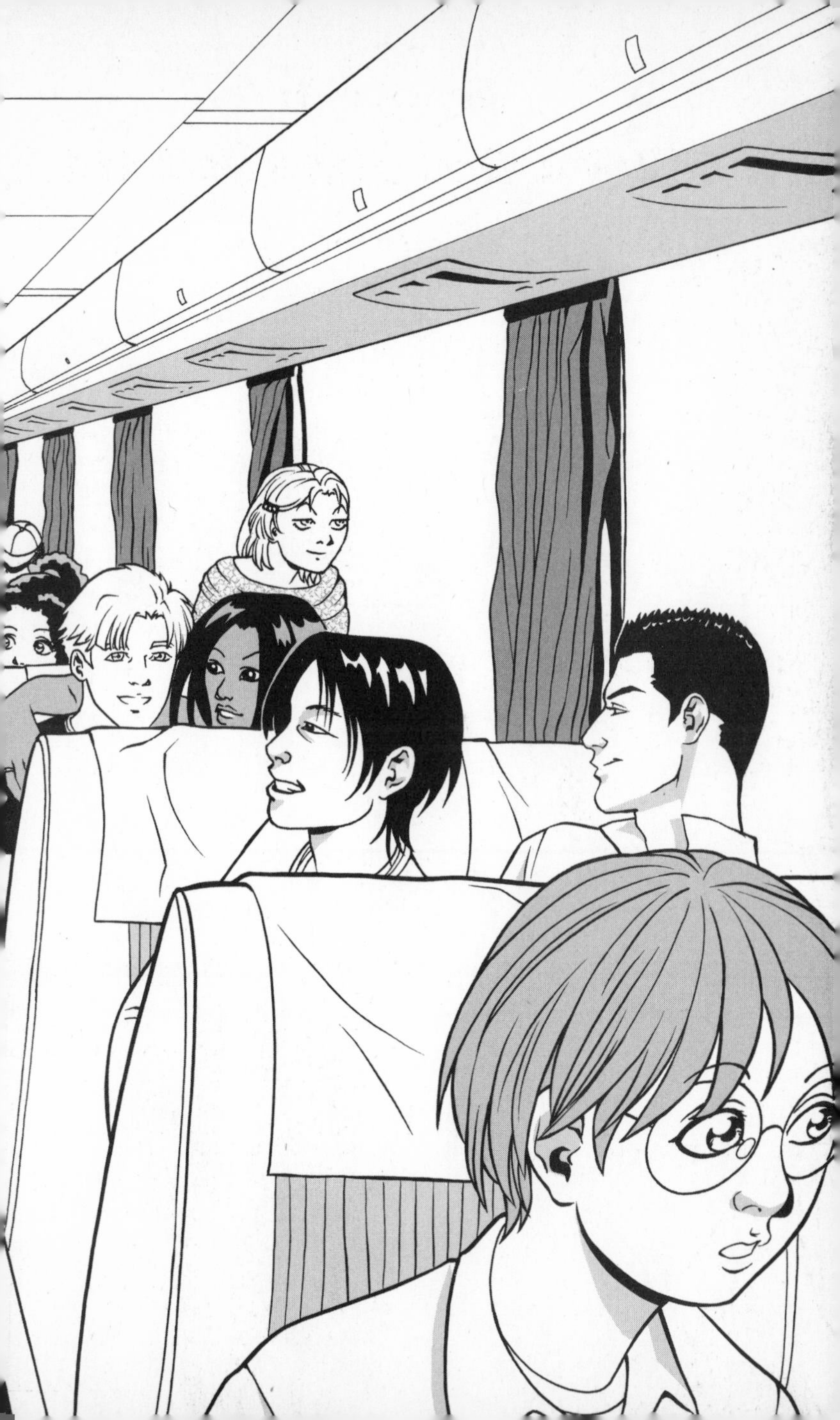

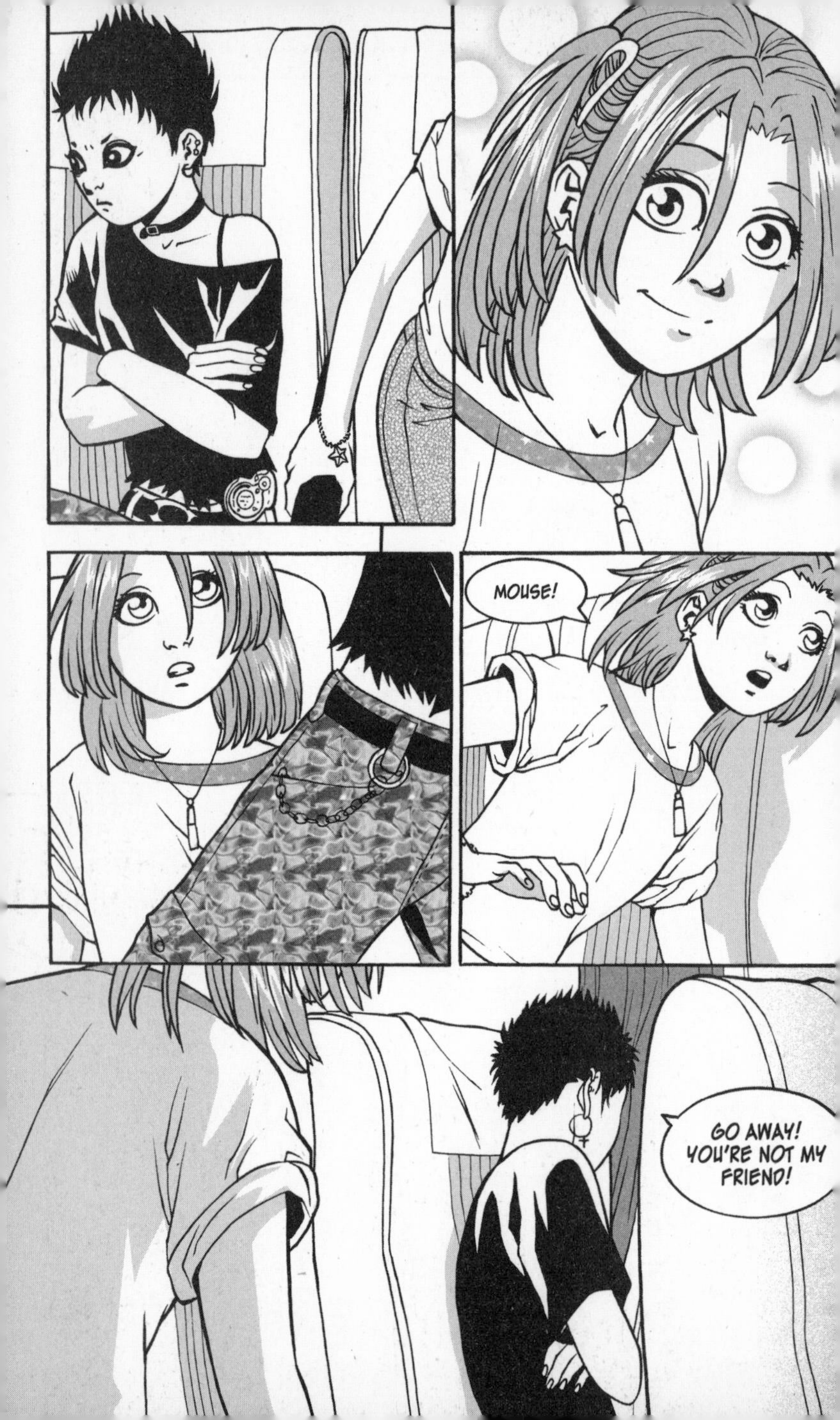
MOUSE!
GO AWAY! YOU'RE NOT MY FRIEND!

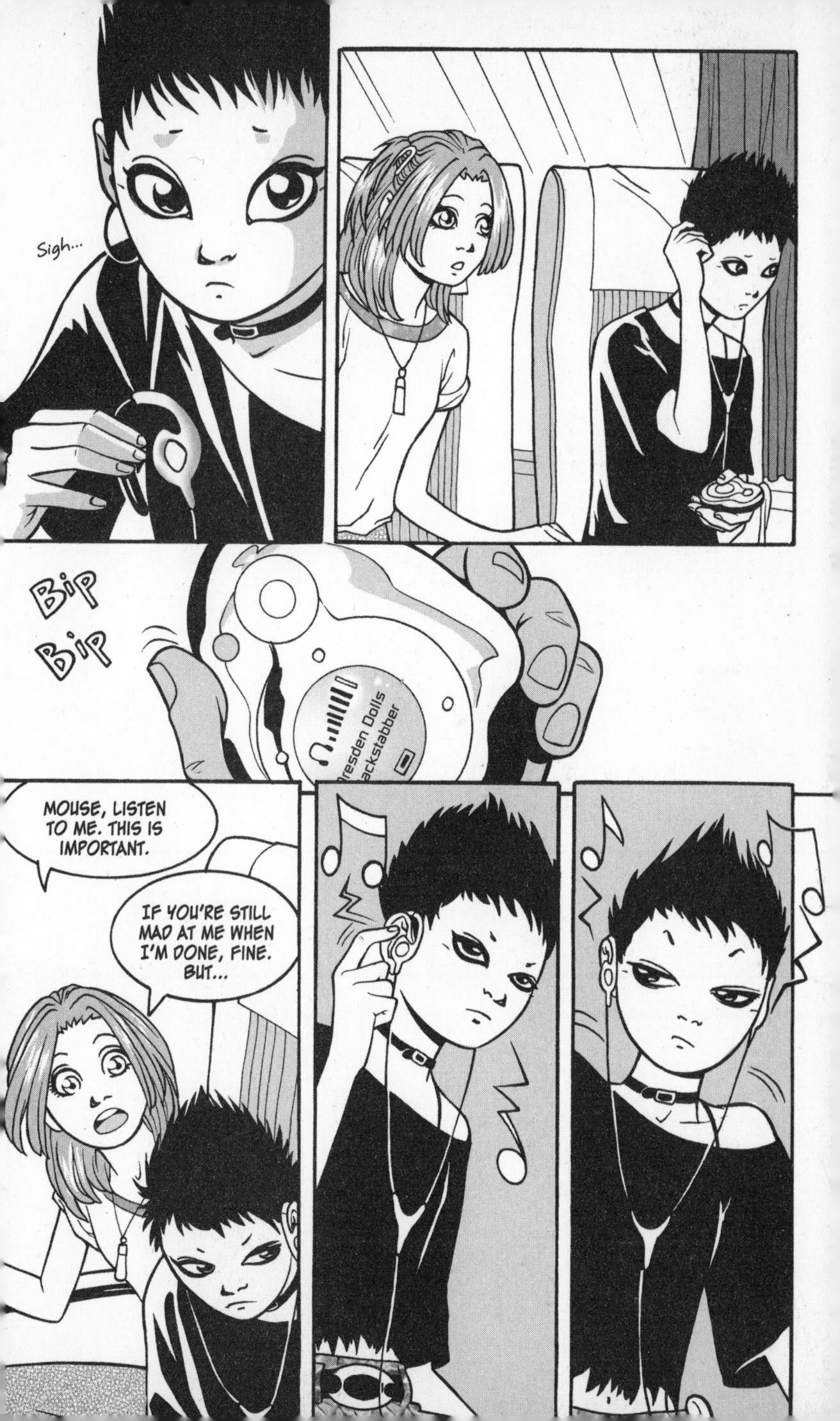
Sigh...
Bip
Bip
resden Dolls
ackstabber
MOUSE, LISTEN TO ME. THIS IS IMPORTANT.
IF YOU'RE STILL MAD AT ME WHEN I'M DONE, FINE. BUT...

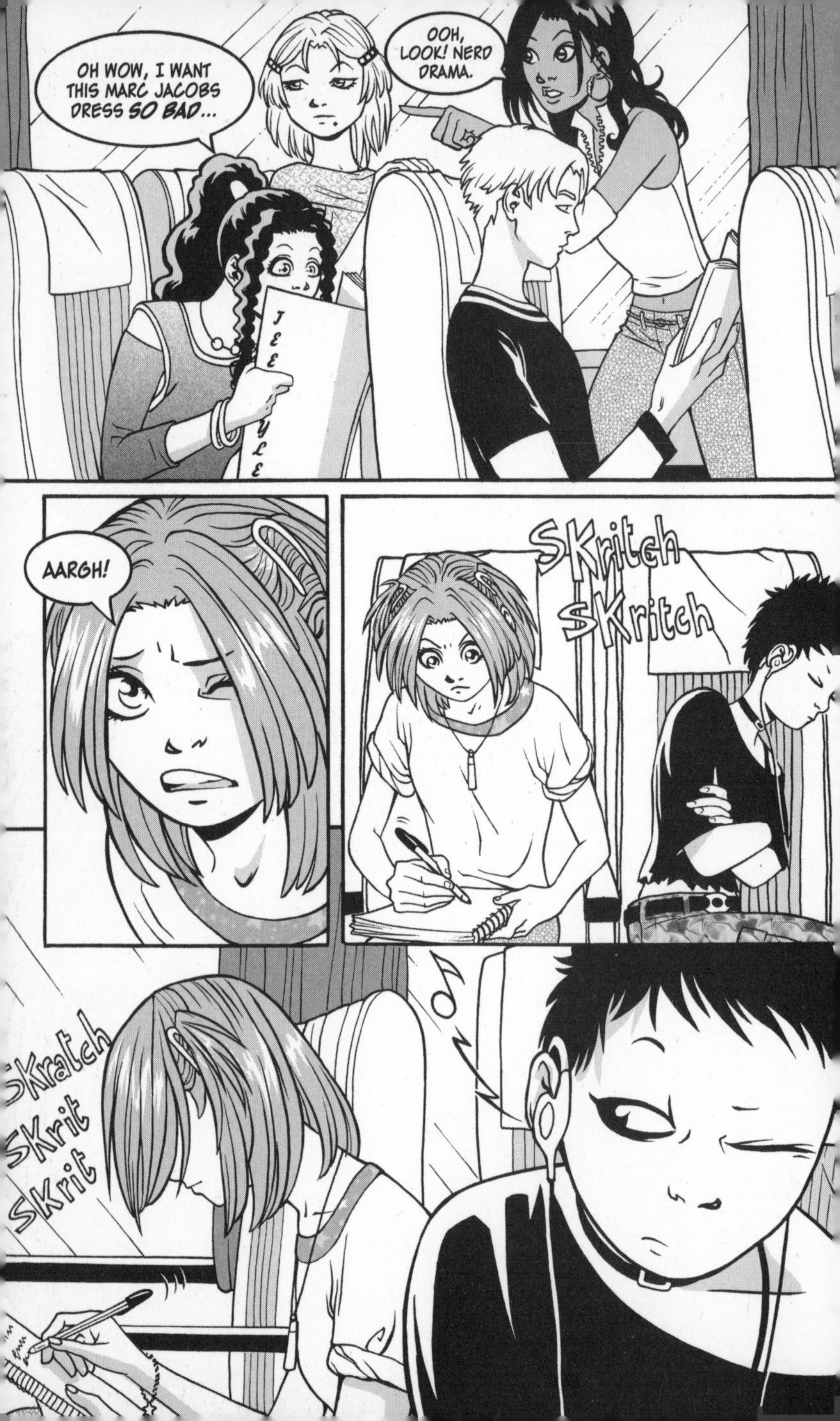
OH WOW, I WANT THIS MARC JACOBS DRESS SO BAD...
OOH, LOOK! NERD DRAMA.
AARGH!
SKritch
sKritch
SKratch
SKrit
SKrit

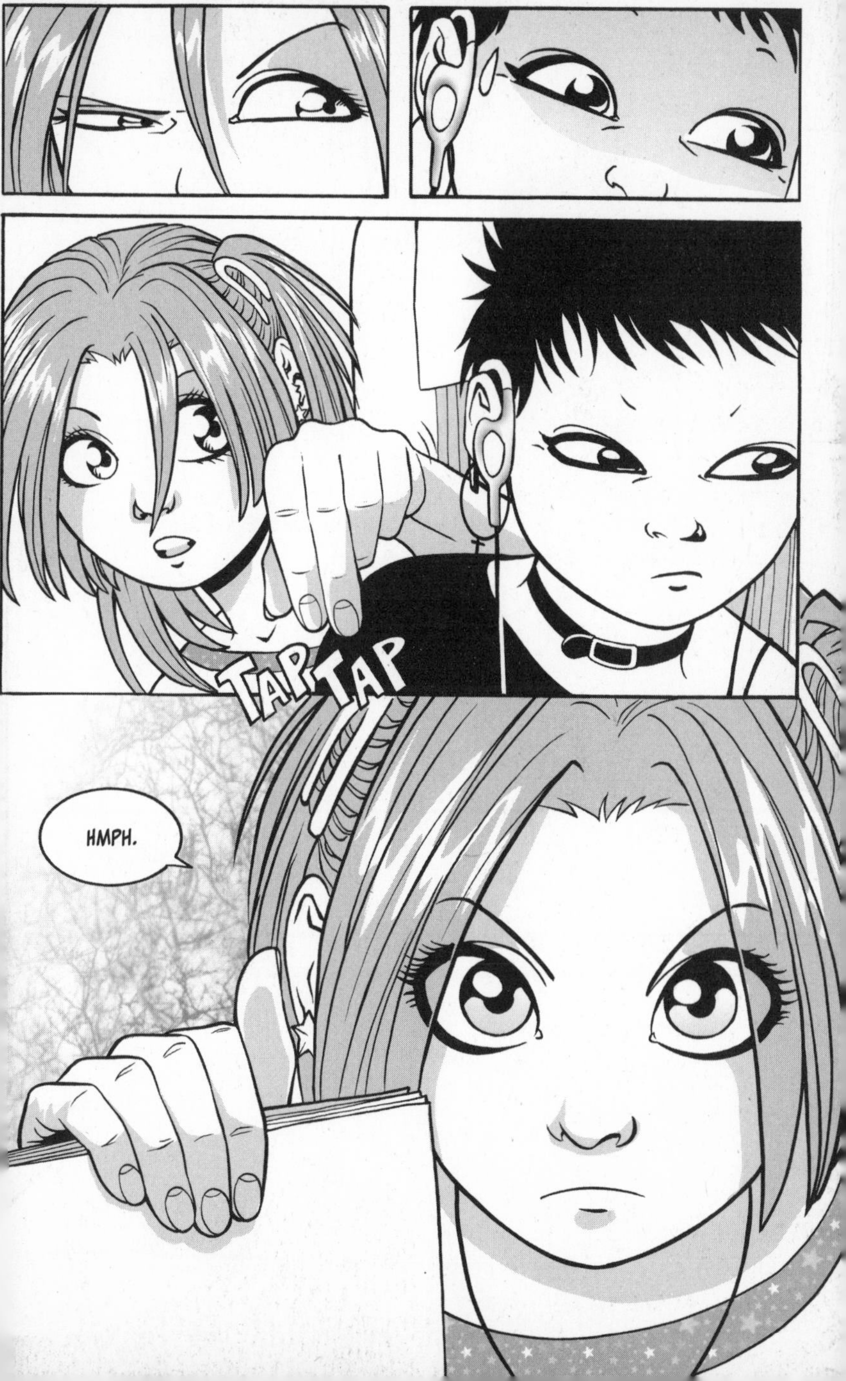
TAP TAP
HMPH.

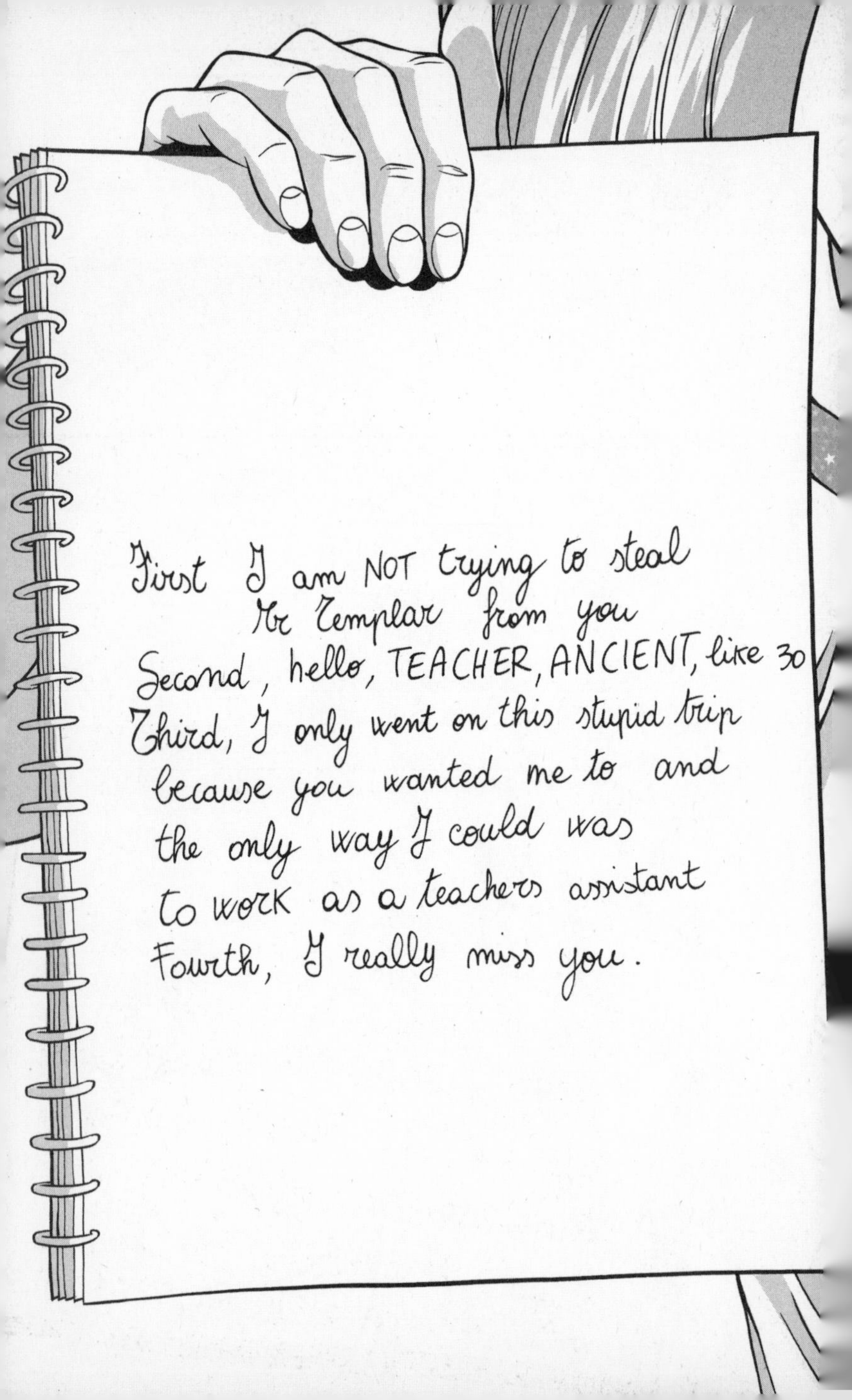
First I am NOT trying to steal
Mr Templar from you
Second, hello, TEACHER, ANCIENT, like 30
Third, I only went on this stupid trip
because you wanted me to and
the only way I could was
to WORK as a teachers assistant
Fourth, I really miss you.

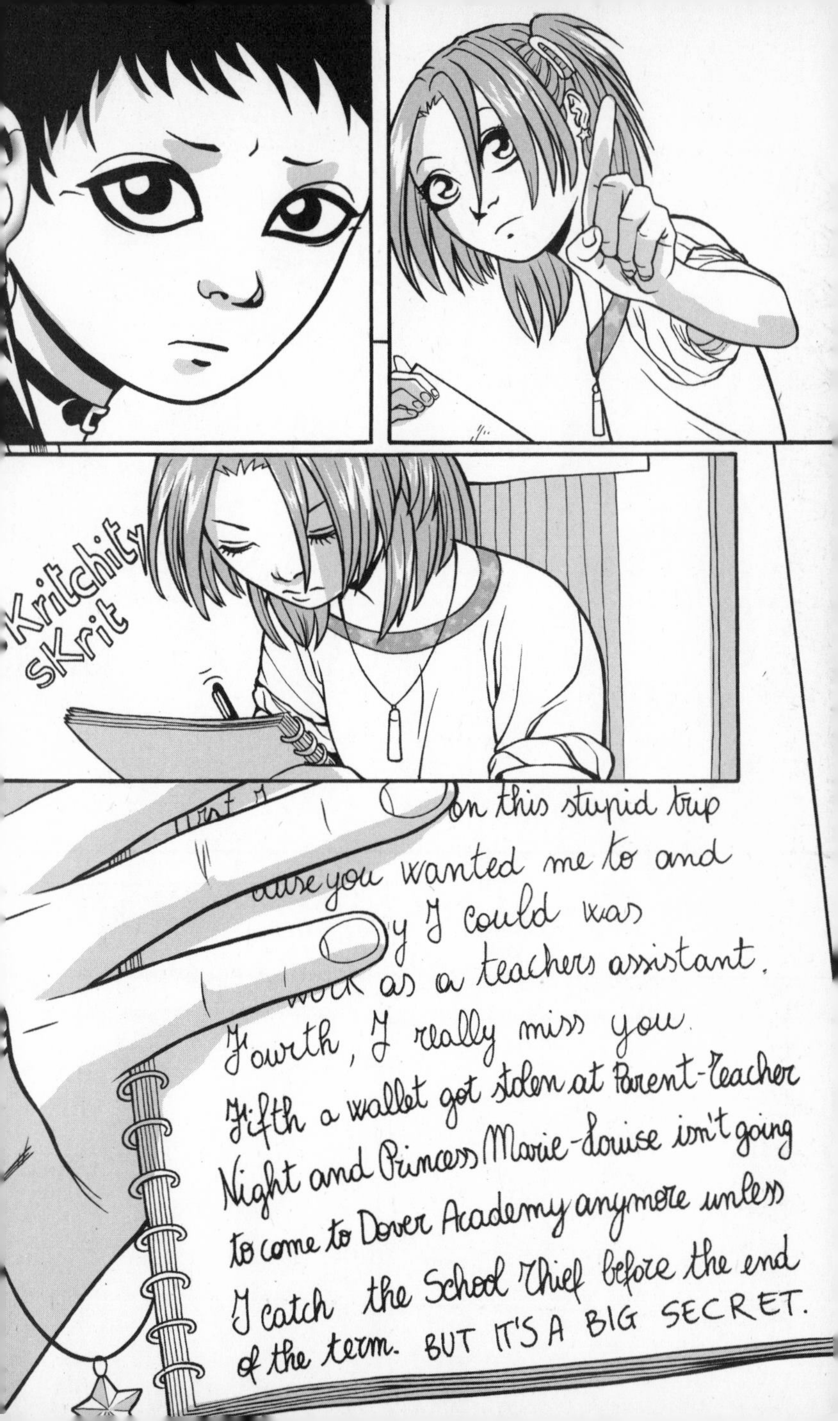
Kritchity sKrit
on this stupid trip
you wanted me to and
I could was
as a teachers assistant.
Fourth, I really miss you.
Fifth a wallet got stolen at Parent-Teacher
Night and Princess Marie-Louise isn't going
to come to Dover Academy anymore unless
I catch the School Thief before the end
of the term. BUT IT'S A BIG SECRET.

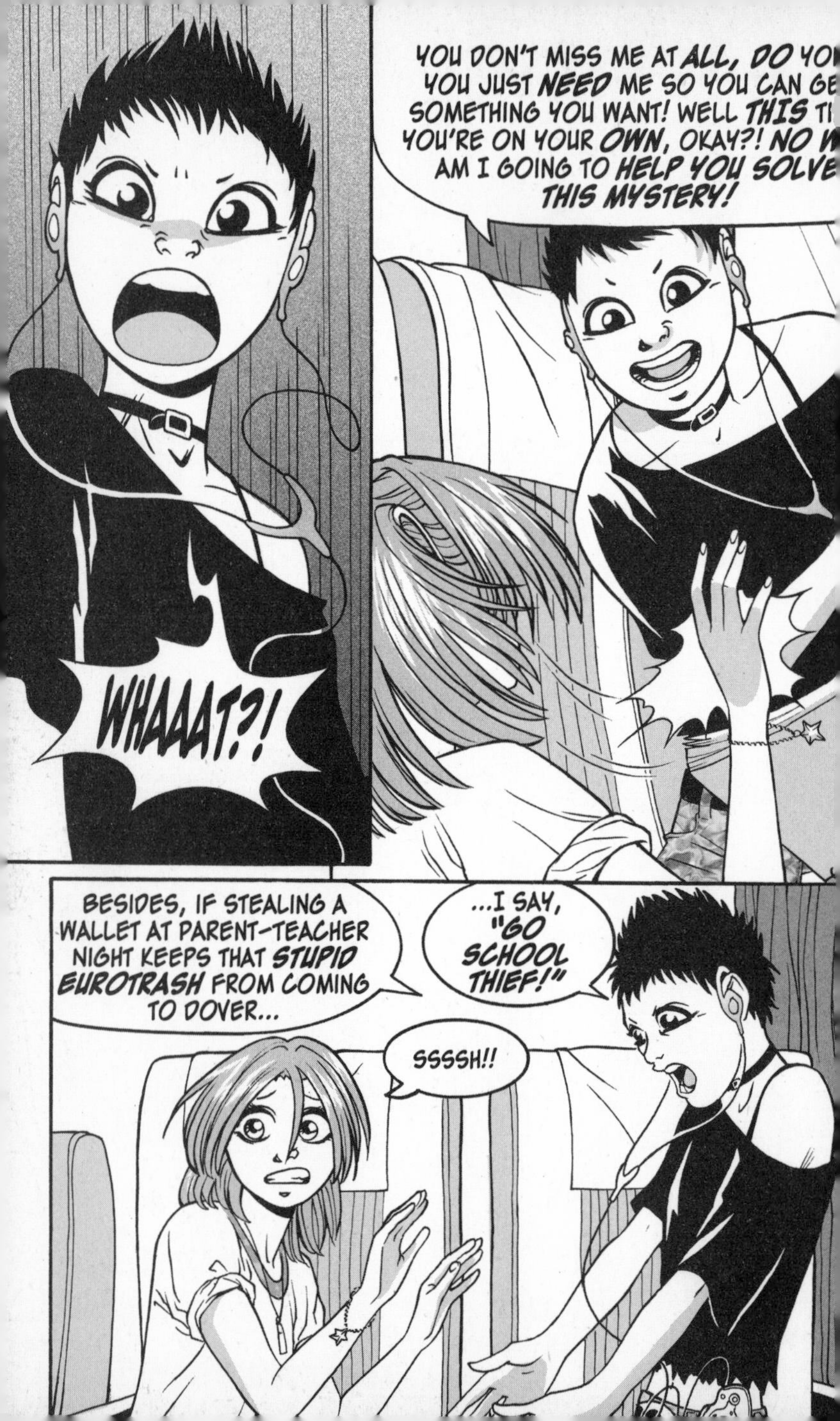
WHAAAT?!
YOU DON'T MISS ME AT ALL, DO YO YOU JUST NEED ME SO YOU CAN GE SOMETHING YOU WANT! WELL THIS TI YOU'RE ON YOUR OWN, OKAY?! NO W AM I GOING TO HELP YOU SOLVE THIS MYSTERY!
BESIDES, IF STEALING A WALLET AT PARENT-TEACHER NIGHT KEEPS THAT STUPID EUROTRASH FROM COMING TO DOVER...
...I SAY, "GO SCHOOL THIEF!"
SSSSH!!

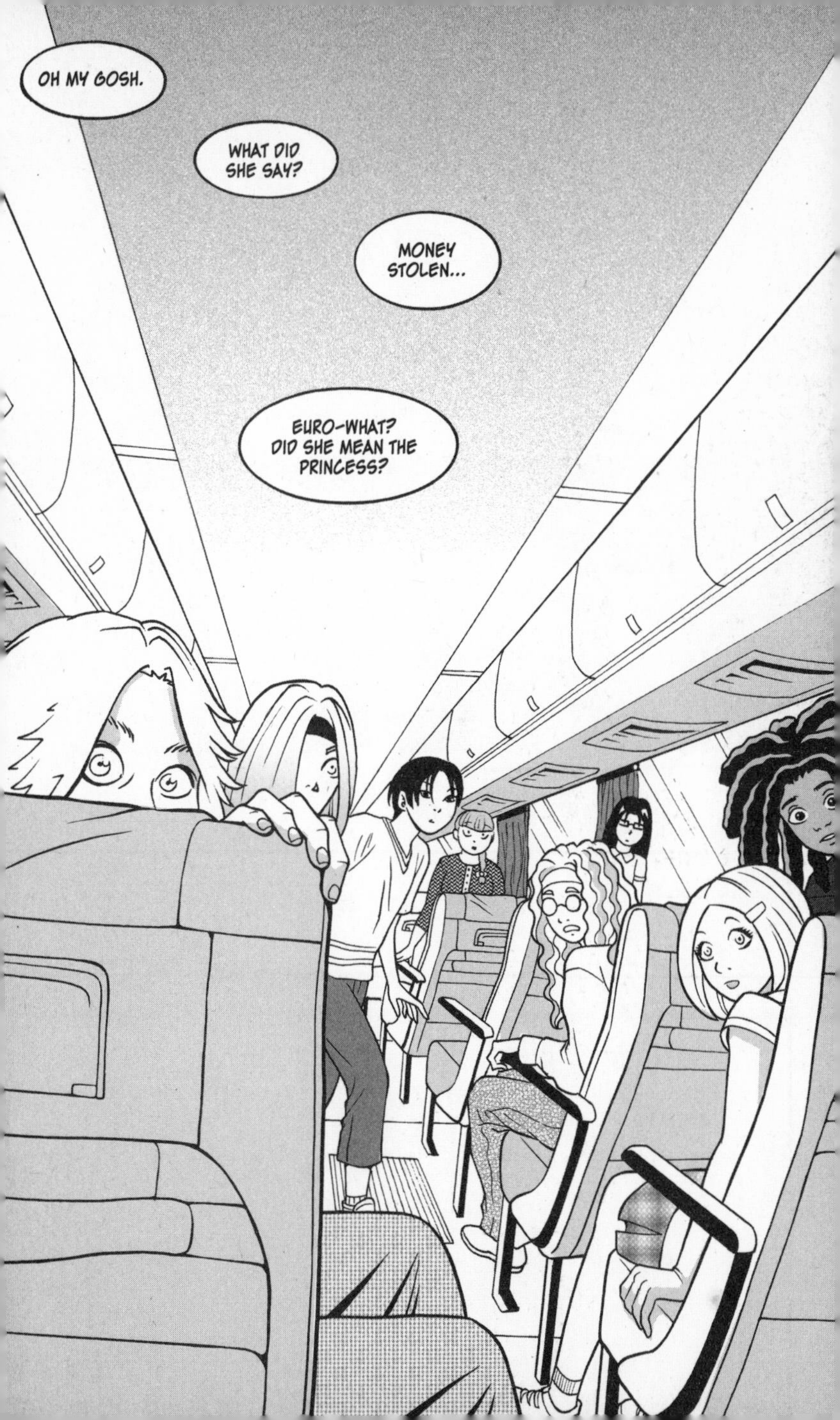
OH MY GOSH.
WHAT DID SHE SAY?
MONEY STOLEN...
EURO-WHAT? DID SHE MEAN THE PRINCESS?

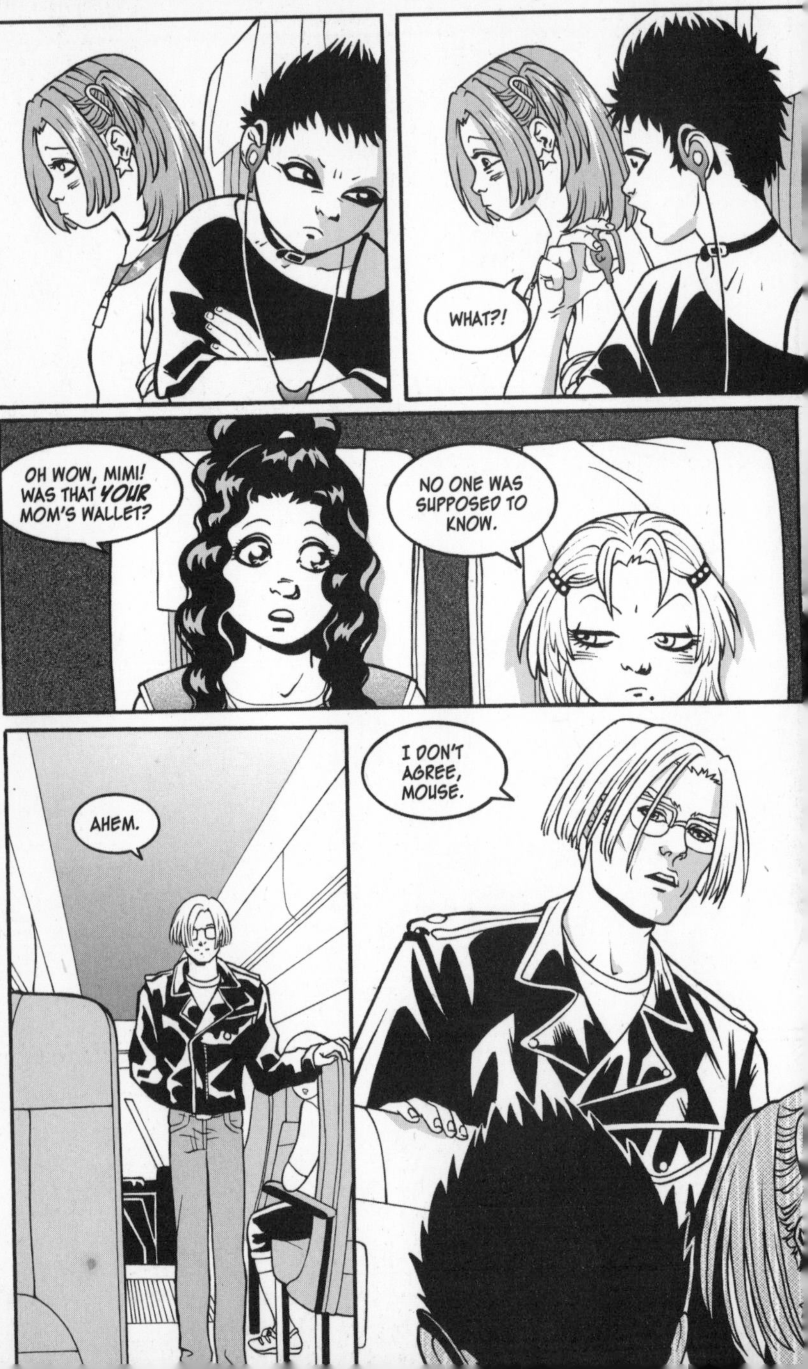
WHAT?!
OH WOW, MIMI! WAS THAT *YOUR* MOM'S WALLET?
NO ONE WAS SUPPOSED TO KNOW.
AHEM.
I DON'T AGREE, MOUSE.

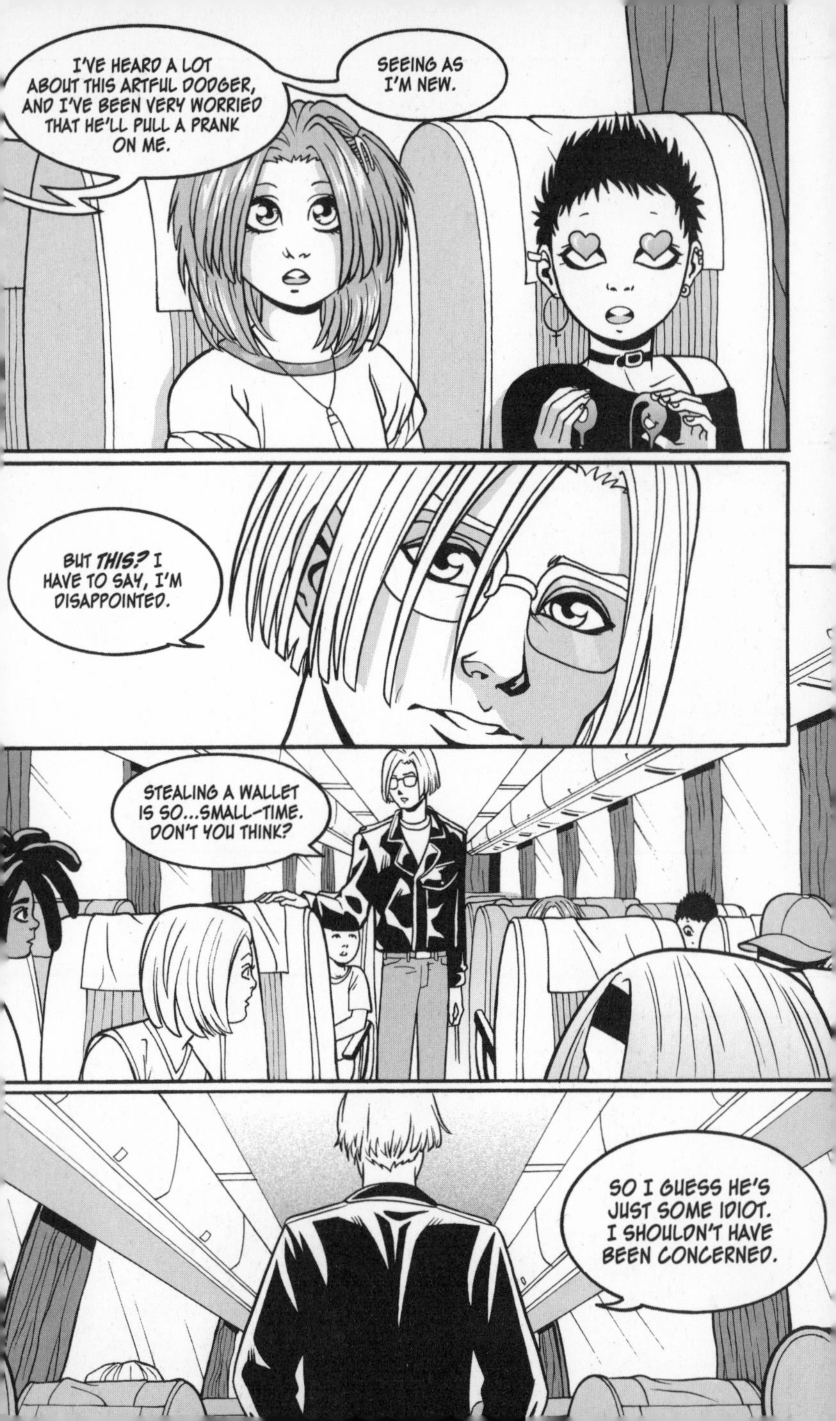
I'VE HEARD A LOT ABOUT THIS ARTFUL DODGER, AND I'VE BEEN VERY WORRIED THAT HE'LL PULL A PRANK ON ME.
SEEING AS I'M NEW.
BUT *THIS?* I HAVE TO SAY, I'M DISAPPOINTED.
STEALING A WALLET IS SO...SMALL-TIME. DON'T YOU THINK?
SO I GUESS HE'S JUST SOME IDIOT. I SHOULDN'T HAVE BEEN CONCERNED.

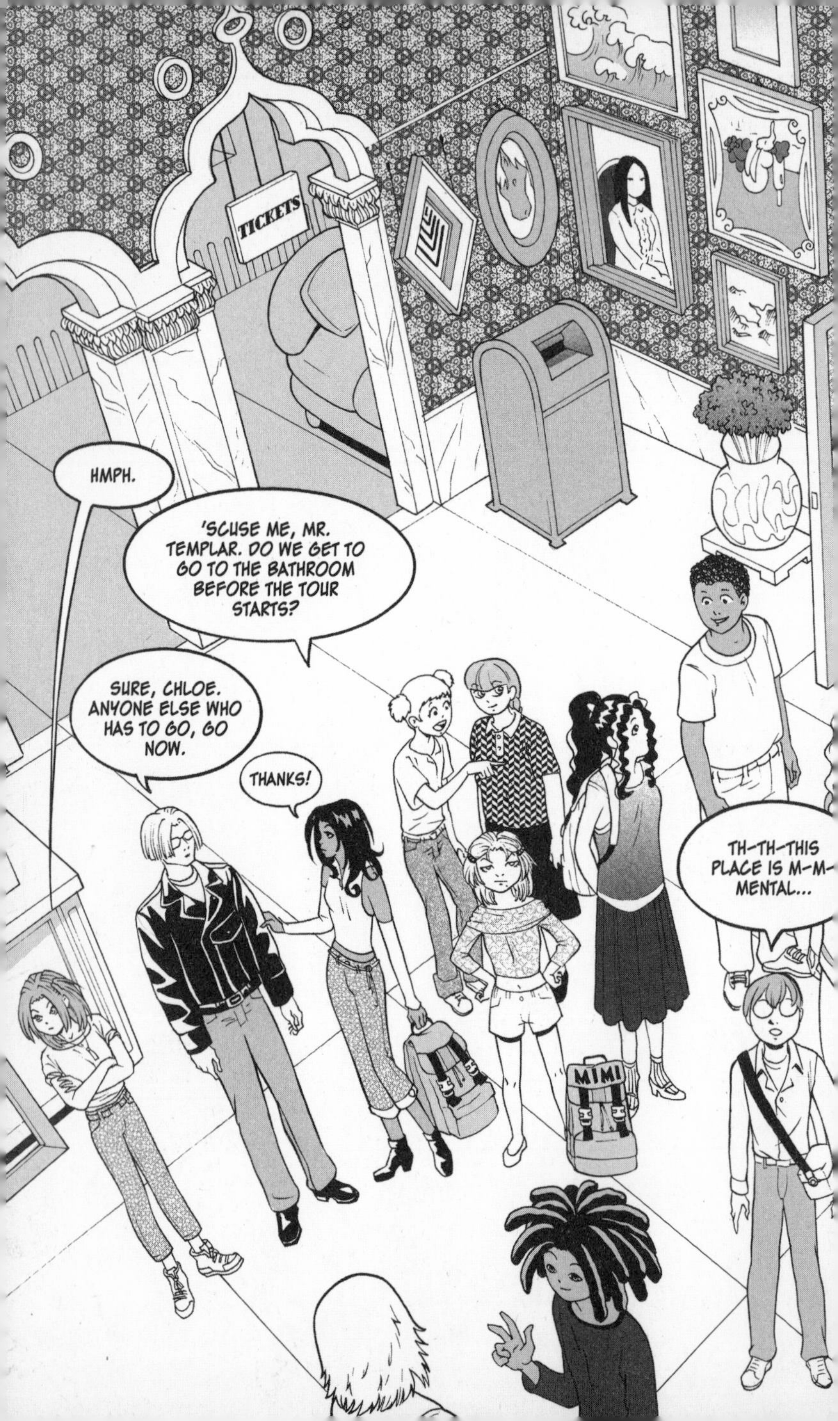
TICKETS
HMPH.
'SCUSE ME, MR. TEMPLAR. DO WE GET TO GO TO THE BATHROOM BEFORE THE TOUR STARTS?
SURE, CHLOE. ANYONE ELSE WHO HAS TO GO, GO NOW.
THANKS!
TH-TH-THIS PLACE IS M-M-MENTAL...
MIMI

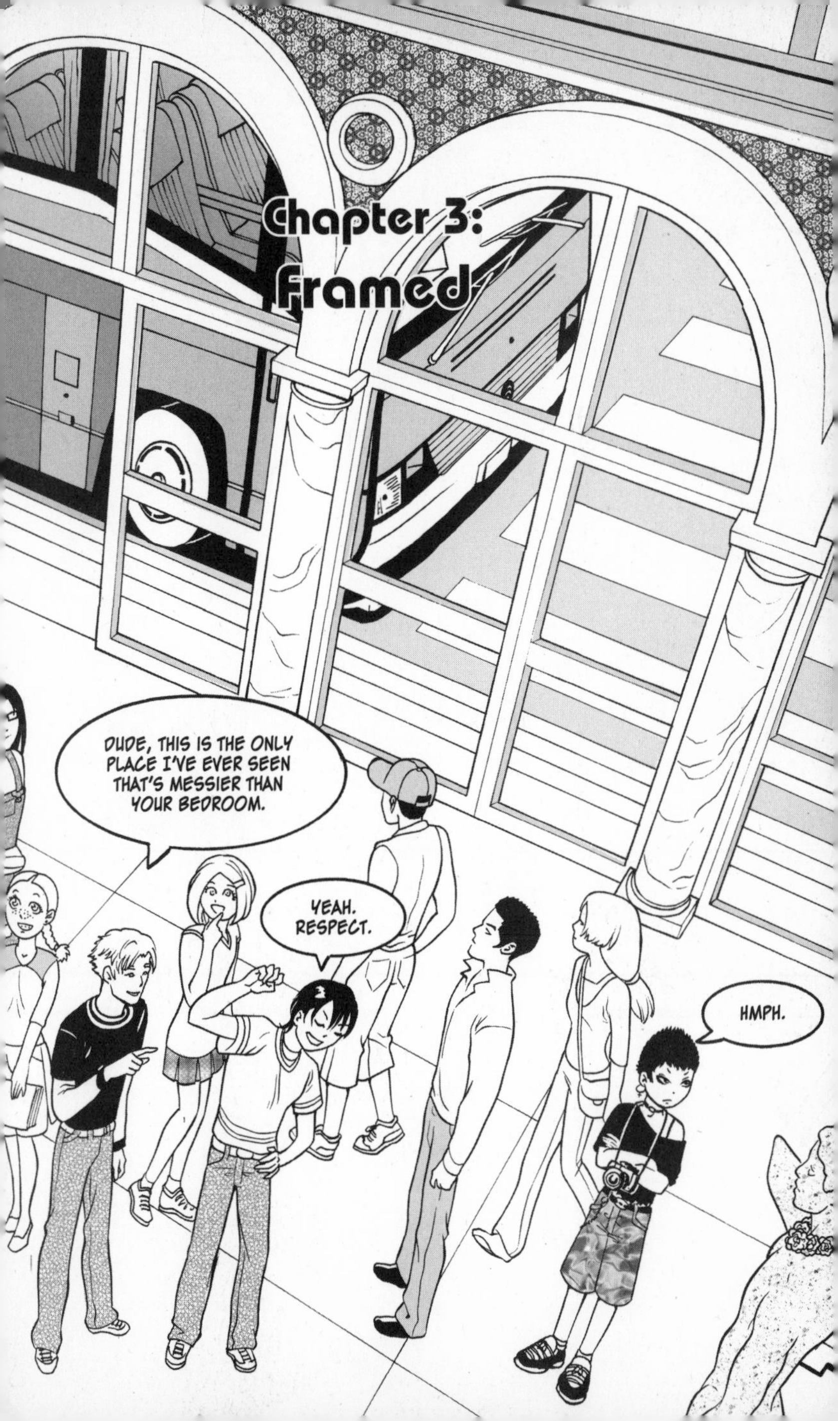
Chapter 3:
Framed
DUDE, THIS IS THE ONLY PLACE I'VE EVER SEEN THAT'S MESSIER THAN YOUR BEDROOM.
YEAH. RESPECT.
HMPH.

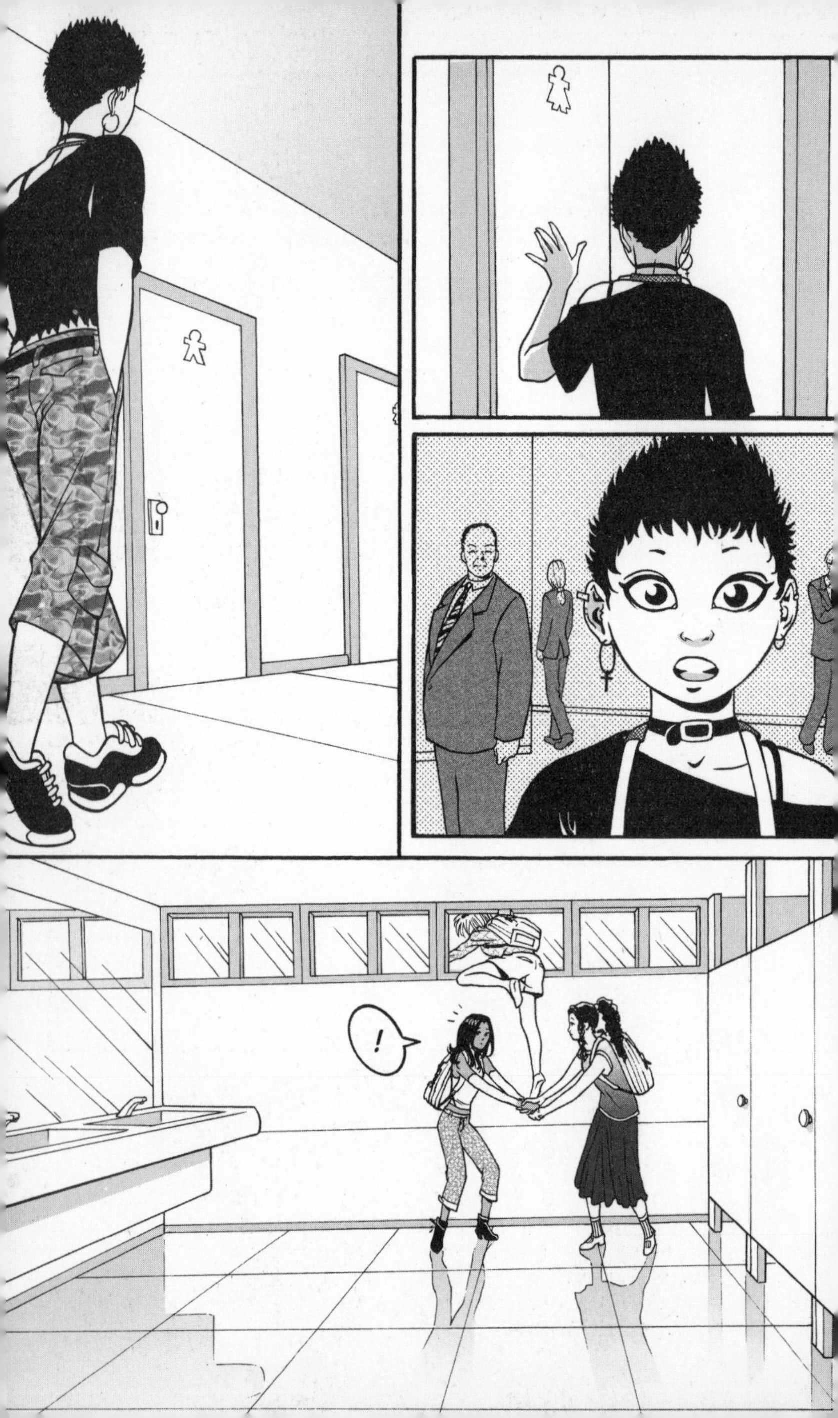
!

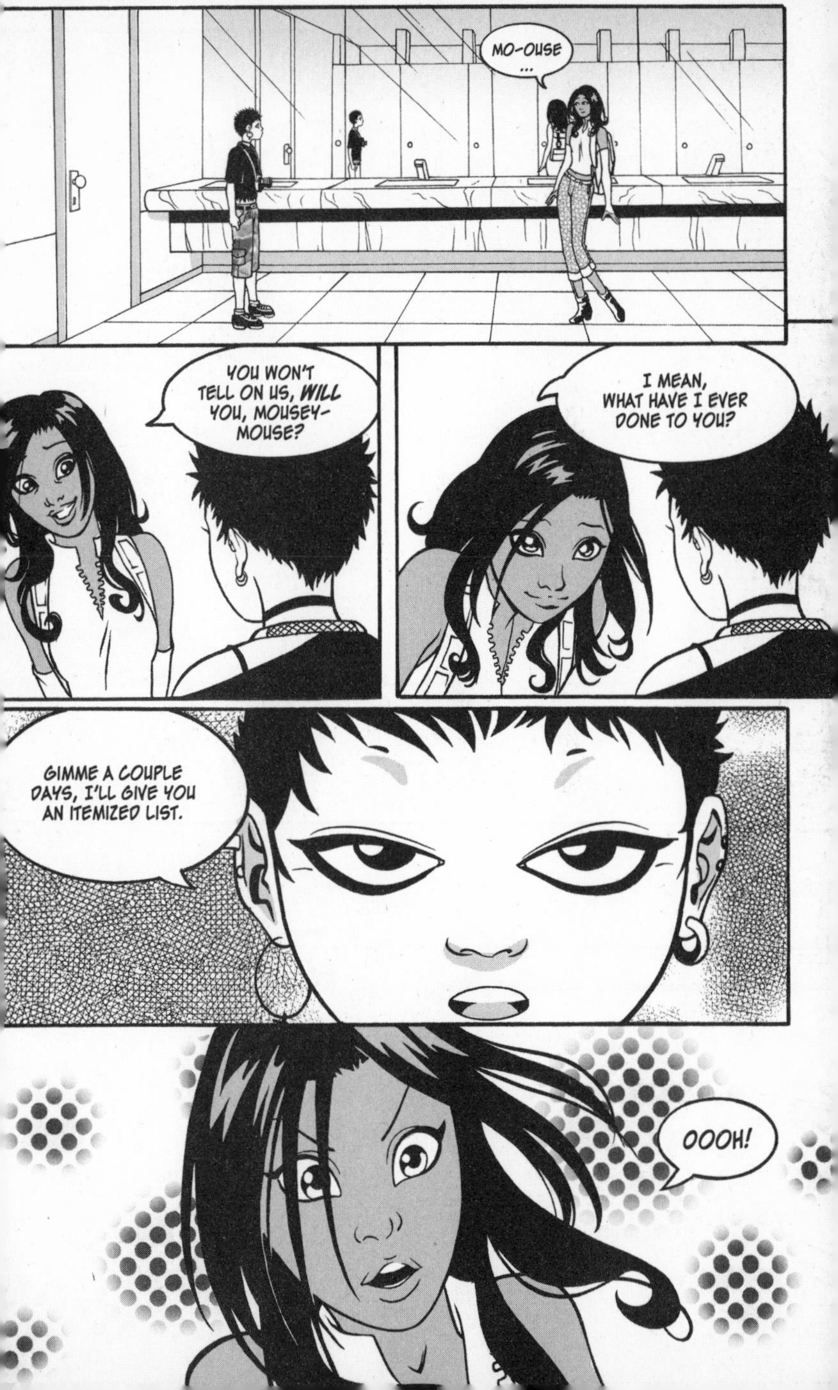
MO-OUSE ...
YOU WON'T TELL ON US, *WILL* YOU, MOUSEY-MOUSE?
I MEAN, WHAT HAVE I EVER DONE TO YOU?
GIMME A COUPLE DAYS, I'LL GIVE YOU AN ITEMIZED LIST.
OOOH!

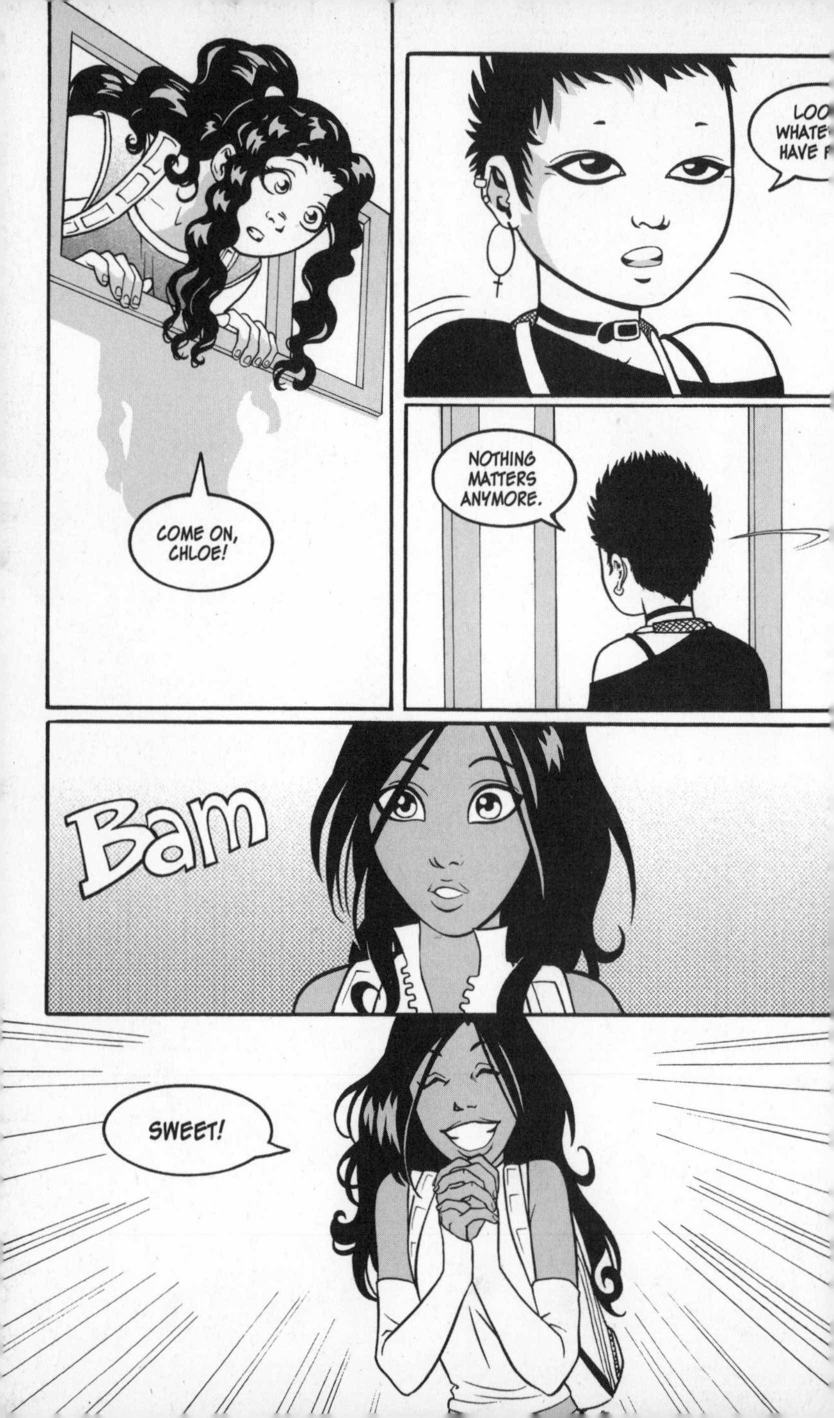
COME ON, CHLOE!
NOTHING MATTERS ANYMORE.
Bam
SWEET!

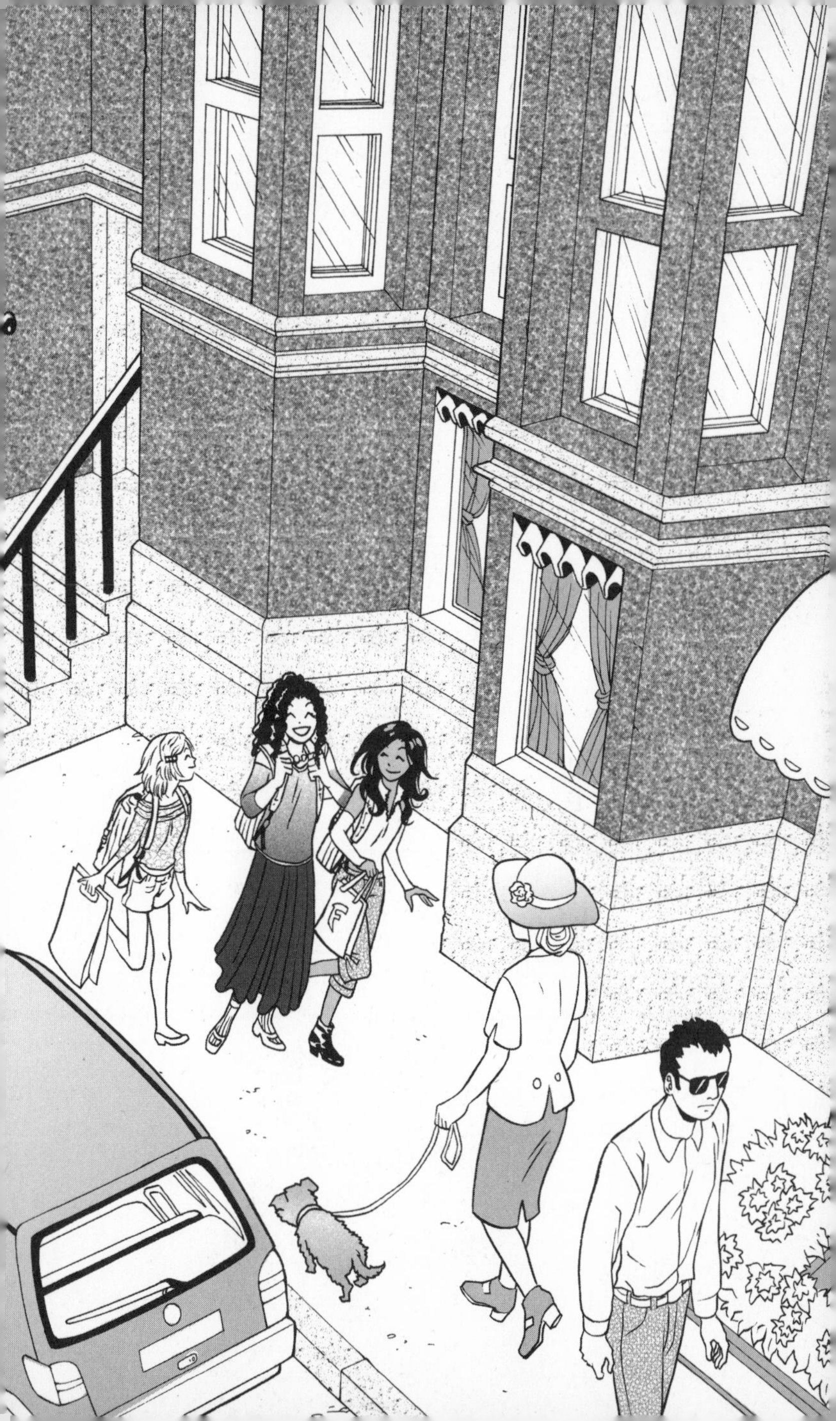

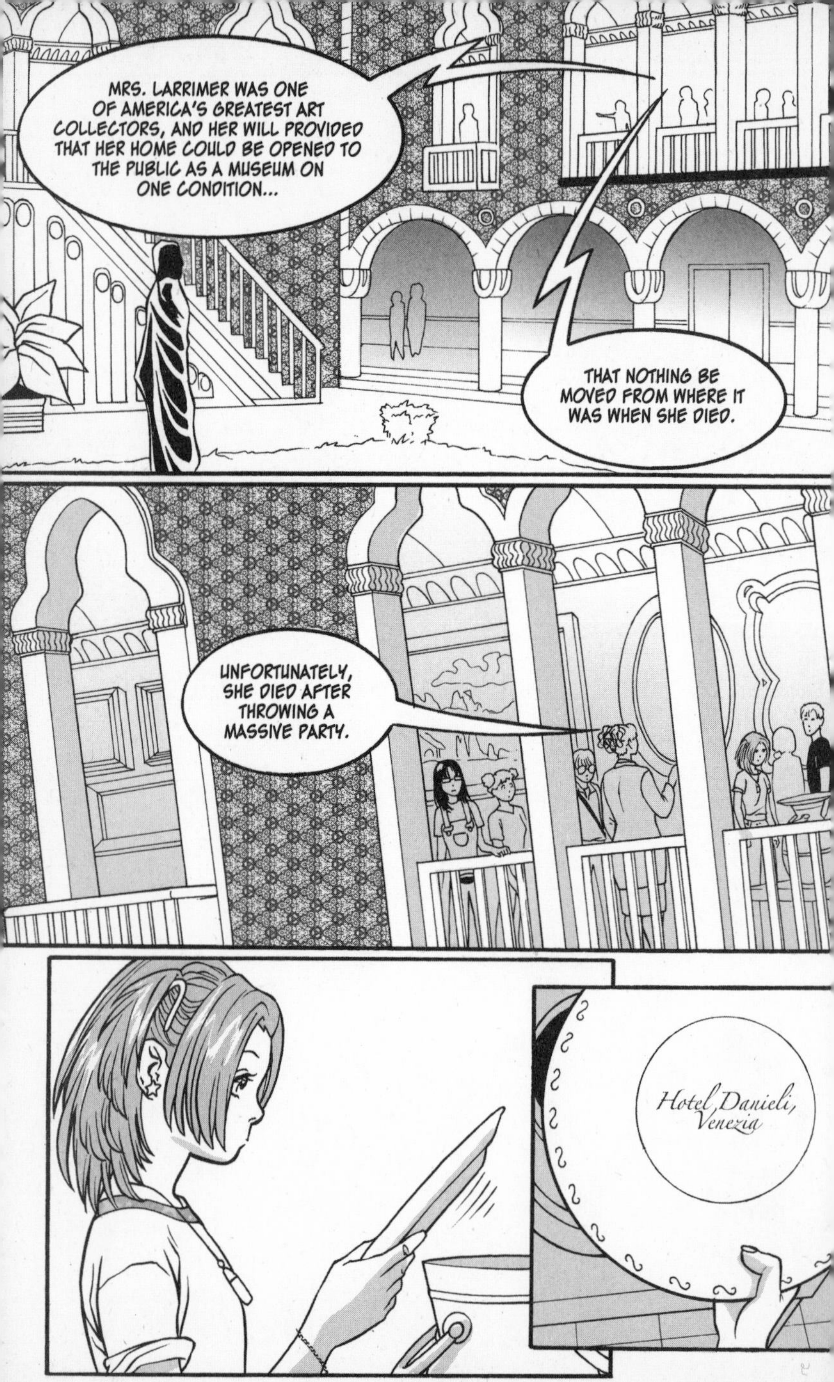
MRS. LARRIMER WAS ONE OF AMERICA'S GREATEST ART COLLECTORS, AND HER WILL PROVIDED THAT HER HOME COULD BE OPENED TO THE PUBLIC AS A MUSEUM ON ONE CONDITION...
THAT NOTHING BE MOVED FROM WHERE IT WAS WHEN SHE DIED.
UNFORTUNATELY, SHE DIED AFTER THROWING A MASSIVE PARTY.
Hotel Danieli, Venezia

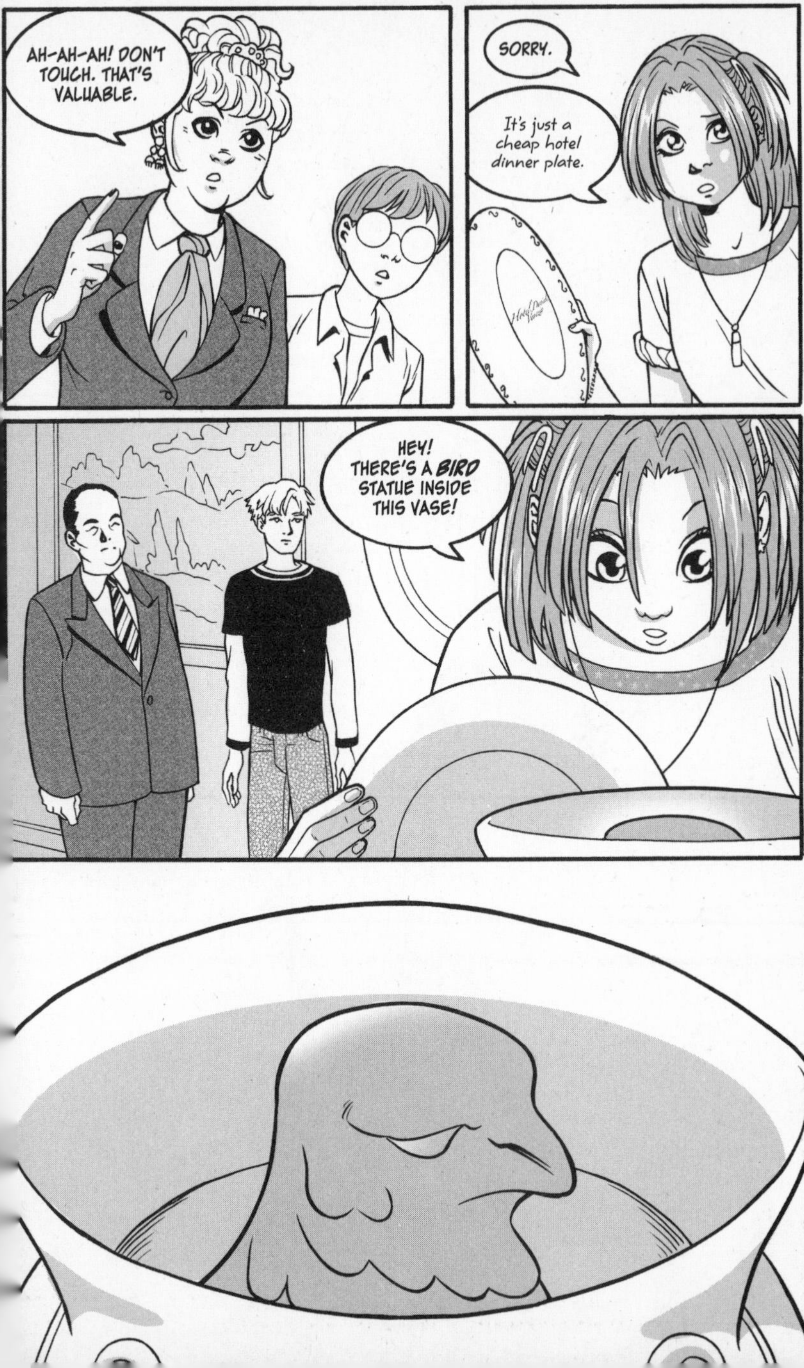
AH-AH-AH! DON'T TOUCH. THAT'S VALUABLE.
SORRY.
It's just a cheap hotel dinner plate.
HEY! THERE'S A BIRD STATUE INSIDE THIS VASE!

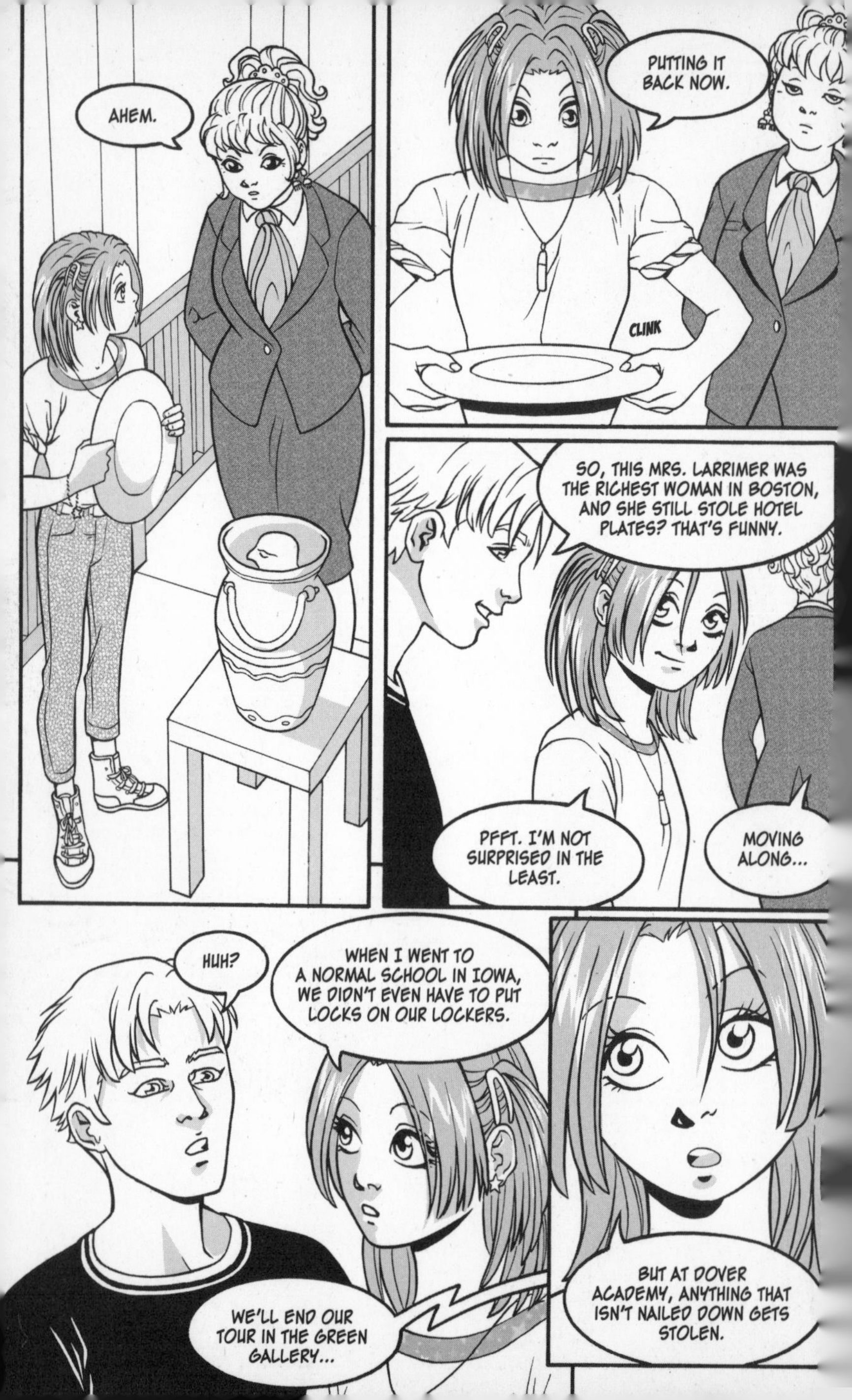
AHEM.
PUTTING IT BACK NOW.
CLINK
SO, THIS MRS. LARRIMER WAS THE RICHEST WOMAN IN BOSTON, AND SHE STILL STOLE HOTEL PLATES? THAT'S FUNNY.
PFFT. I'M NOT SURPRISED IN THE LEAST.
MOVING ALONG...
HUH?
WHEN I WENT TO A NORMAL SCHOOL IN IOWA, WE DIDN'T EVEN HAVE TO PUT LOCKS ON OUR LOCKERS.
WE'LL END OUR TOUR IN THE GREEN GALLERY...
BUT AT DOVER ACADEMY, ANYTHING THAT ISN'T NAILED DOWN GETS STOLEN.

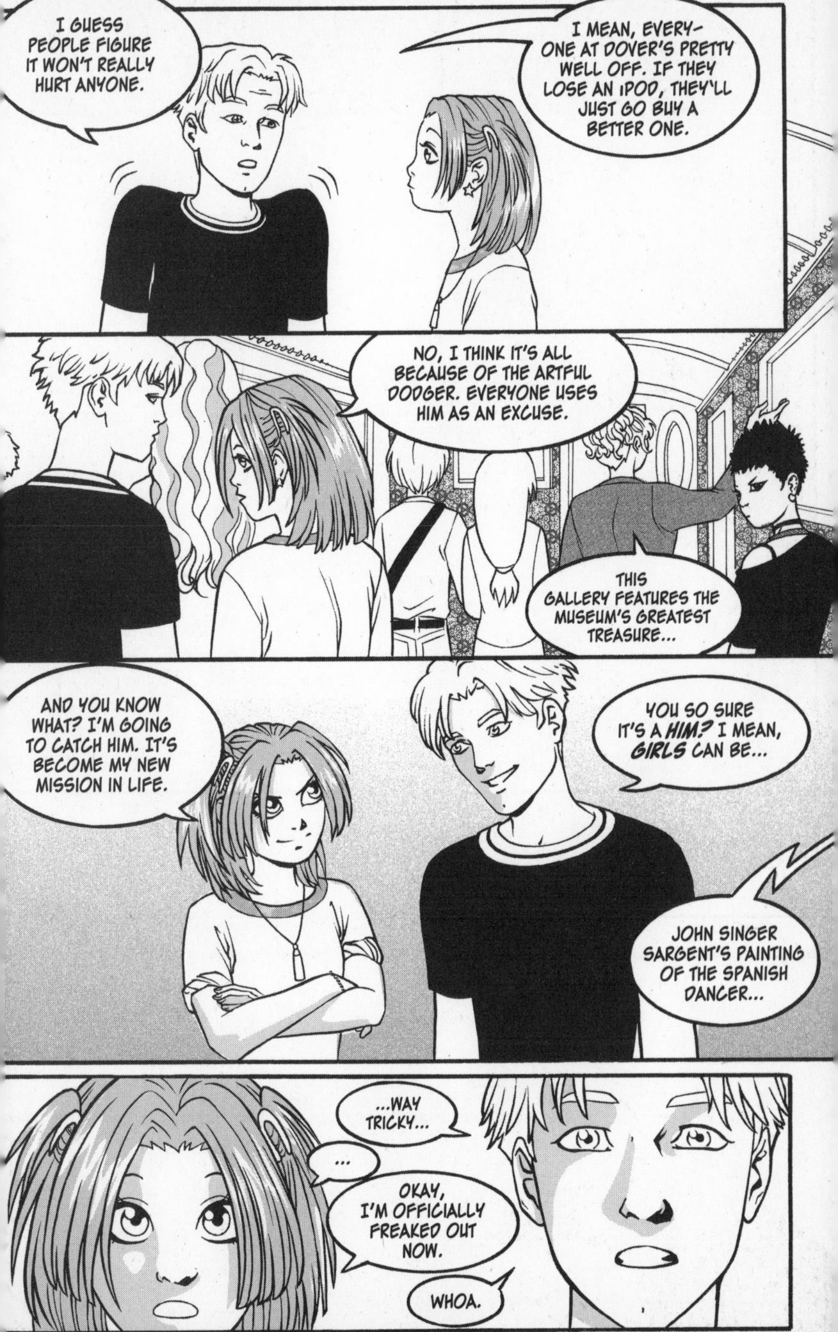
I GUESS PEOPLE FIGURE IT WON'T REALLY HURT ANYONE.
I MEAN, EVERY-ONE AT DOVER'S PRETTY WELL OFF. IF THEY LOSE AN IPOD, THEY'LL JUST GO BUY A BETTER ONE.
NO, I THINK IT'S ALL BECAUSE OF THE ARTFUL DODGER. EVERYONE USES HIM AS AN EXCUSE.
THIS GALLERY FEATURES THE MUSEUM'S GREATEST TREASURE...
AND YOU KNOW WHAT? I'M GOING TO CATCH HIM. IT'S BECOME MY NEW MISSION IN LIFE.
YOU SO SURE IT'S A ***HIM?*** I MEAN, ***GIRLS*** CAN BE...
JOHN SINGER SARGENT'S PAINTING OF THE SPANISH DANCER...
...WAY TRICKY...
...
OKAY, I'M OFFICIALLY FREAKED OUT NOW.
WHOA.

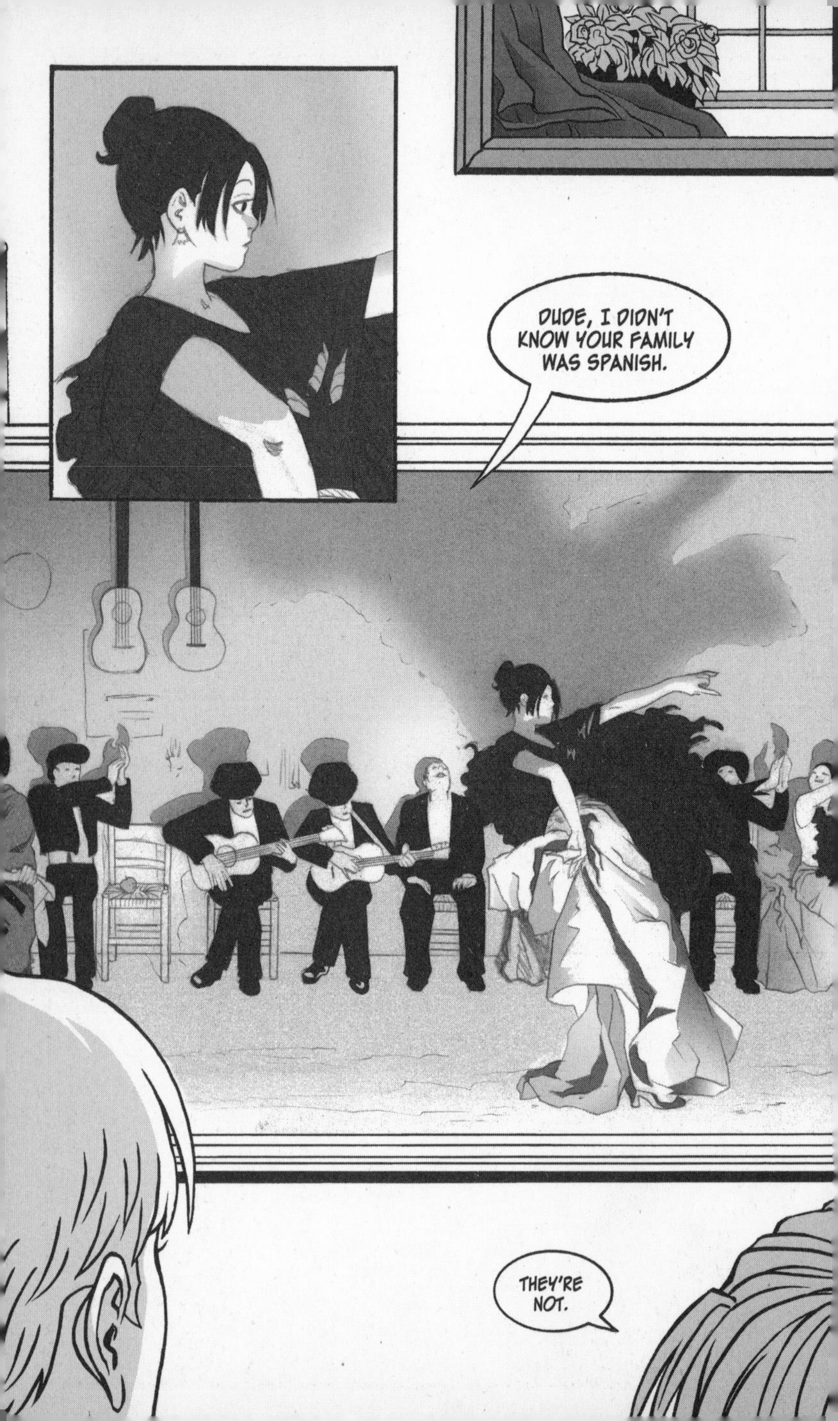
DUDE, I DIDN'T KNOW YOUR FAMILY WAS SPANISH.
THEY'RE NOT.

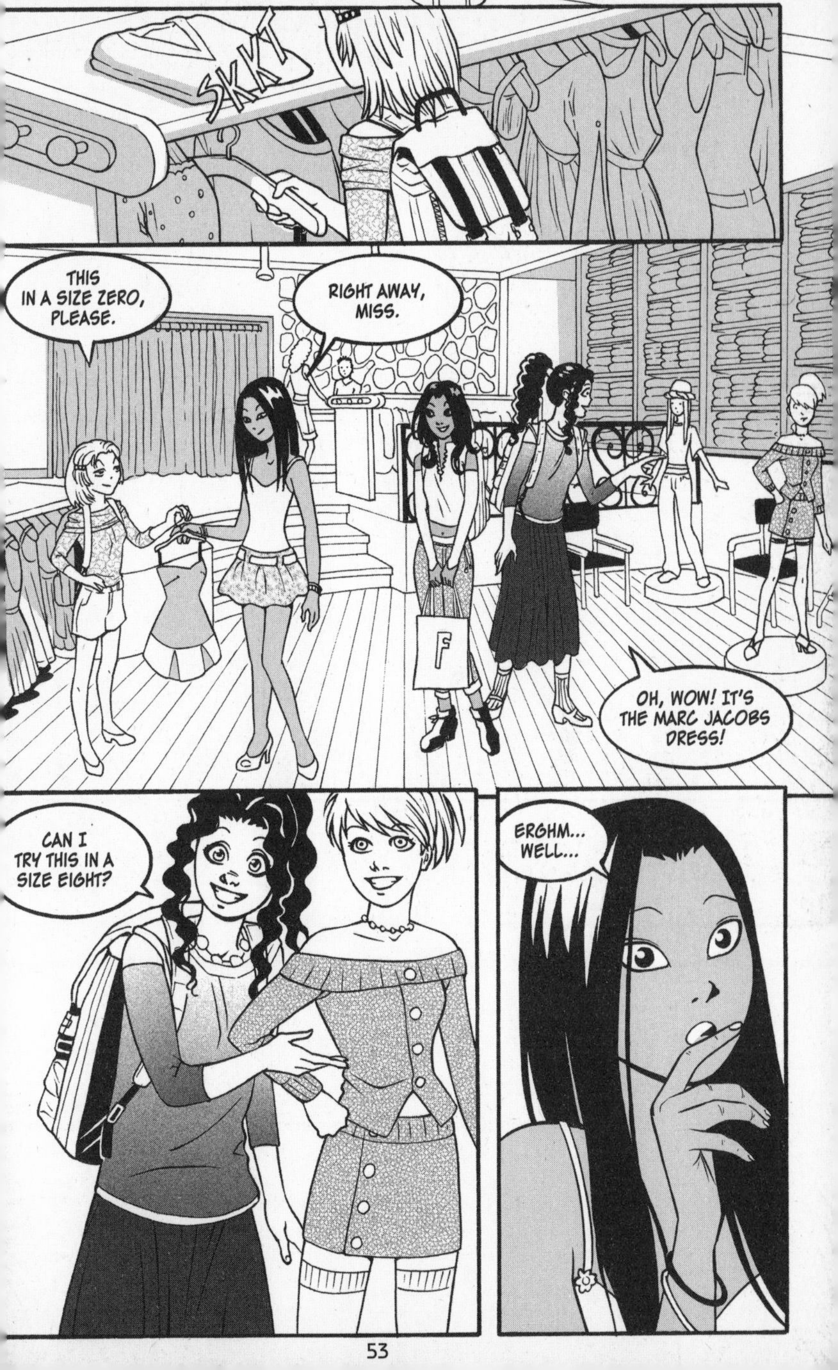
SKKT
THIS IN A SIZE ZERO, PLEASE.
RIGHT AWAY, MISS.
F
OH, WOW! IT'S THE MARC JACOBS DRESS!
CAN I TRY THIS IN A SIZE EIGHT?
ERGHM... WELL...

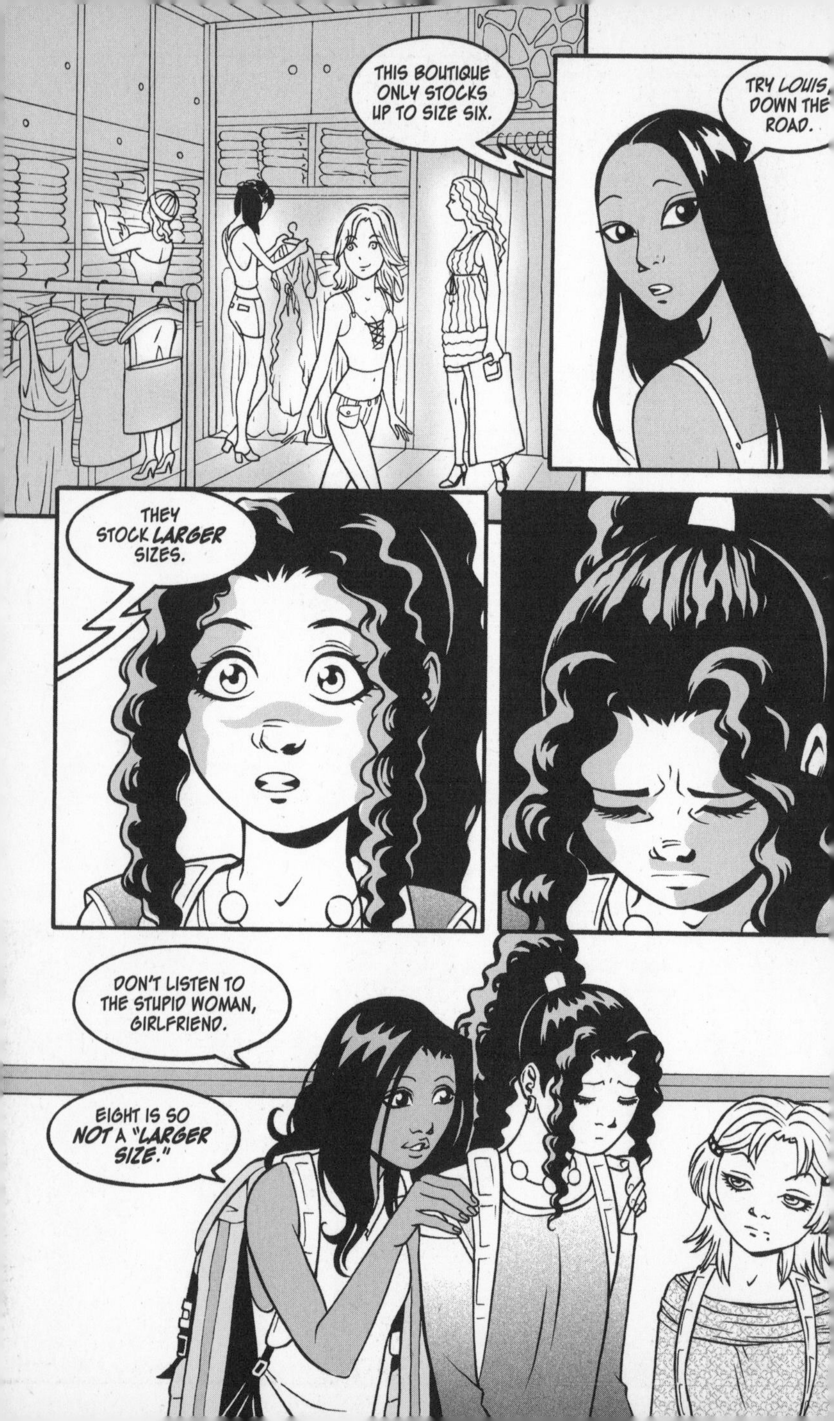
THIS BOUTIQUE ONLY STOCKS UP TO SIZE SIX.
TRY LOUIS, DOWN THE ROAD.
THEY STOCK LARGER SIZES.
DON'T LISTEN TO THE STUPID WOMAN, GIRLFRIEND.
EIGHT IS SO NOT A "LARGER SIZE."

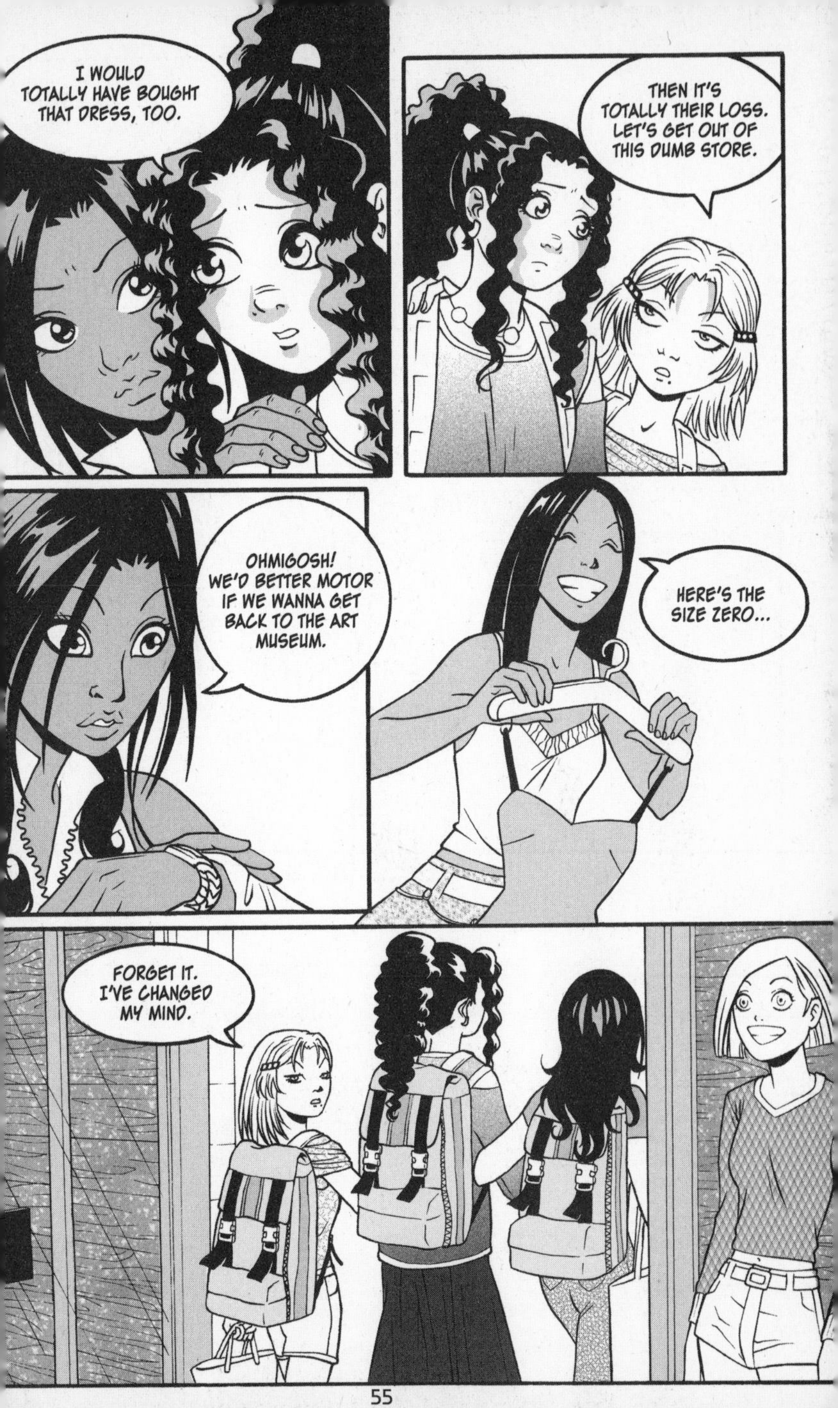
I WOULD TOTALLY HAVE BOUGHT THAT DRESS, TOO.
THEN IT'S TOTALLY THEIR LOSS. LET'S GET OUT OF THIS DUMB STORE.
OHMIGOSH! WE'D BETTER MOTOR IF WE WANNA GET BACK TO THE ART MUSEUM.
HERE'S THE SIZE ZERO...
FORGET IT. I'VE CHANGED MY MIND.

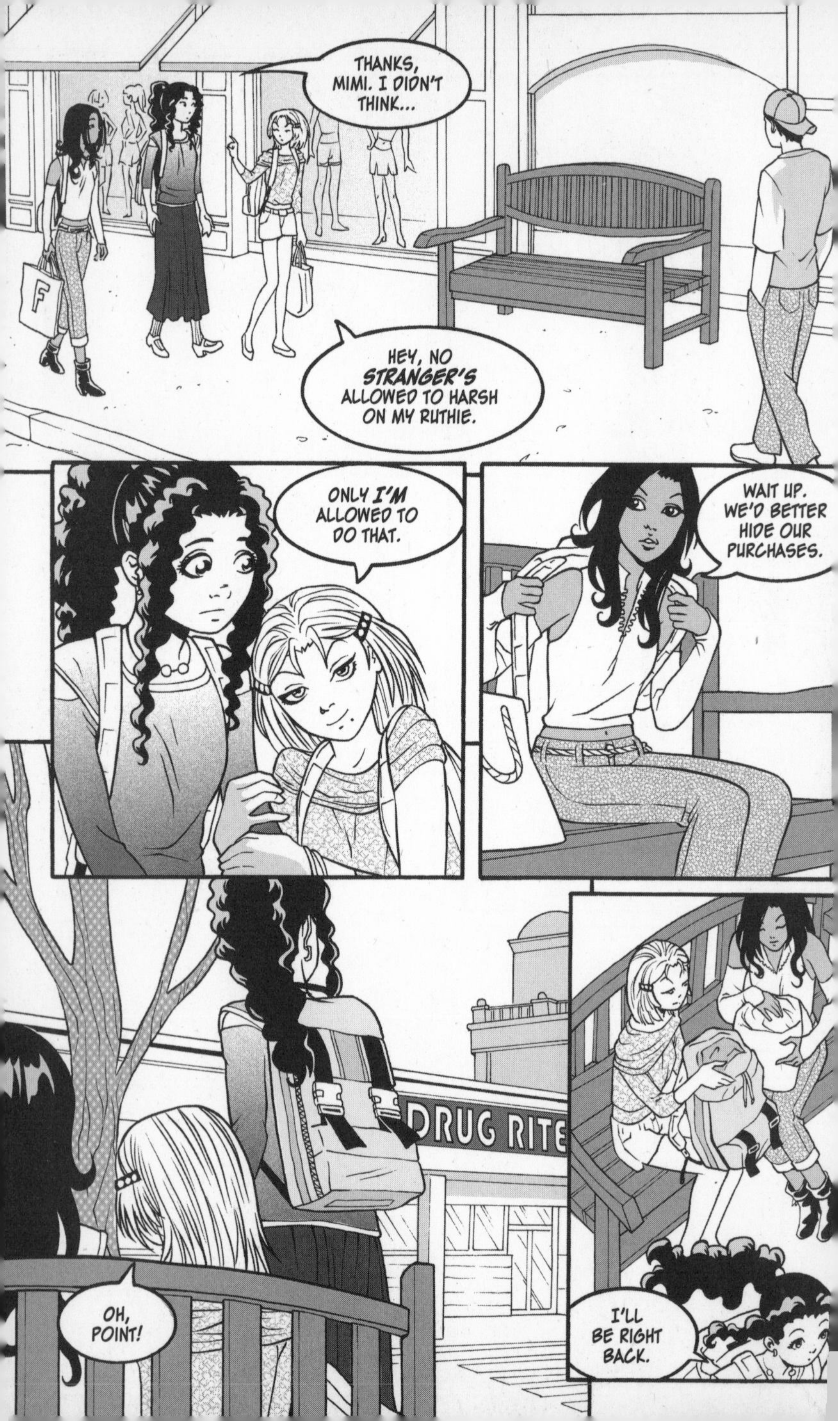
THANKS, MIMI. I DIDN'T THINK...
HEY, NO STRANGER'S ALLOWED TO HARSH ON MY RUTHIE.
ONLY I'M ALLOWED TO DO THAT.
WAIT UP. WE'D BETTER HIDE OUR PURCHASES.
DRUG RITE
OH, POINT!
I'LL BE RIGHT BACK.

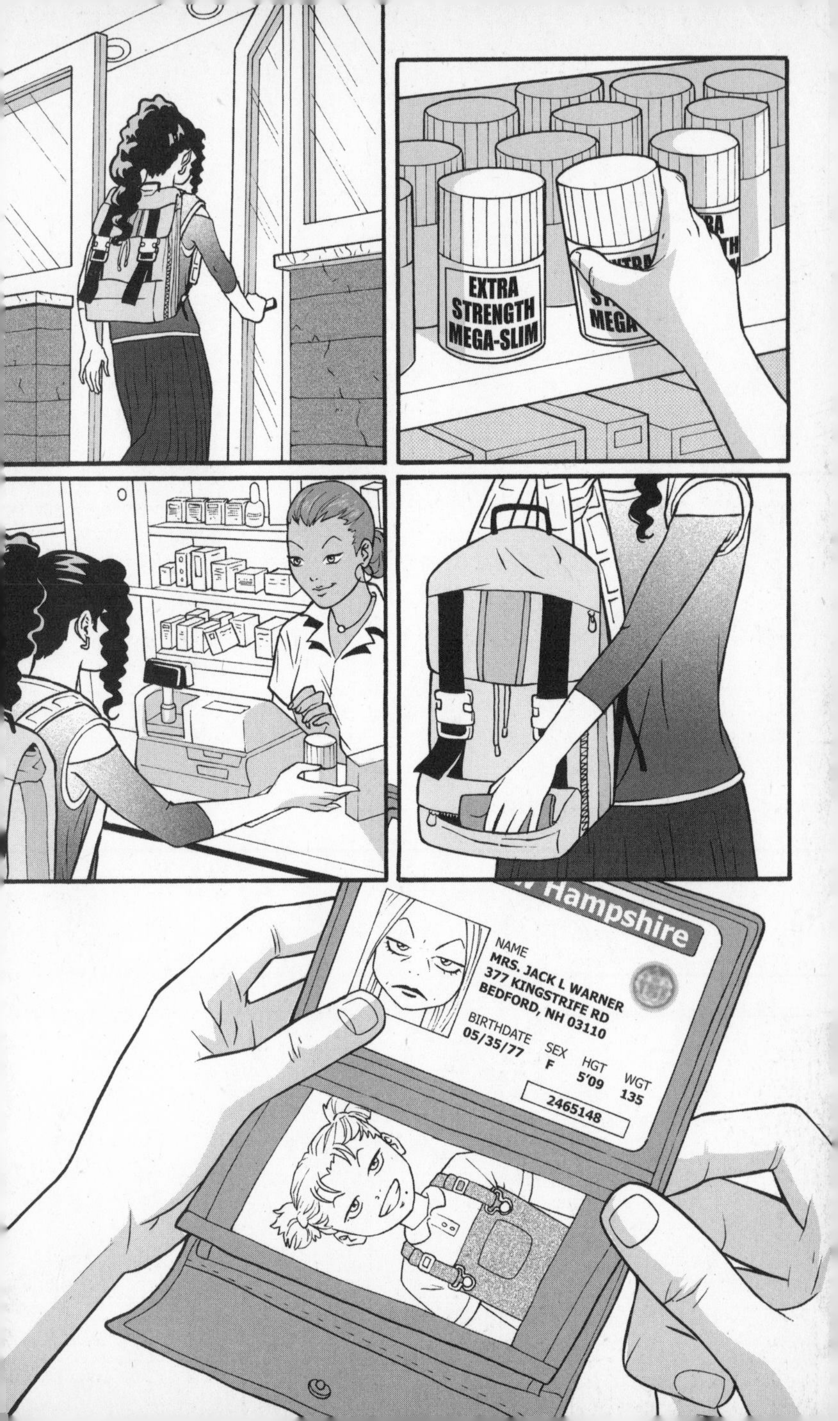
EXTRA
STRENGTH
MEGA-SLIM
Hampshire
NAME
MRS. JACK L WARNER
377 KINGSTRIFE RD
BEDFORD, NH 03110
BIRTHDATE
05/35/77
SEX
F
HGT
5'09
WGT
135
2465148

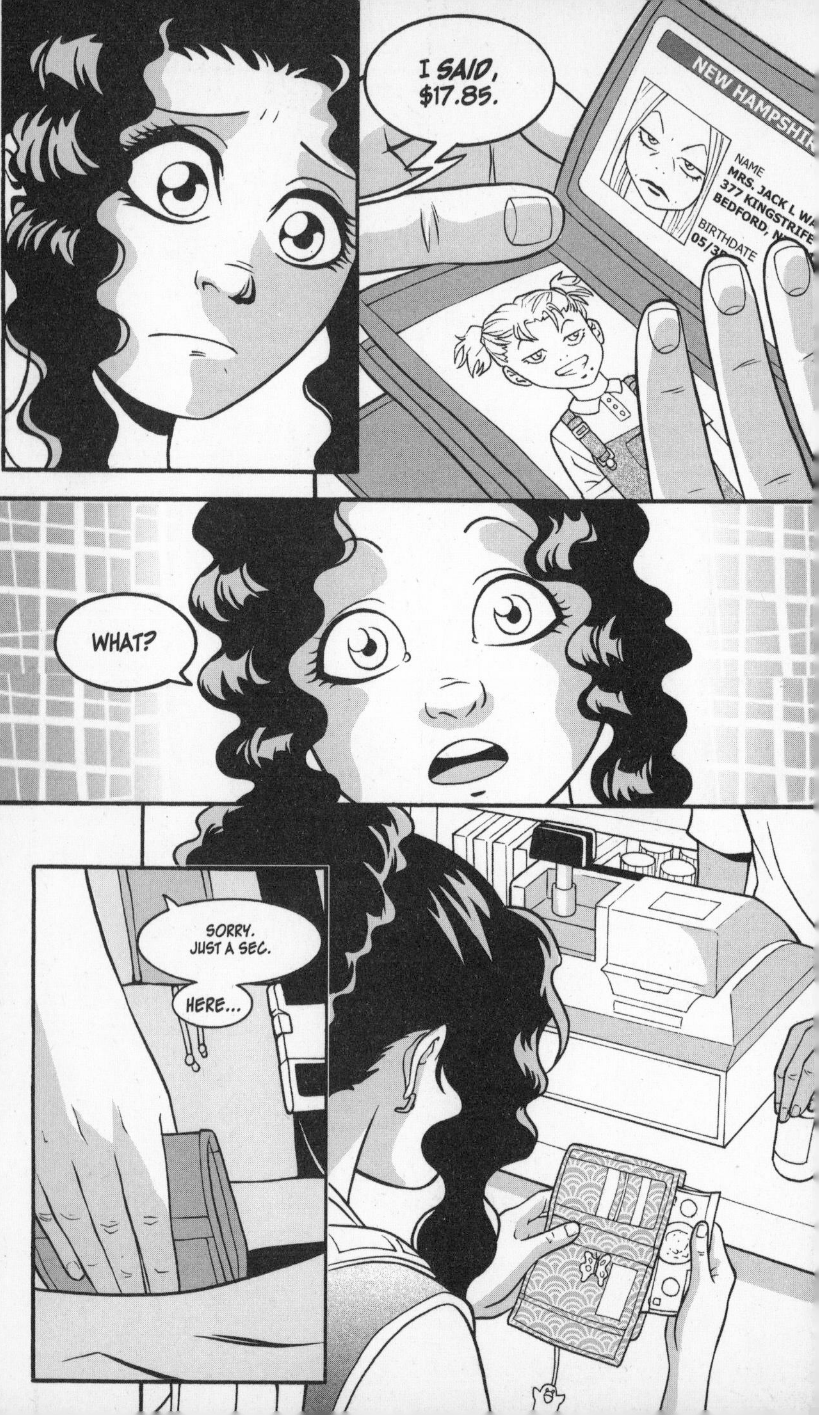
I SAID, $17.85.
NEW HAMPSHI
NAME
MRS. JACK L WA
377 KINGSTRIFE
BEDFORD, N
BIRTHDATE
05/3
WHAT?
SORRY. JUST A SEC.
HERE...

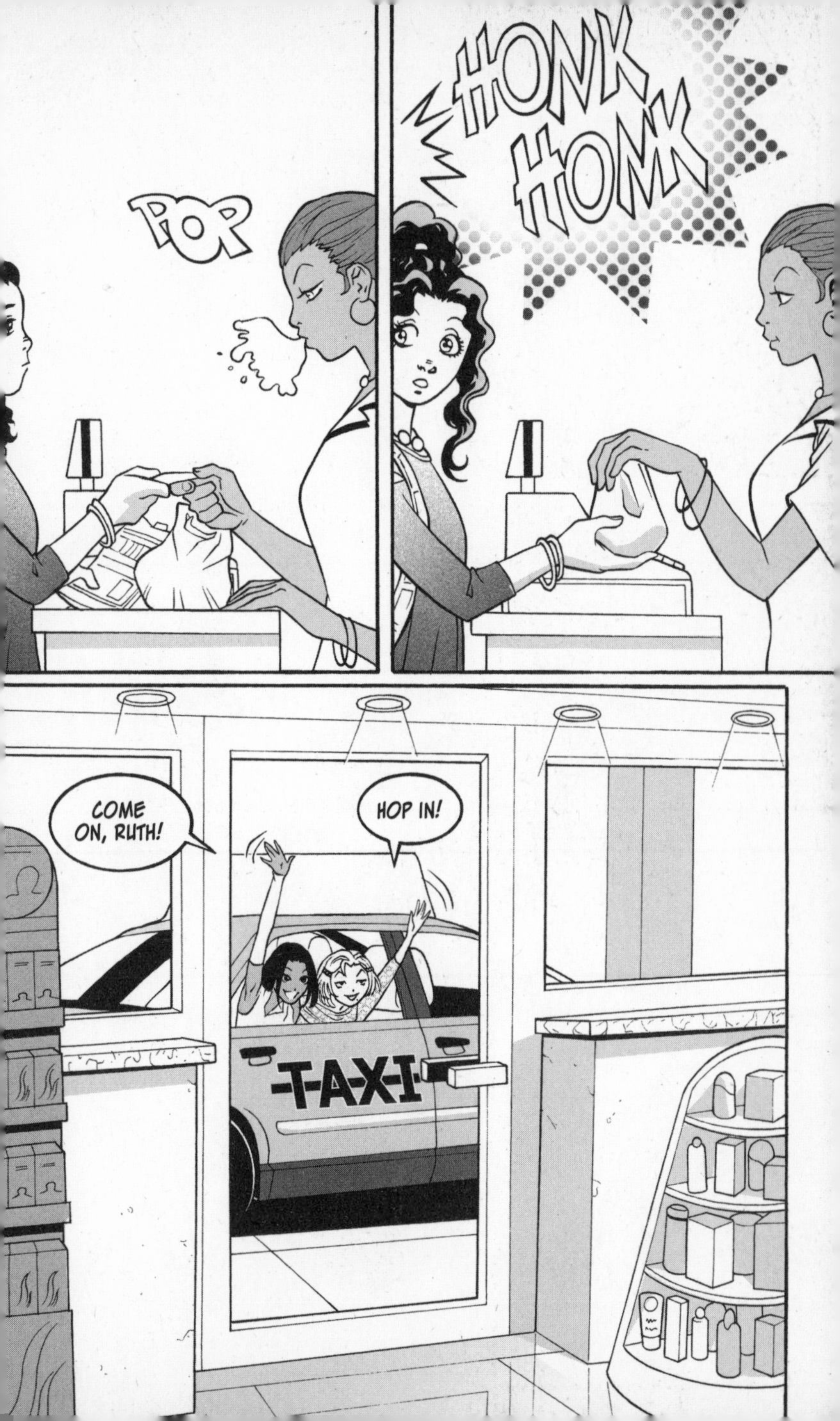
POP
HONK HONK
COME ON, RUTH!
HOP IN!

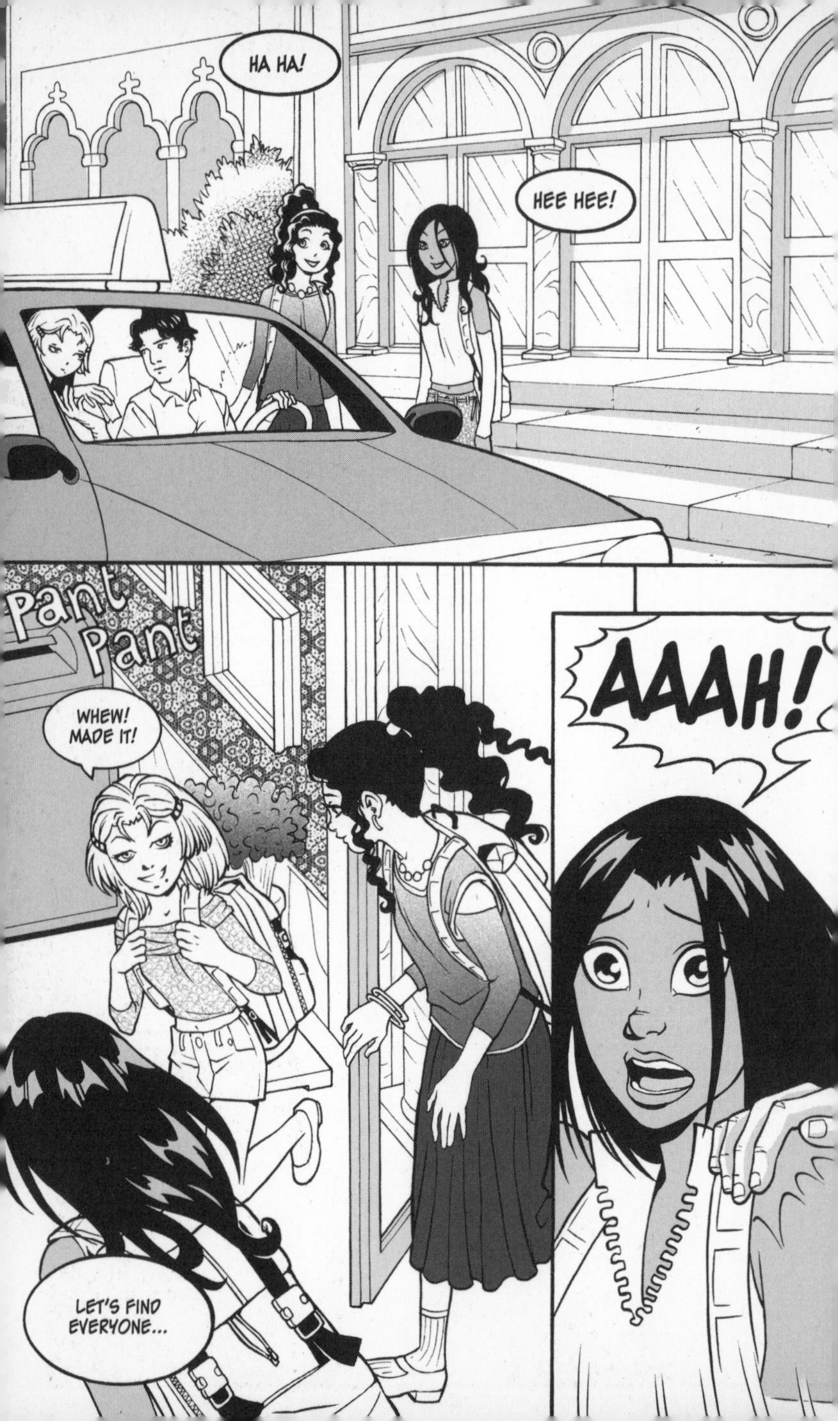
HA HA!
HEE HEE!
Pant Pant
WHEW! MADE IT!
LET'S FIND EVERYONE...
AAAH!

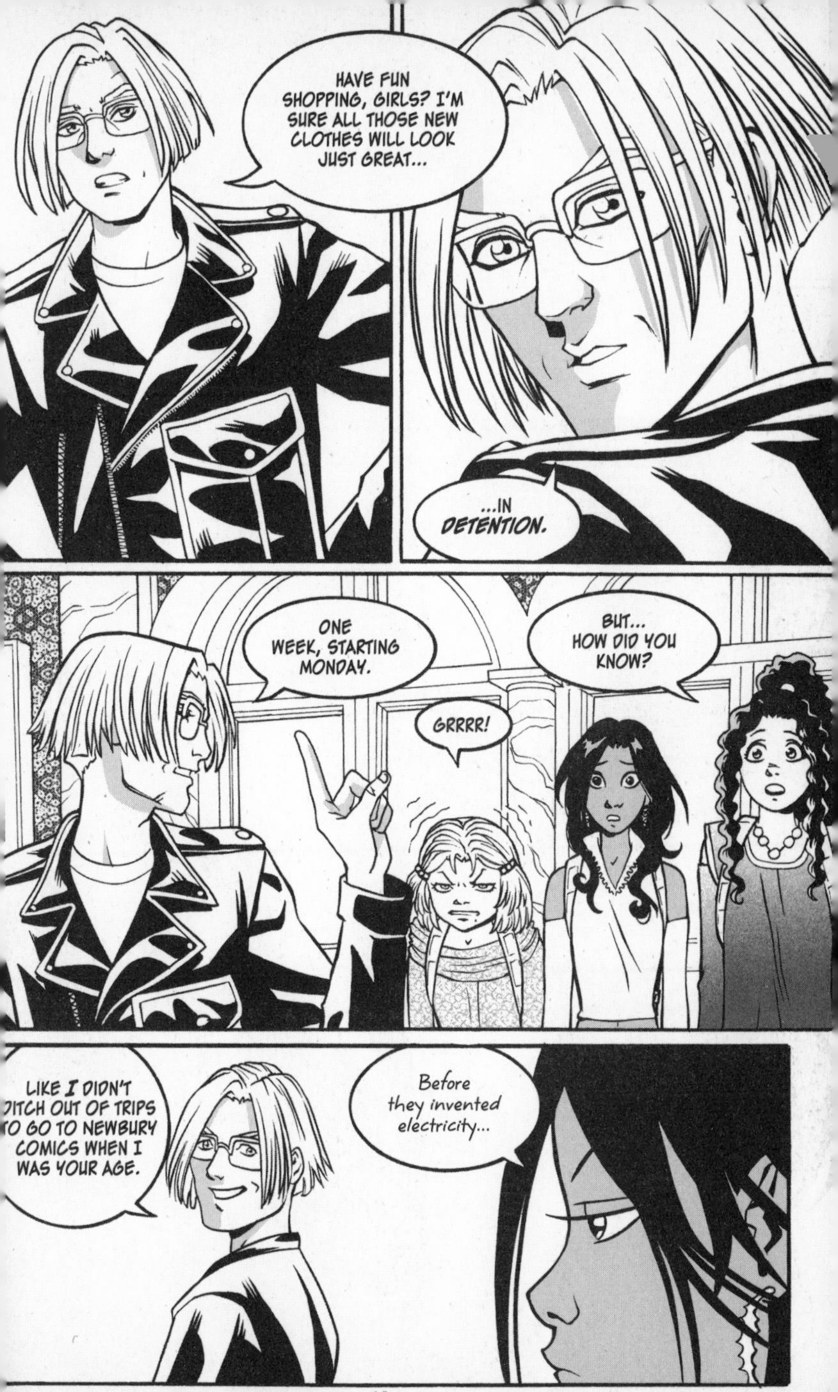
HAVE FUN SHOPPING, GIRLS? I'M SURE ALL THOSE NEW CLOTHES WILL LOOK JUST GREAT...
...IN *DETENTION.*
ONE WEEK, STARTING MONDAY.
BUT... HOW DID YOU KNOW?
GRRRR!
LIKE *I* DIDN'T DITCH OUT OF TRIPS TO GO TO NEWBURY COMICS WHEN I WAS YOUR AGE.
Before they invented electricity...

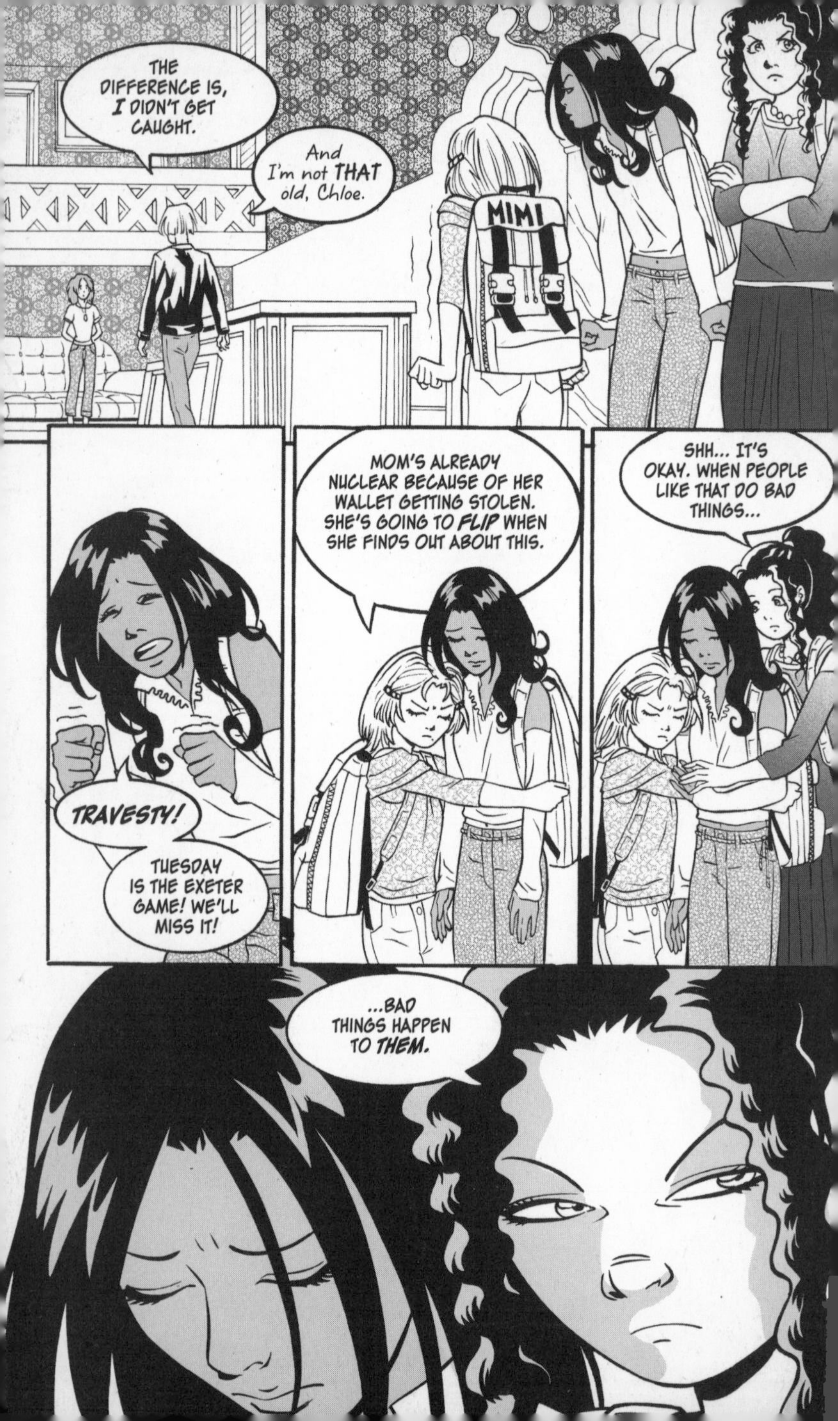
THE DIFFERENCE IS, I DIDN'T GET CAUGHT.
And I'm not THAT old, Chloe.
MIMI
TRAVESTY!
TUESDAY IS THE EXETER GAME! WE'LL MISS IT!
MOM'S ALREADY NUCLEAR BECAUSE OF HER WALLET GETTING STOLEN. SHE'S GOING TO FLIP WHEN SHE FINDS OUT ABOUT THIS.
SHH... IT'S OKAY. WHEN PEOPLE LIKE THAT DO BAD THINGS...
...BAD THINGS HAPPEN TO THEM.

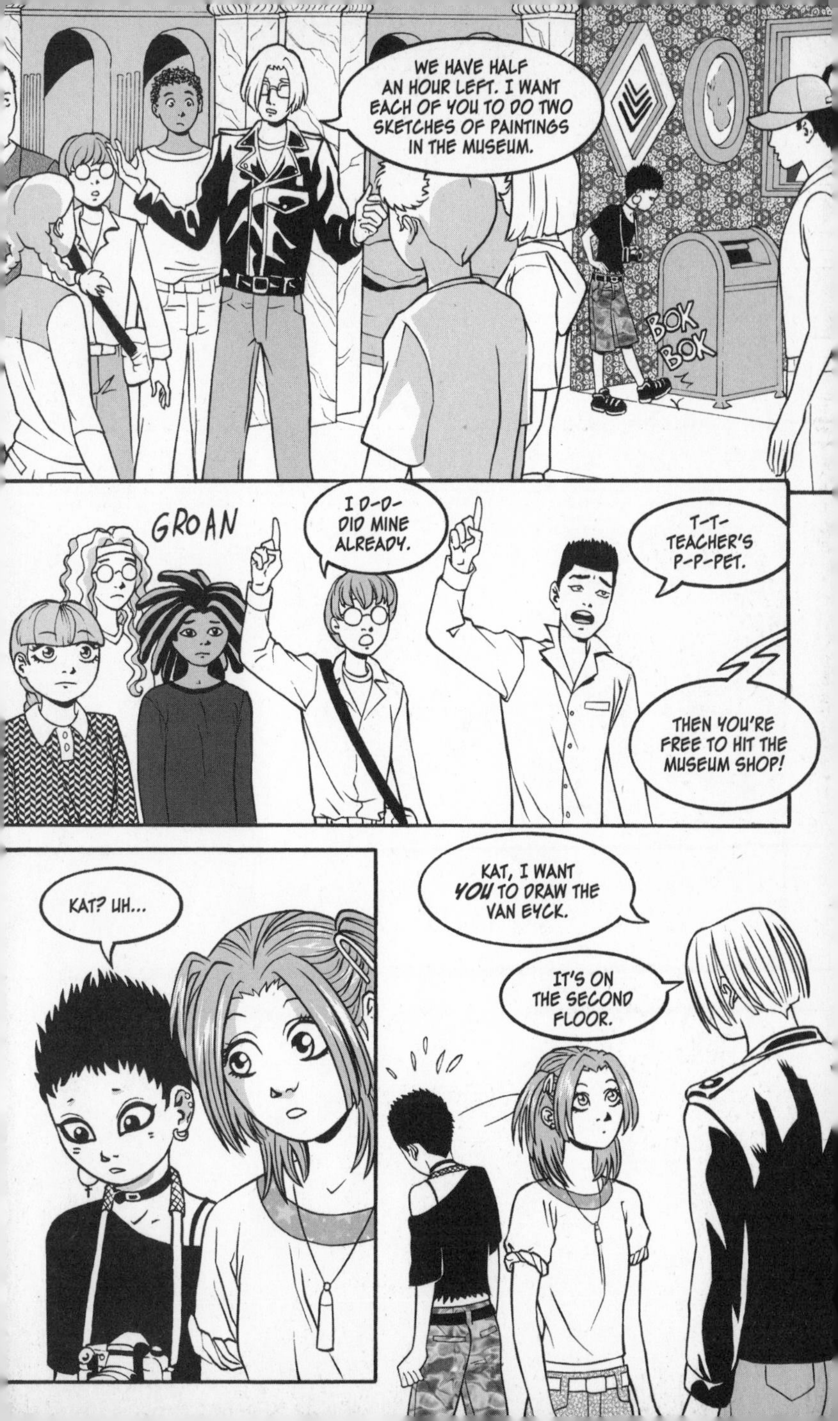
WE HAVE HALF AN HOUR LEFT. I WANT EACH OF YOU TO DO TWO SKETCHES OF PAINTINGS IN THE MUSEUM.
BOK BOK
GROAN
I D-D-DID MINE ALREADY.
T-T-TEACHER'S P-P-PET.
THEN YOU'RE FREE TO HIT THE MUSEUM SHOP!
KAT? UH...
KAT, I WANT YOU TO DRAW THE VAN EYCK.
IT'S ON THE SECOND FLOOR.

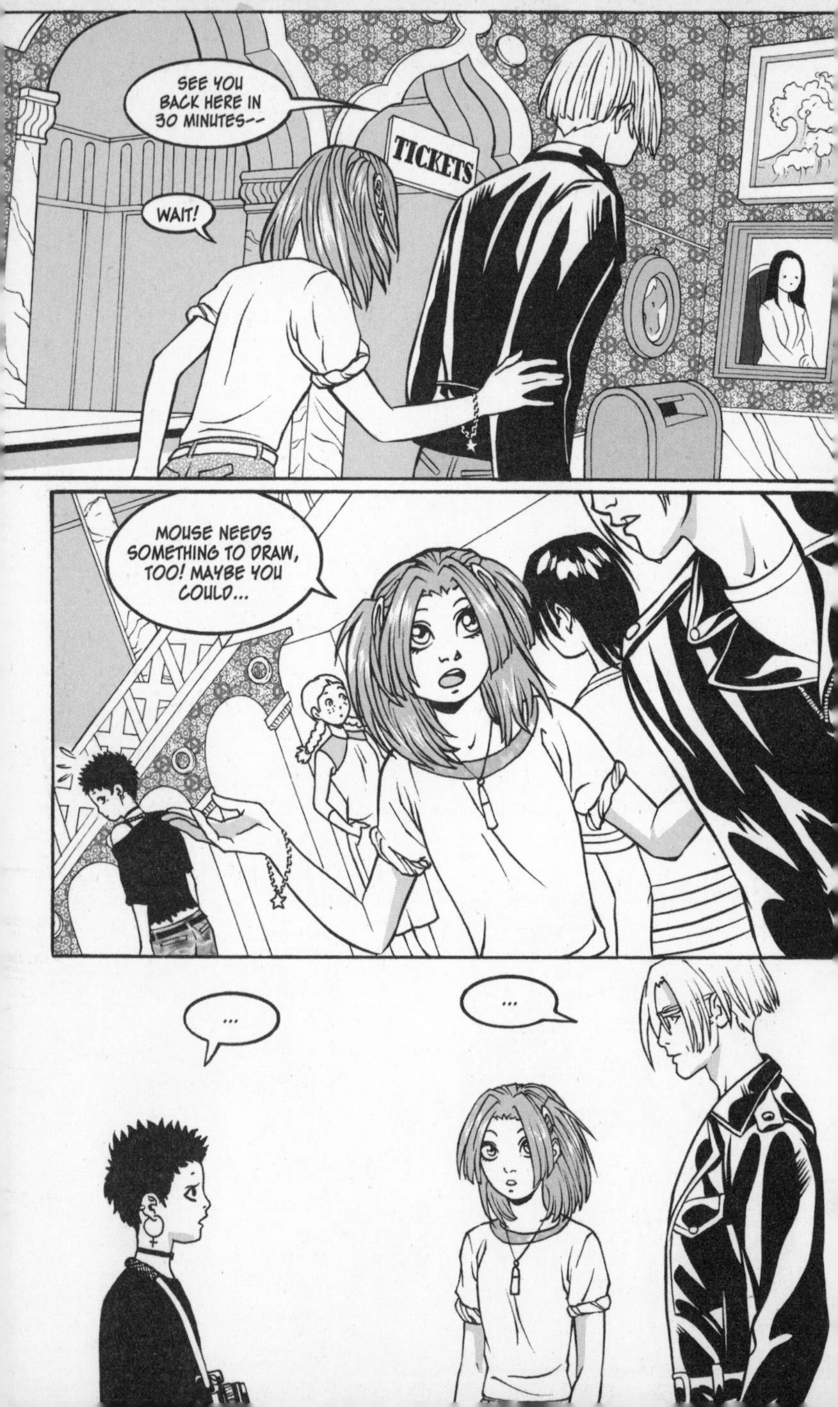

SEE YOU BACK HERE IN 30 MINUTES--
TICKETS
WAIT!
MOUSE NEEDS SOMETHING TO DRAW, TOO! MAYBE YOU COULD...
...
...

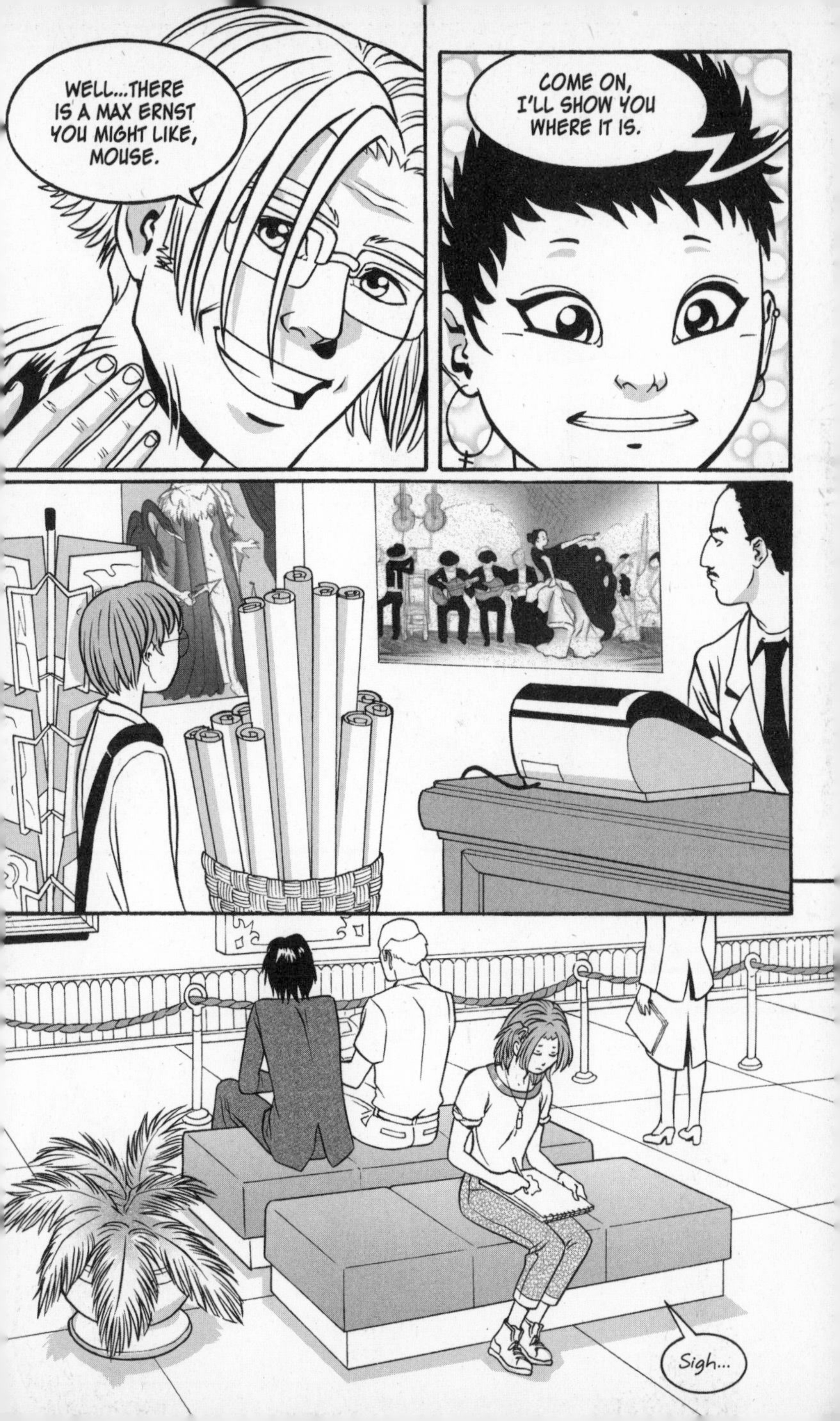
WELL...THERE IS A MAX ERNST YOU MIGHT LIKE, MOUSE.
COME ON, I'LL SHOW YOU WHERE IT IS.
Sigh...

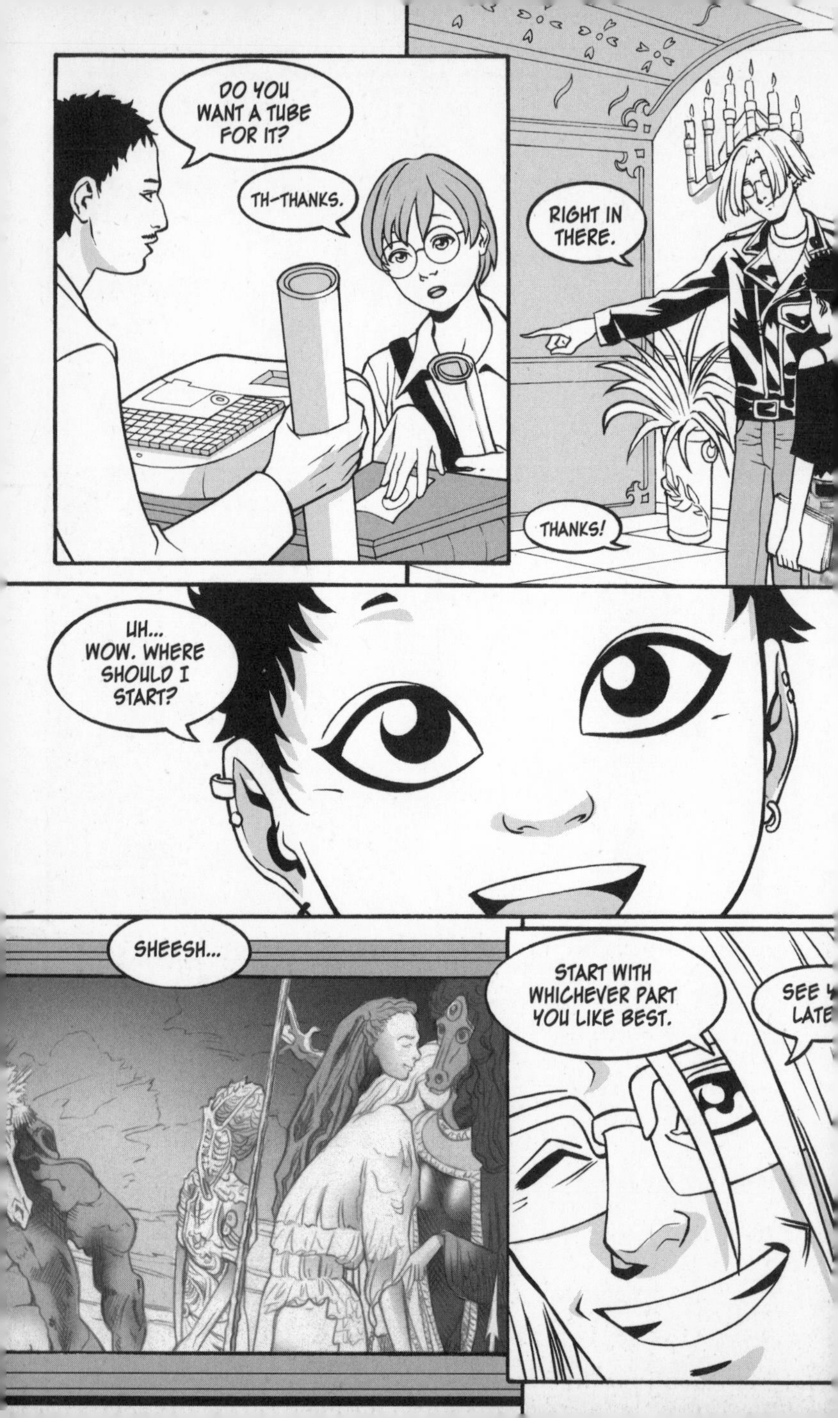
DO YOU WANT A TUBE FOR IT?
TH-THANKS.
RIGHT IN THERE.
THANKS!
UH... WOW. WHERE SHOULD I START?
SHEESH...
START WITH WHICHEVER PART YOU LIKE BEST.

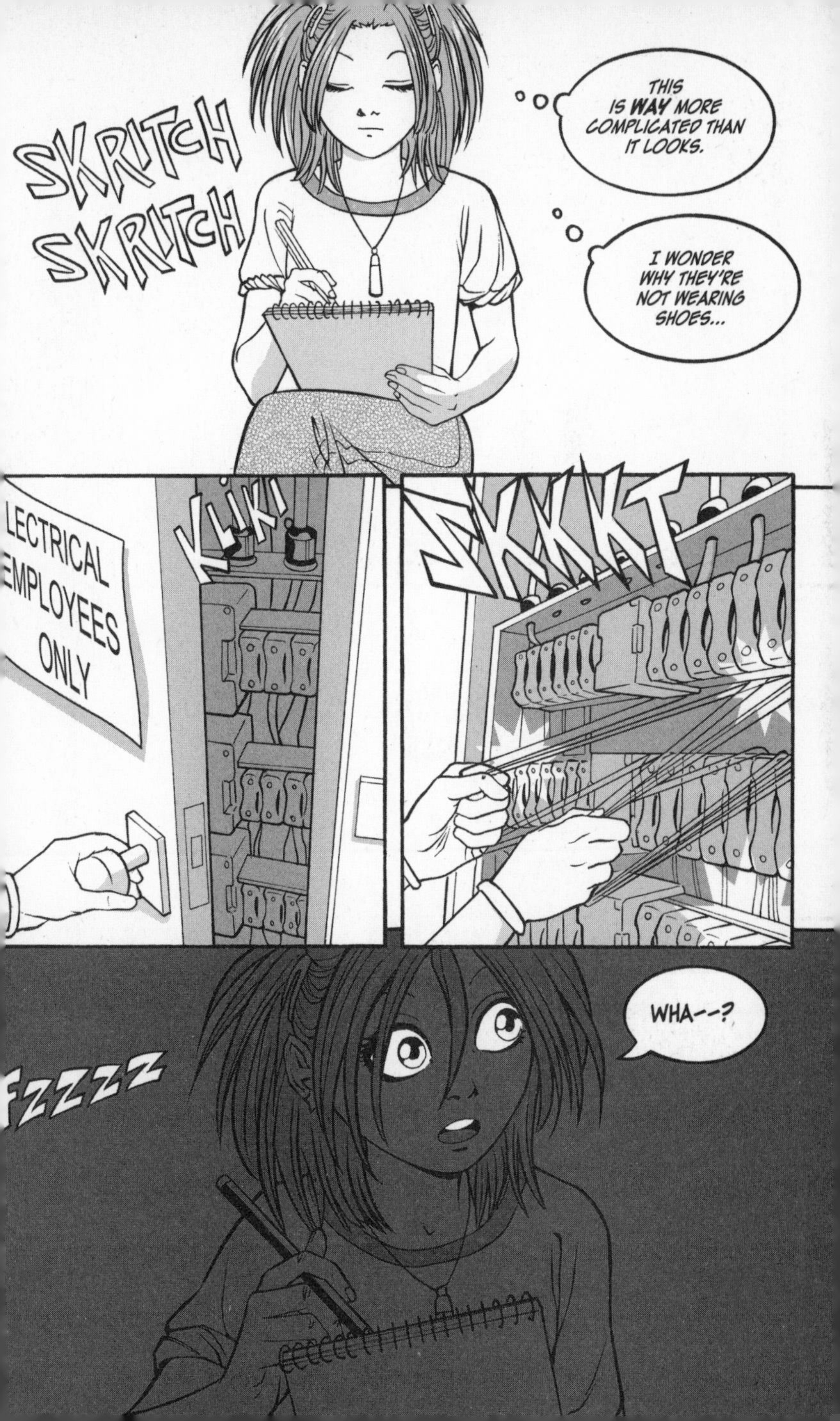
SKRITCH SKRITCH
THIS IS **WAY** MORE COMPLICATED THAN IT LOOKS.
I WONDER WHY THEY'RE NOT WEARING SHOES...
LECTRICAL EMPLOYEES ONLY
KLIK
SKKKT
FZZZZ
WHA--?

RRRRRIP!
AAAAAH!

Chapter 4:
The Spanish Prisoner

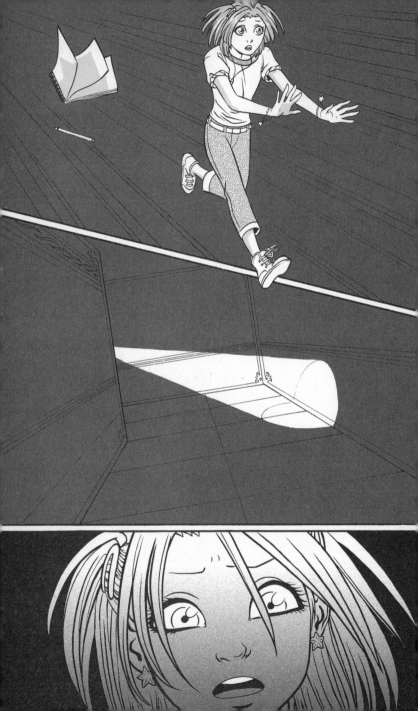

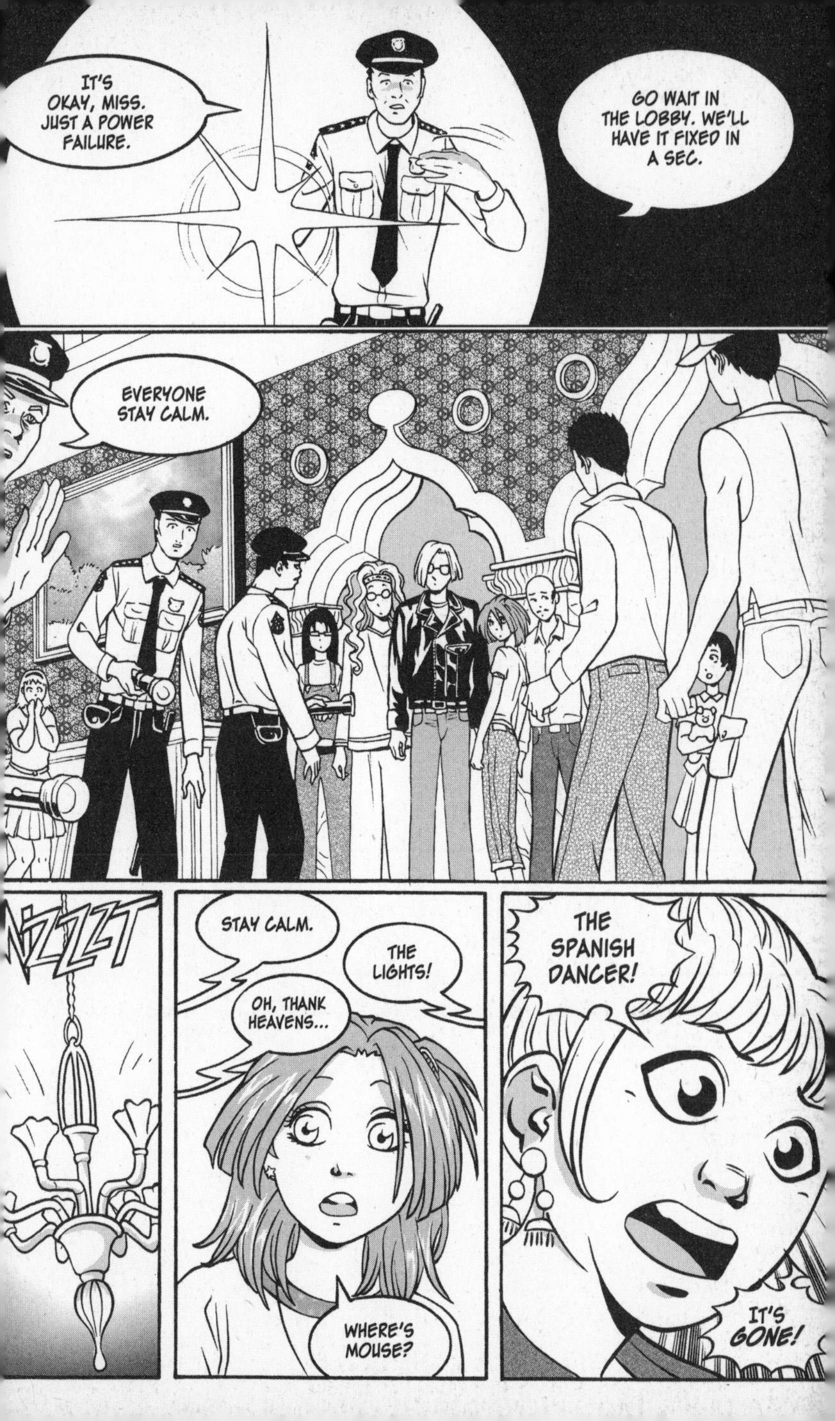
IT'S OKAY, MISS. JUST A POWER FAILURE.
GO WAIT IN THE LOBBY. WE'LL HAVE IT FIXED IN A SEC.
EVERYONE STAY CALM.
ZZZT
STAY CALM.
THE LIGHTS!
OH, THANK HEAVENS...
WHERE'S MOUSE?
THE SPANISH DANCER!
IT'S GONE!

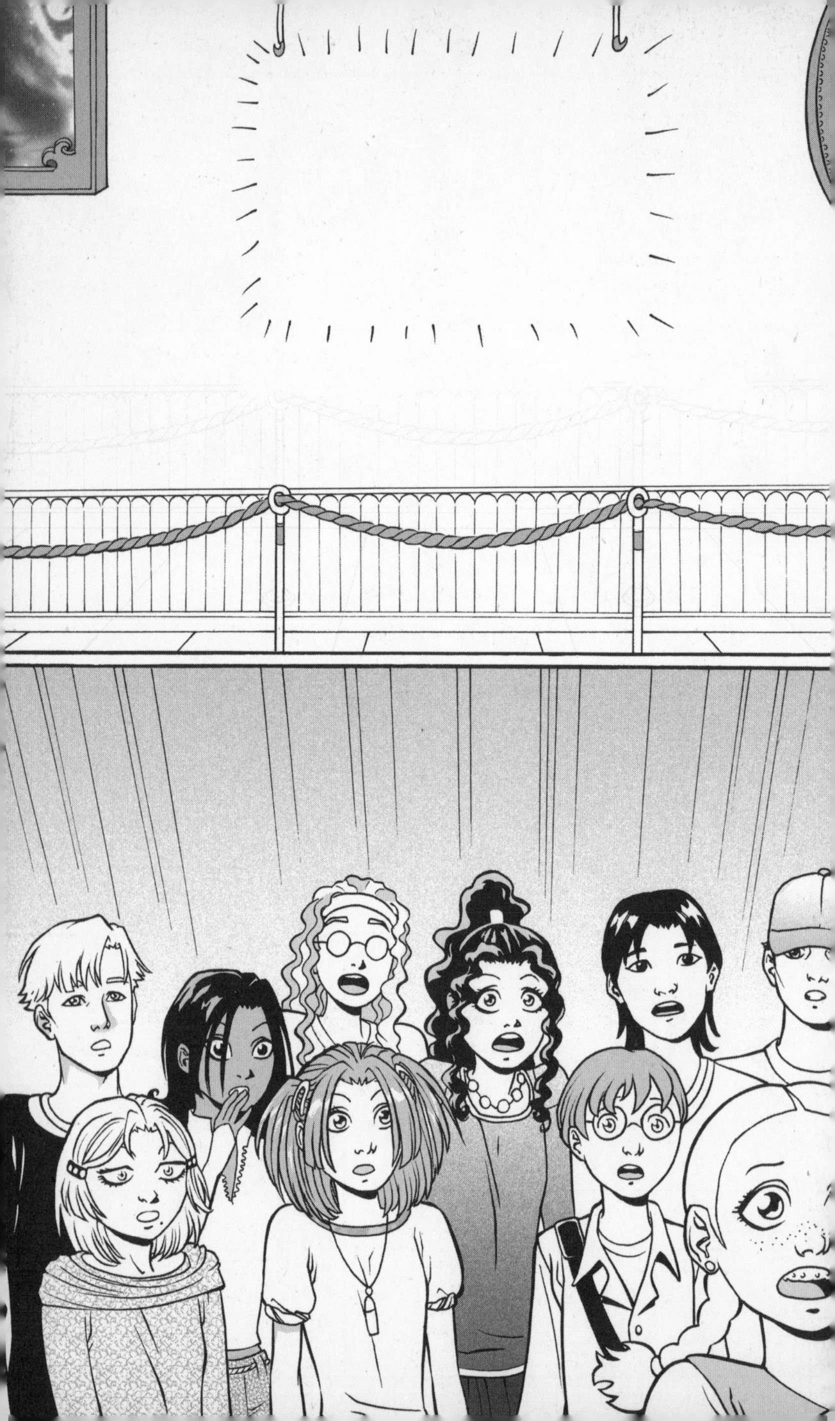

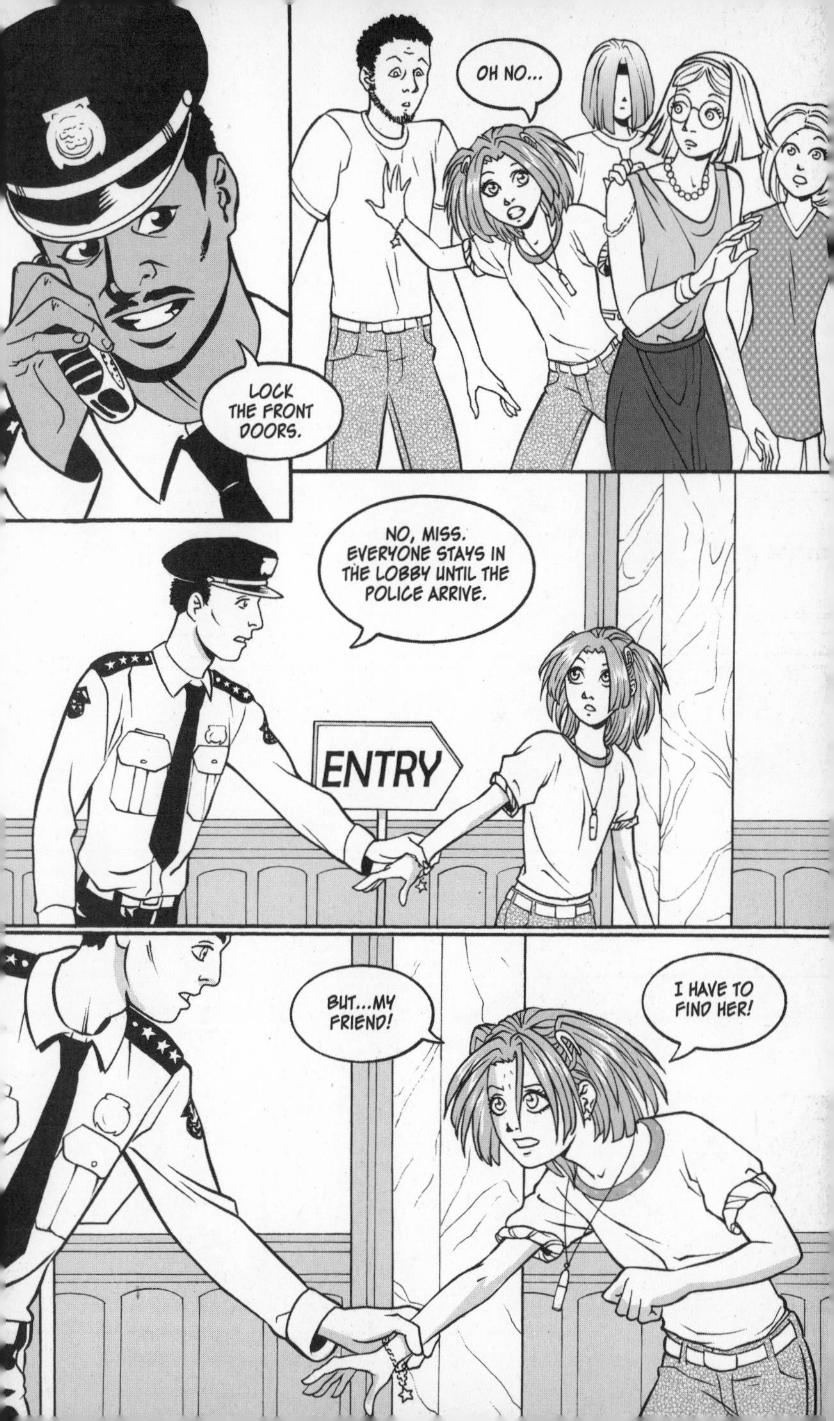
LOCK THE FRONT DOORS.
OH NO...
NO, MISS. EVERYONE STAYS IN THE LOBBY UNTIL THE POLICE ARRIVE.
ENTRY
BUT...MY FRIEND!
I HAVE TO FIND HER!

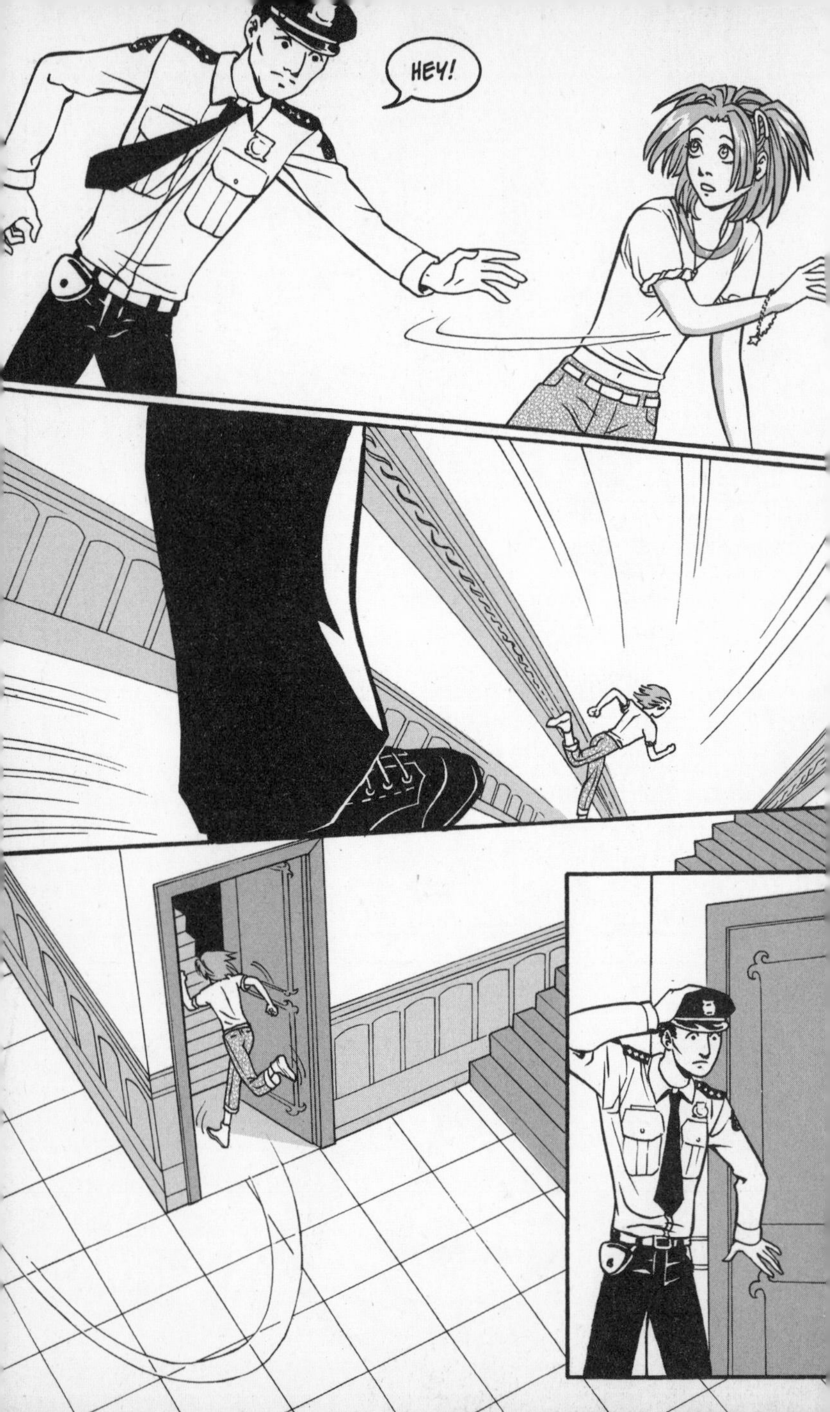
HEY!

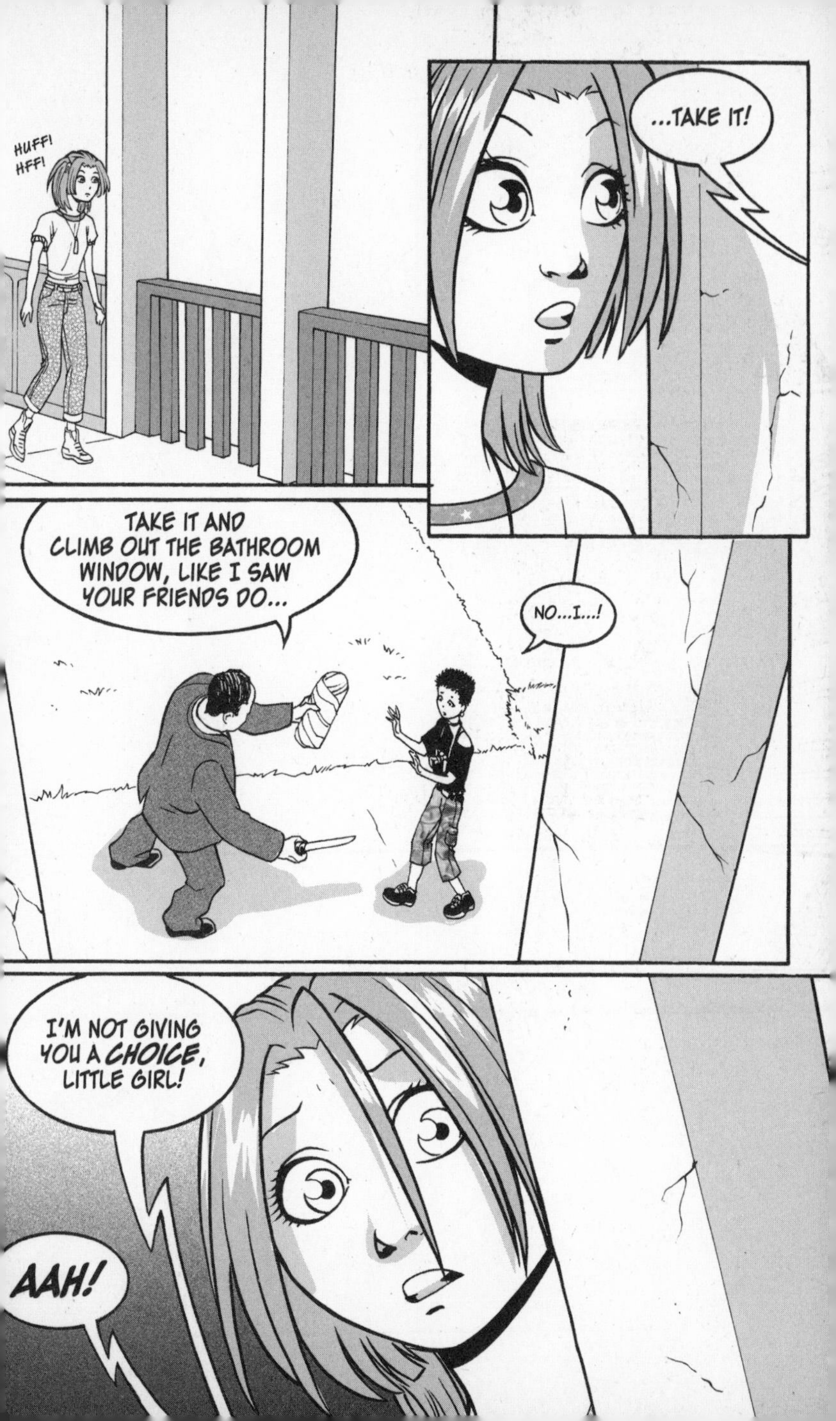
HUFF! HFF!
...TAKE IT!
TAKE IT AND CLIMB OUT THE BATHROOM WINDOW, LIKE I SAW YOUR FRIENDS DO...
NO...I...!
I'M NOT GIVING YOU A *CHOICE*, LITTLE GIRL!
AAH!

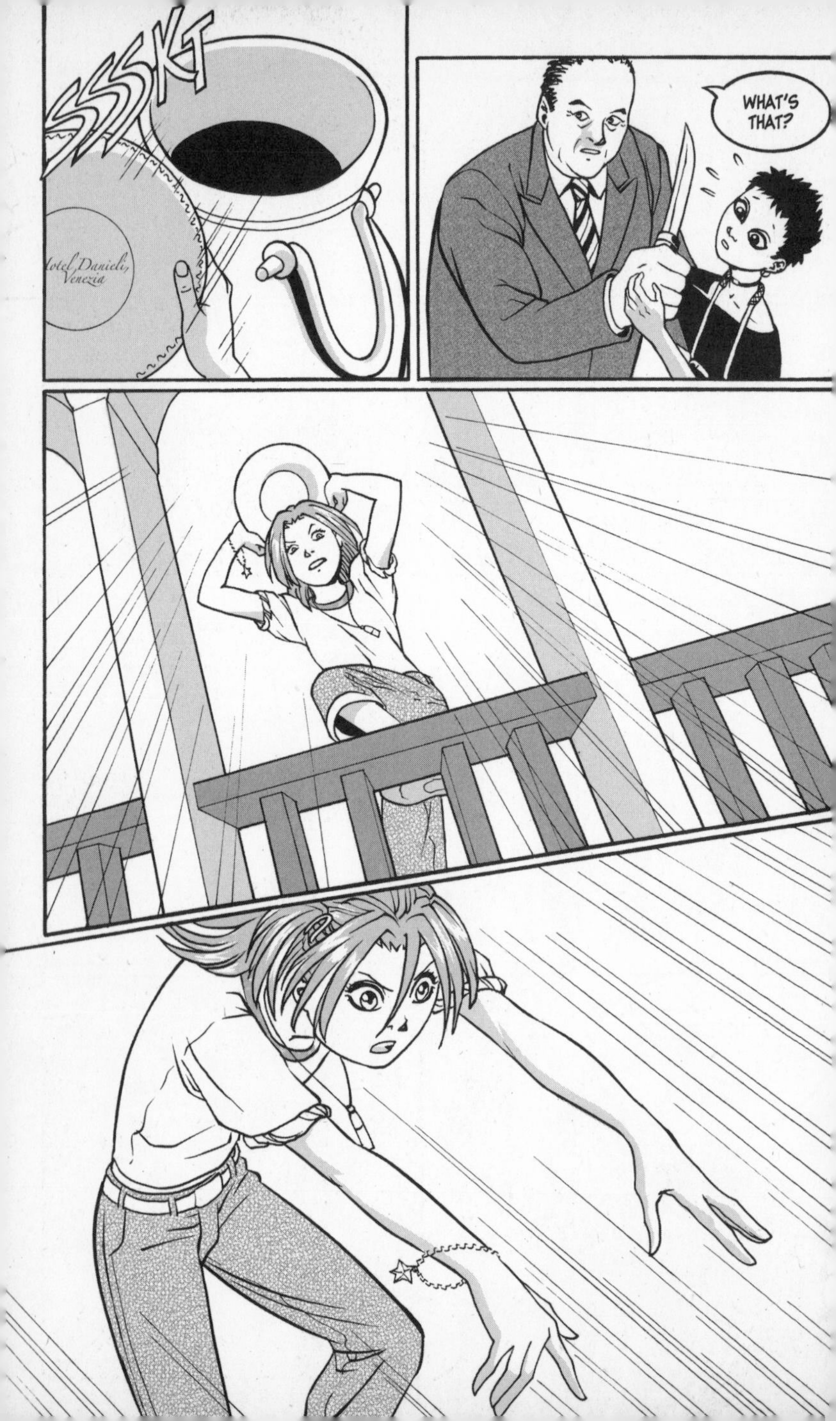
SSSKT
Hotel Danieli, Venezia
WHAT'S THAT?

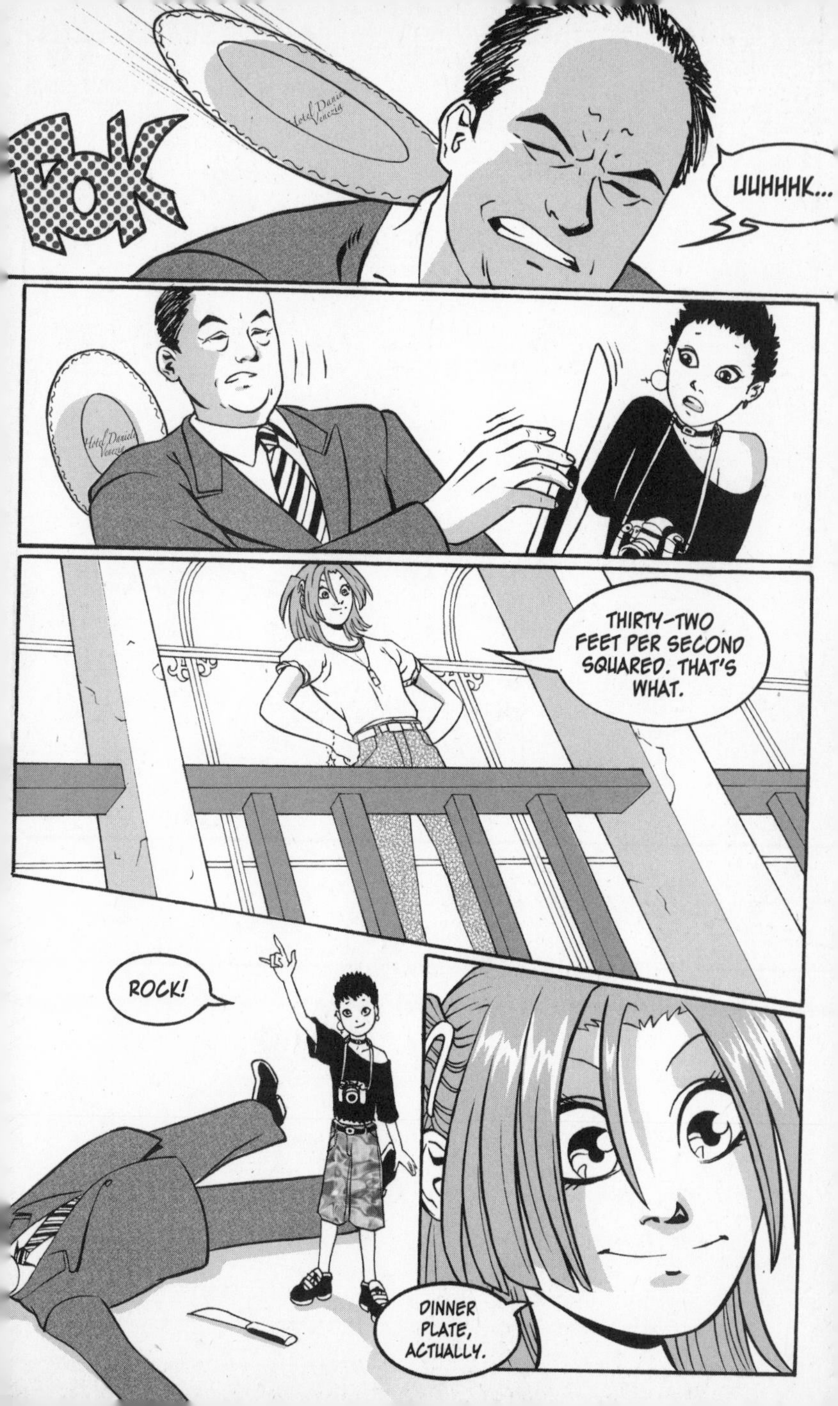
POK
UUHHHK...
THIRTY-TWO FEET PER SECOND SQUARED. THAT'S WHAT.
ROCK!
DINNER PLATE, ACTUALLY.

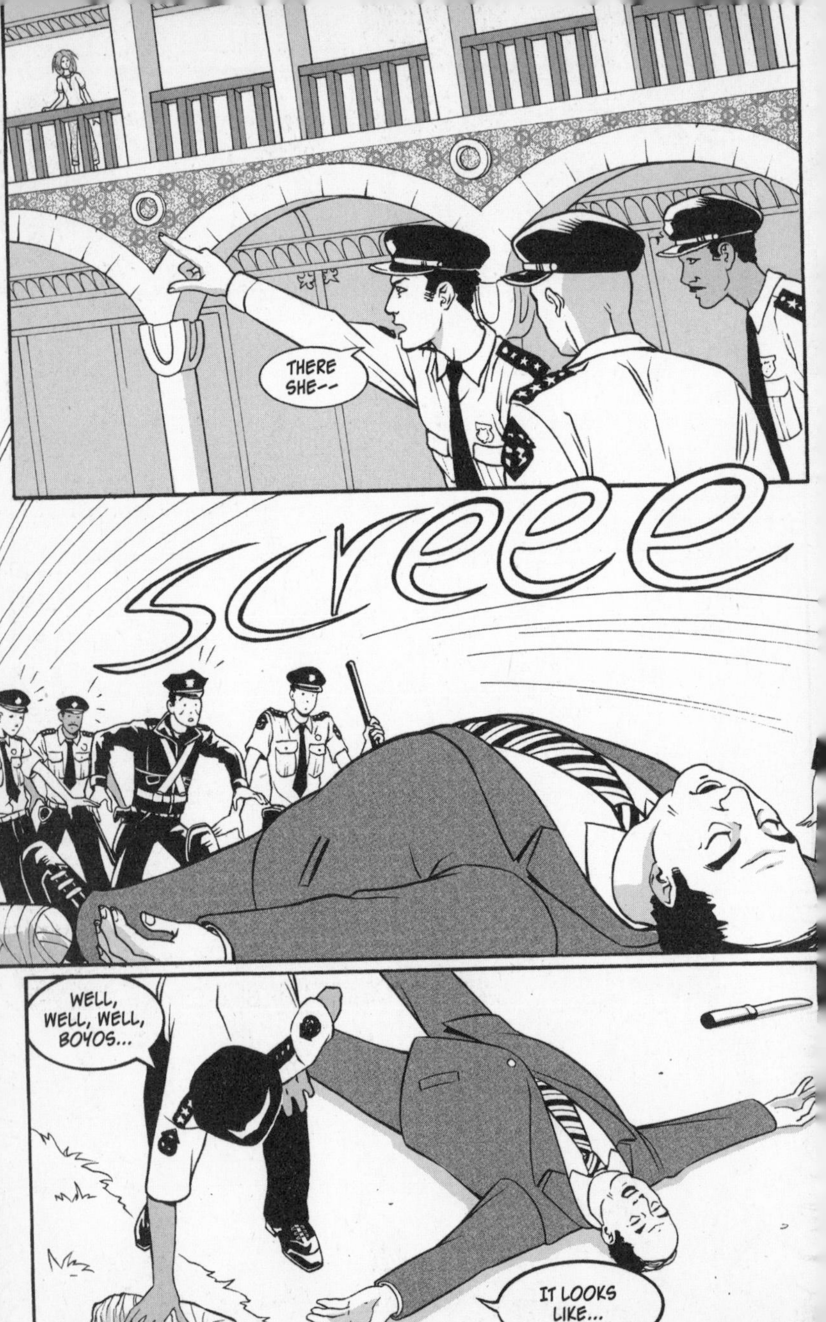
THERE SHE--
SCREEE
WELL, WELL, WELL, BOYOS...
IT LOOKS LIKE...

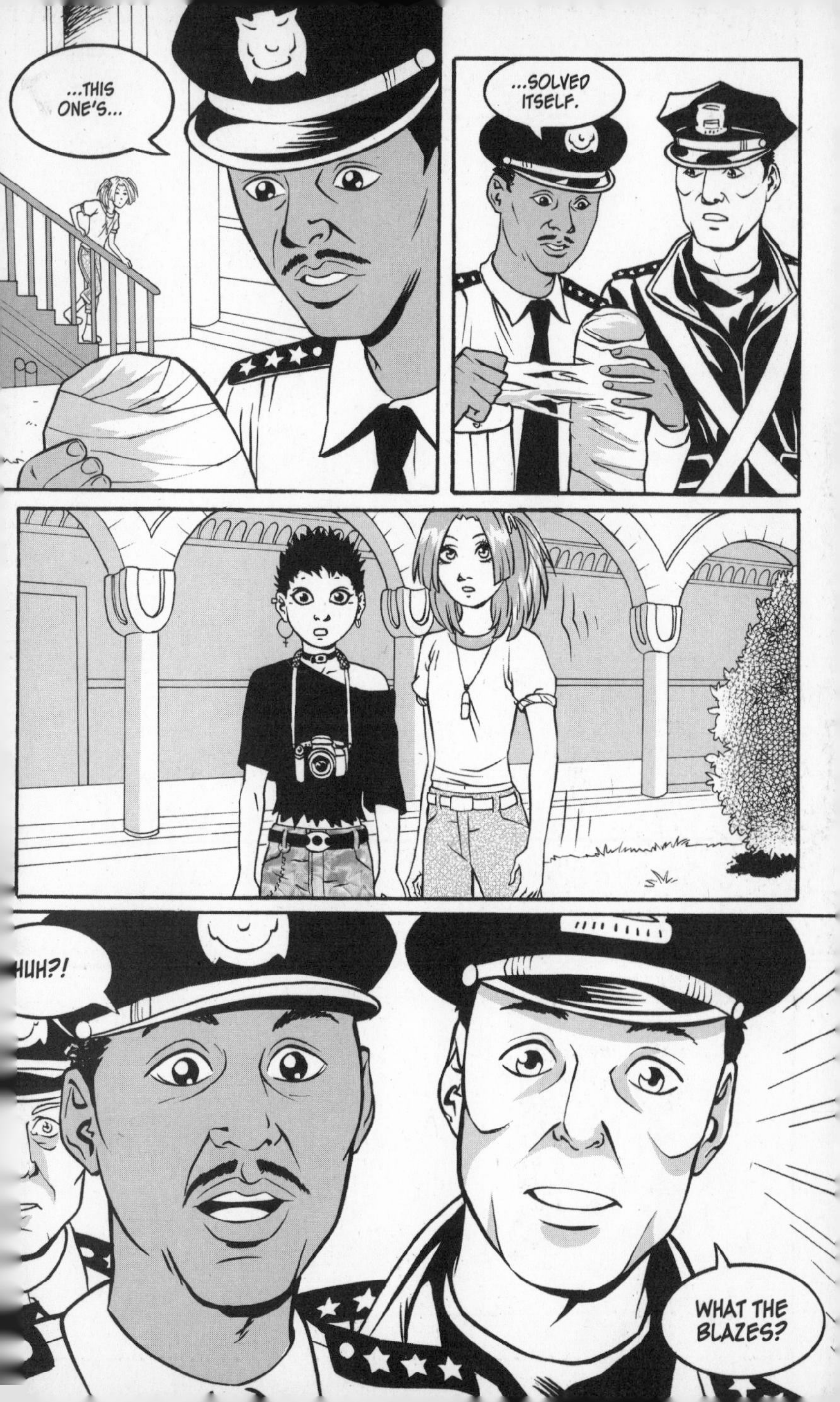
...THIS ONE'S...
...SOLVED ITSELF.
HUH?!
WHAT THE BLAZES?

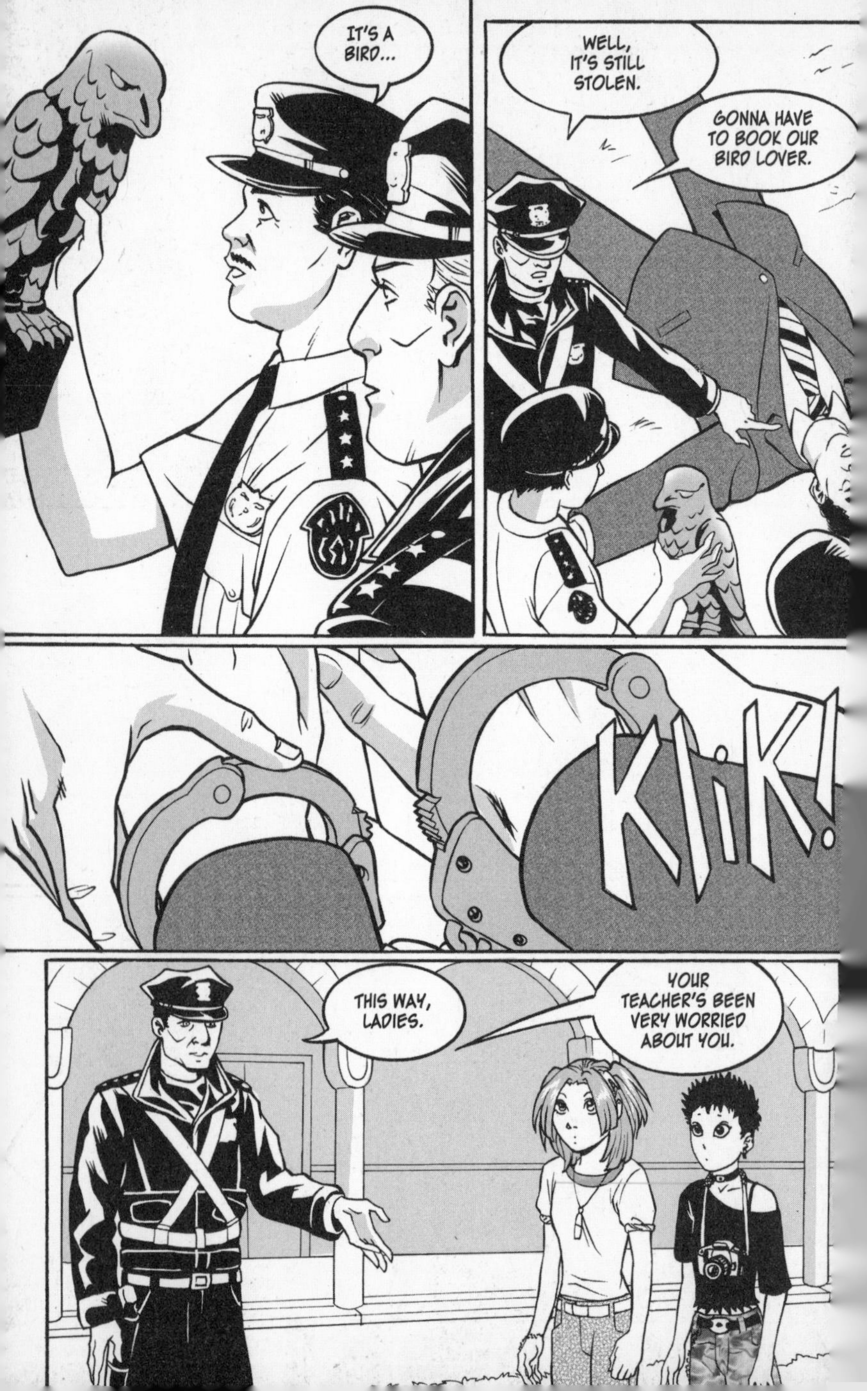
IT'S A BIRD...
WELL, IT'S STILL STOLEN.
GONNA HAVE TO BOOK OUR BIRD LOVER.
KLIK!
THIS WAY, LADIES.
YOUR TEACHER'S BEEN VERY WORRIED ABOUT YOU.

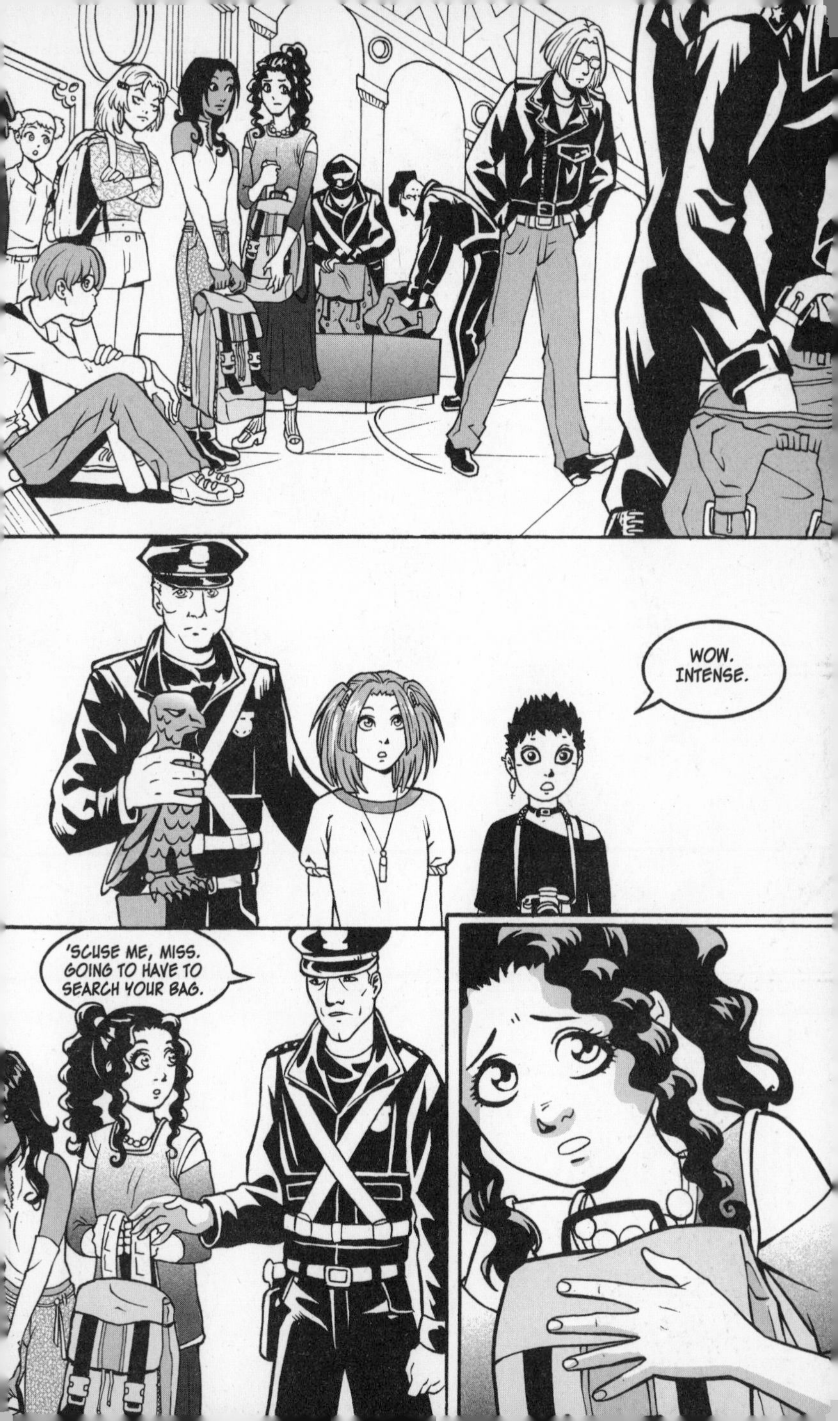
WOW. INTENSE.
'SCUSE ME, MISS. GOING TO HAVE TO SEARCH YOUR BAG.

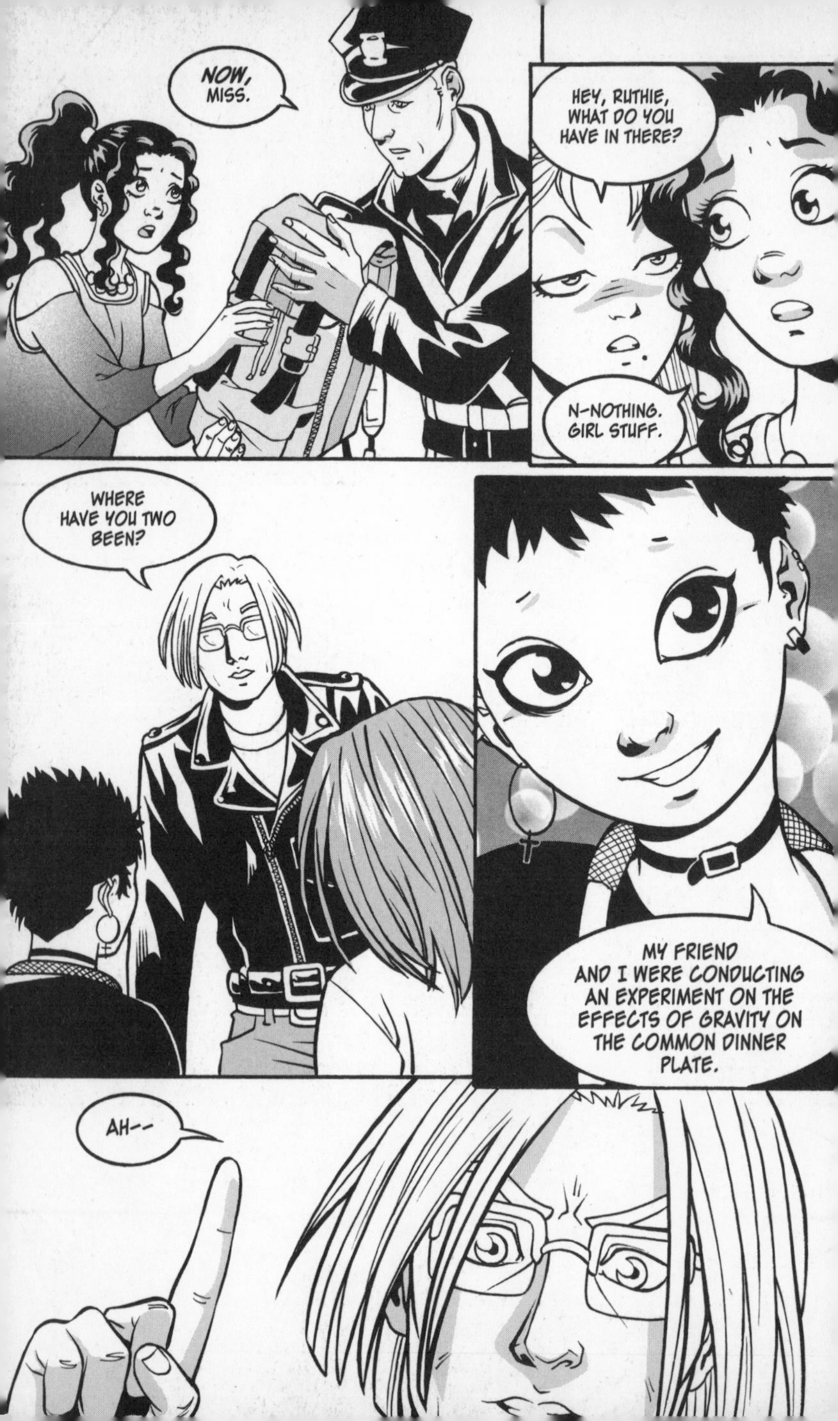
NOW, MISS.
HEY, RUTHIE, WHAT DO YOU HAVE IN THERE?
N-NOTHING. GIRL STUFF.
WHERE HAVE YOU TWO BEEN?
MY FRIEND AND I WERE CONDUCTING AN EXPERIMENT ON THE EFFECTS OF GRAVITY ON THE COMMON DINNER PLATE.
AH--

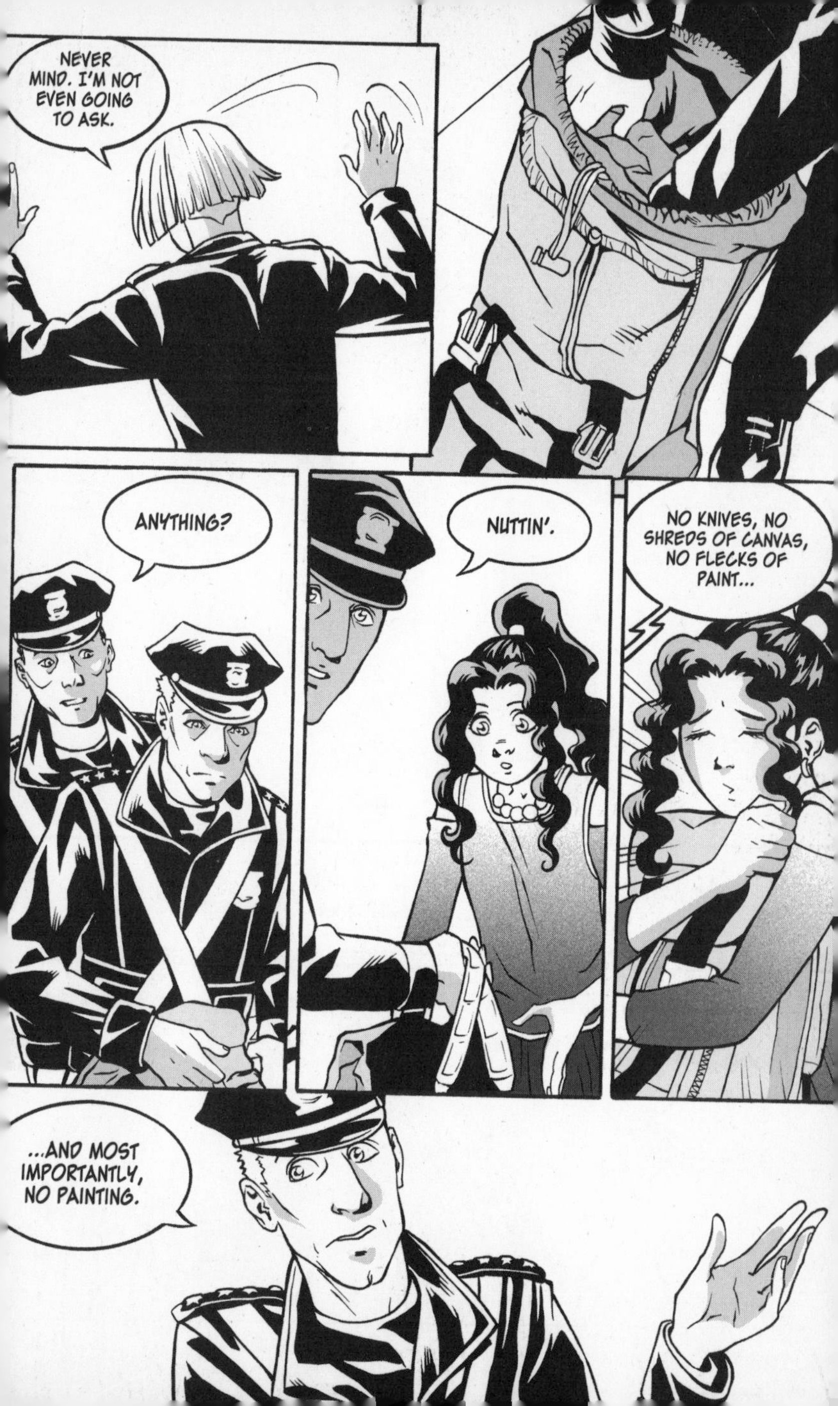
NEVER MIND. I'M NOT EVEN GOING TO ASK.
ANYTHING?
NUTTIN'.
NO KNIVES, NO SHREDS OF CANVAS, NO FLECKS OF PAINT...
...AND MOST IMPORTANTLY, NO PAINTING.

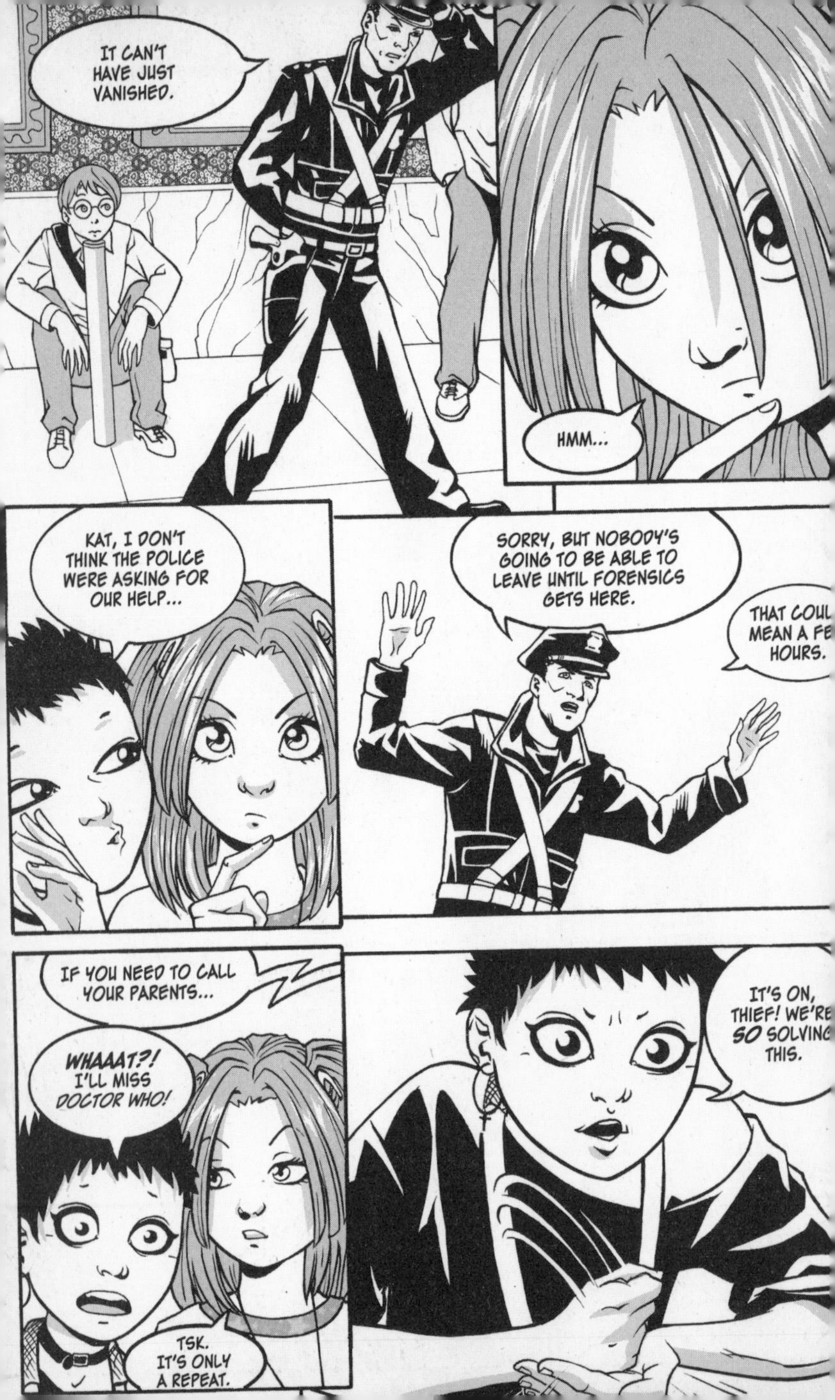
IT CAN'T HAVE JUST VANISHED.
HMM...
KAT, I DON'T THINK THE POLICE WERE ASKING FOR OUR HELP...
SORRY, BUT NOBODY'S GOING TO BE ABLE TO LEAVE UNTIL FORENSICS GETS HERE.
THAT COUL MEAN A FE HOURS.
IF YOU NEED TO CALL YOUR PARENTS...
WHAAAT?! I'LL MISS *DOCTOR WHO!*
TSK. IT'S ONLY A REPEAT.
IT'S ON, THIEF! WE'RE *SO* SOLVING THIS.

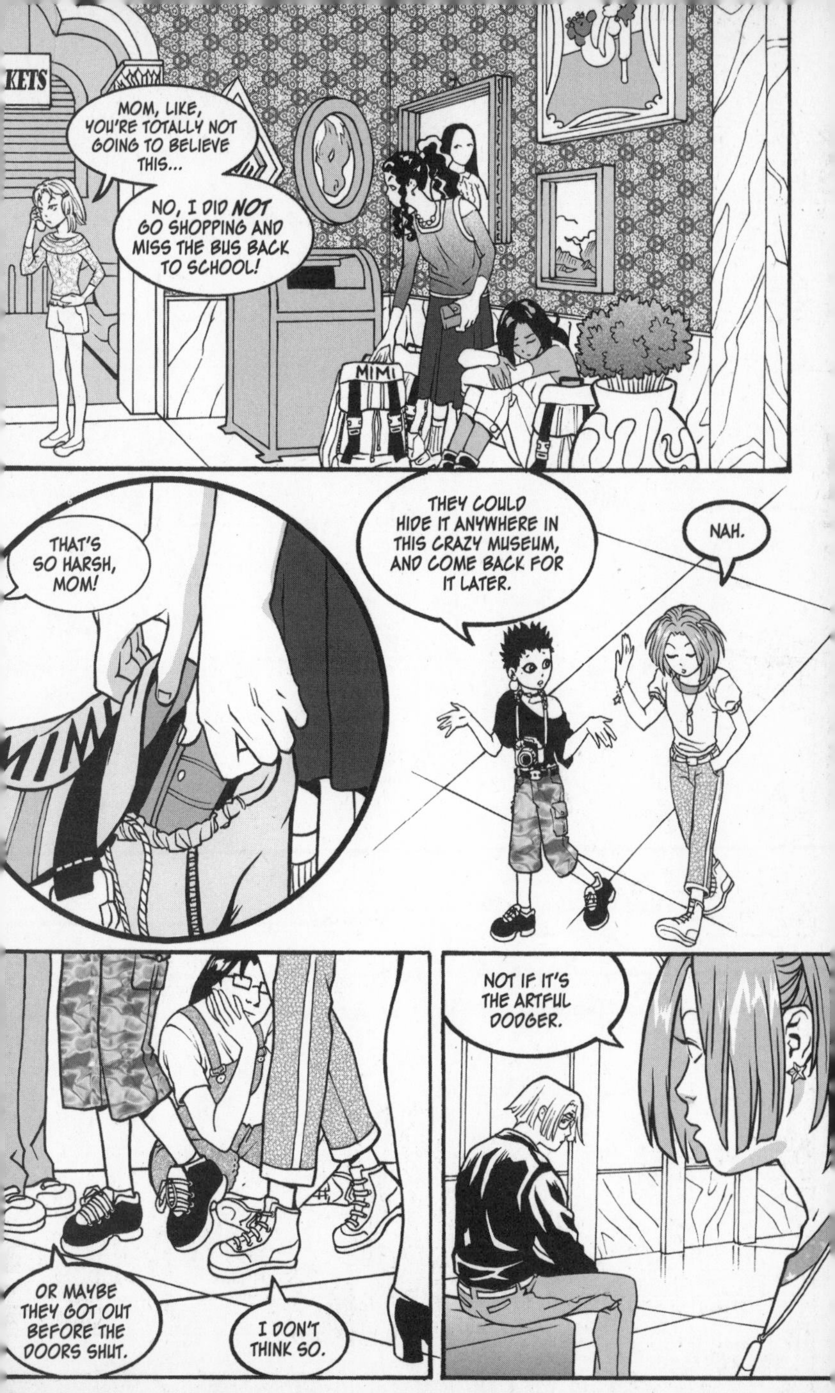
KETS
MOM, LIKE, YOU'RE TOTALLY NOT GOING TO BELIEVE THIS...
NO, I DID **NOT** GO SHOPPING AND MISS THE BUS BACK TO SCHOOL!
MIMI
THAT'S SO HARSH, MOM!
MIMI
THEY COULD HIDE IT ANYWHERE IN THIS CRAZY MUSEUM, AND COME BACK FOR IT LATER.
NAH.
OR MAYBE THEY GOT OUT BEFORE THE DOORS SHUT.
I DON'T THINK SO.
NOT IF IT'S THE ARTFUL DODGER.

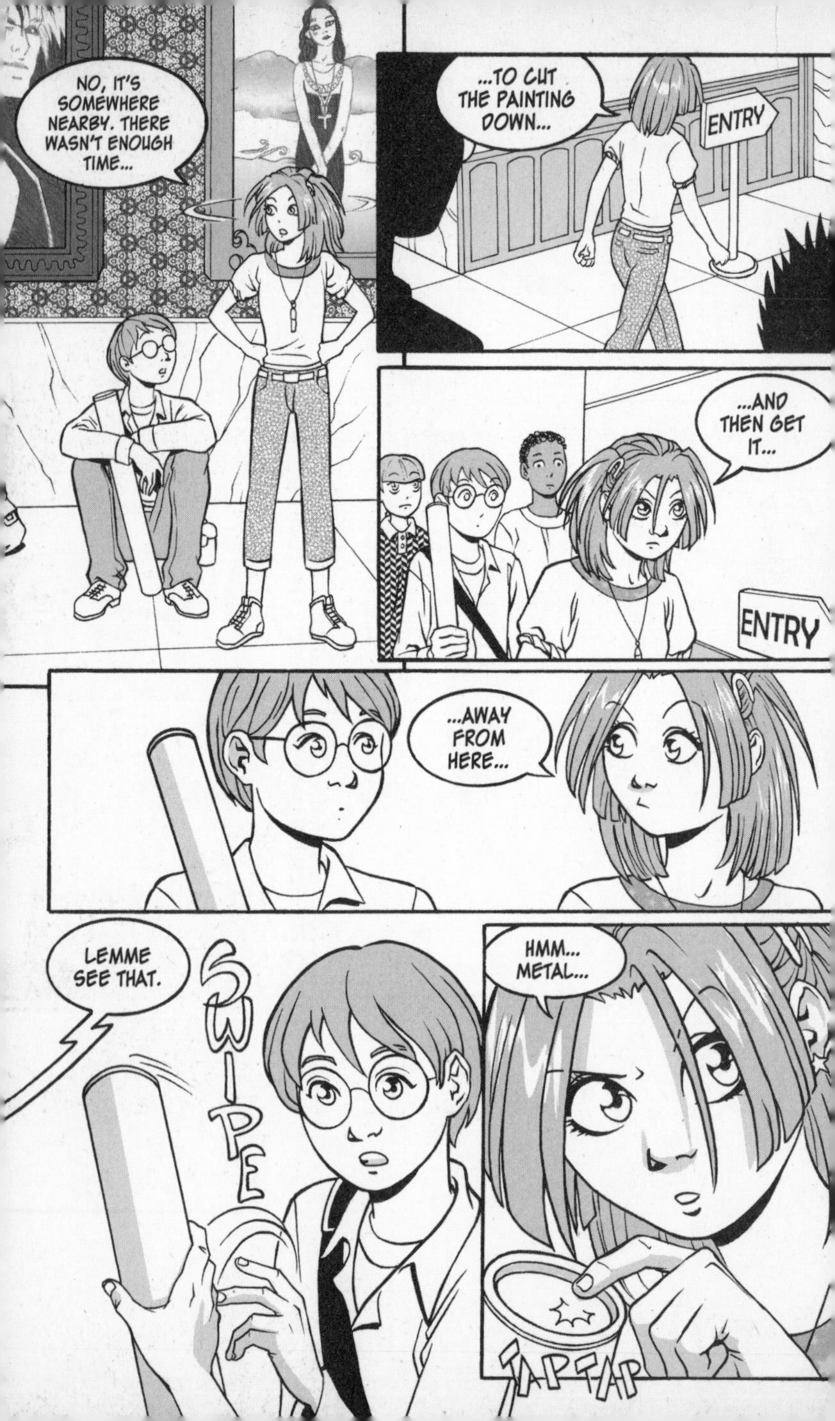

NO, IT'S SOMEWHERE NEARBY. THERE WASN'T ENOUGH TIME...
...TO CUT THE PAINTING DOWN...
ENTRY
...AND THEN GET IT...
ENTRY
...AWAY FROM HERE...
LEMME SEE THAT.
SWIPE
HMM... METAL...
TAPTAP

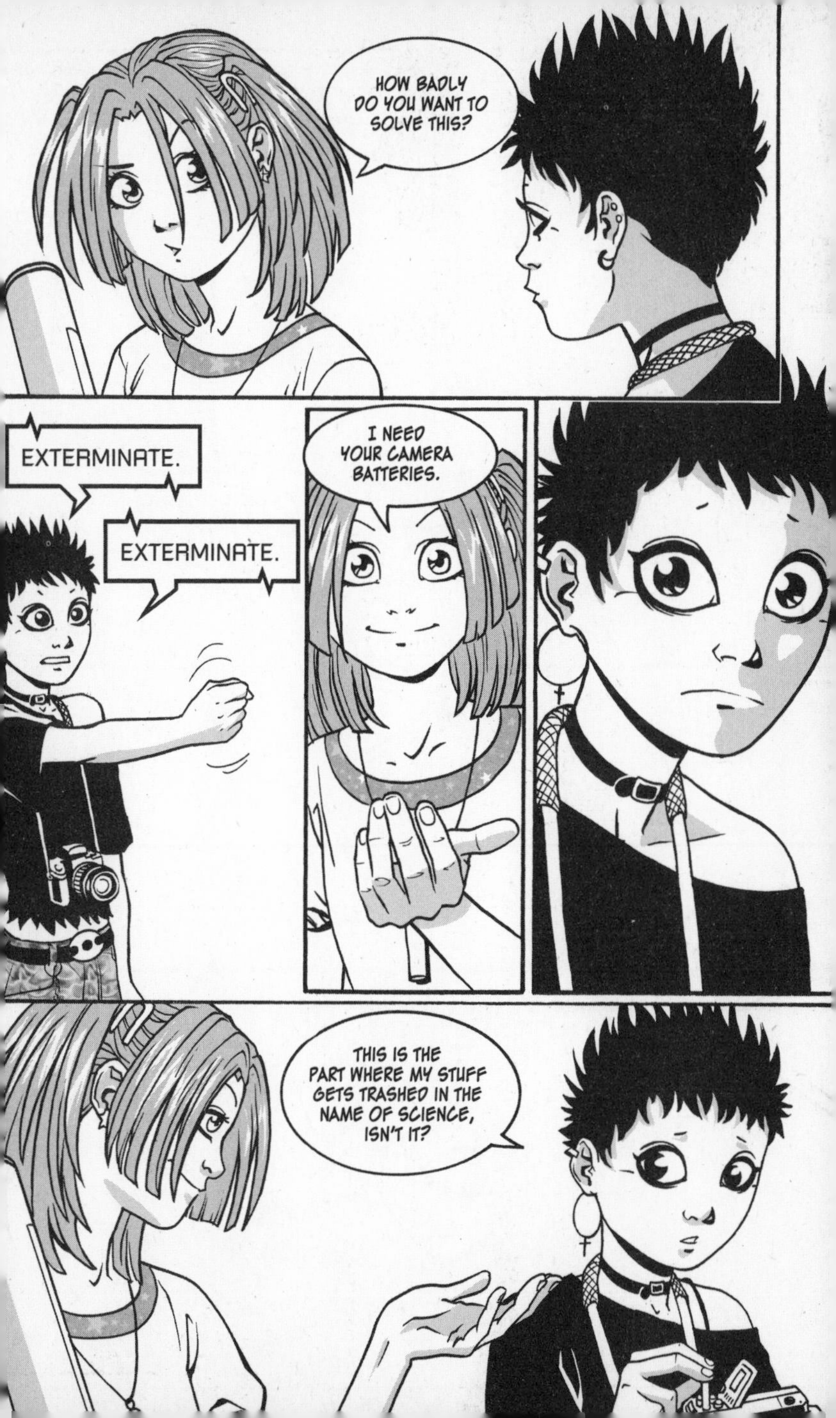
HOW BADLY DO YOU WANT TO SOLVE THIS?
EXTERMINATE.
EXTERMINATE.
I NEED YOUR CAMERA BATTERIES.
THIS IS THE PART WHERE MY STUFF GETS TRASHED IN THE NAME OF SCIENCE, ISN'T IT?

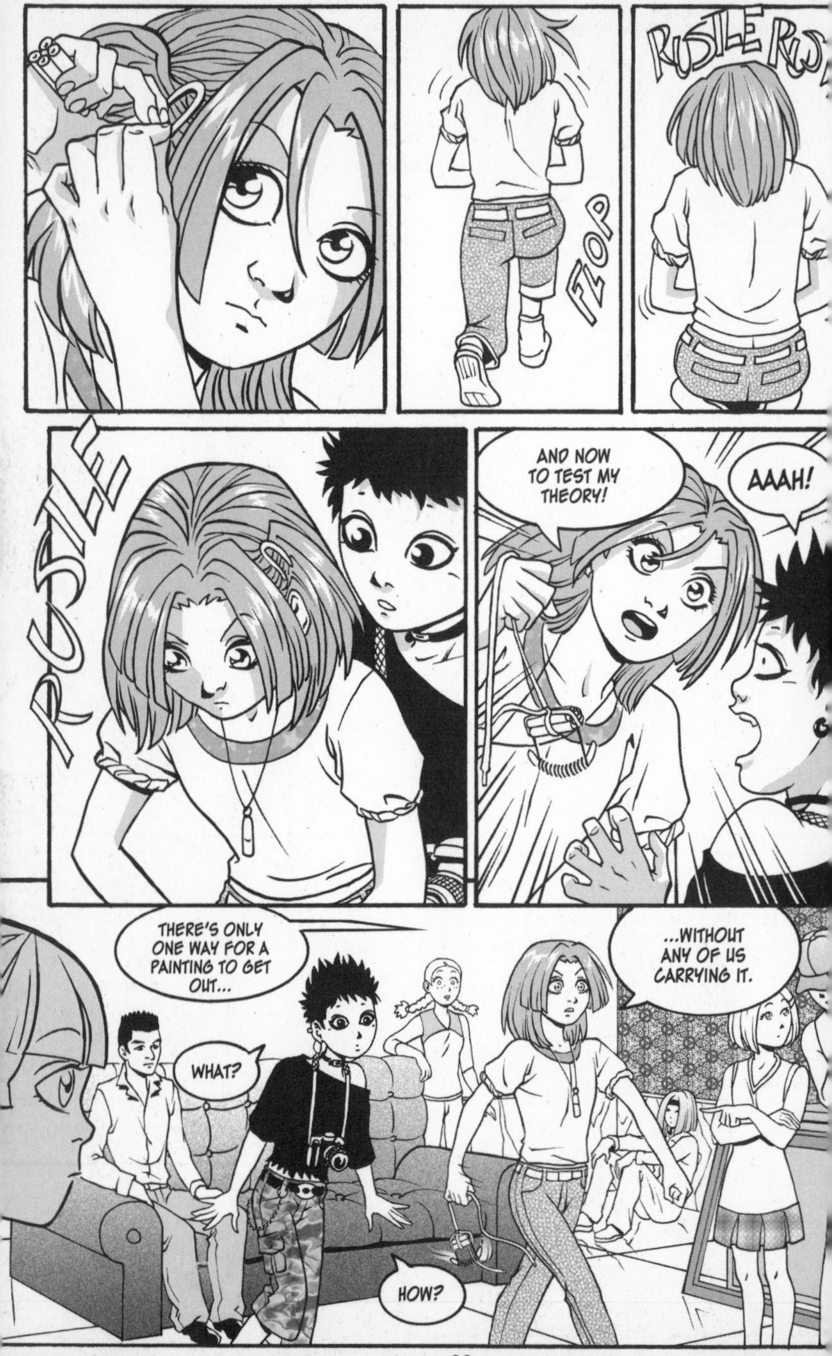
ZOOP
RUSTLE RUS
RUSTLE
AND NOW TO TEST MY THEORY!
AAAH!
THERE'S ONLY ONE WAY FOR A PAINTING TO GET OUT...
...WITHOUT ANY OF US CARRYING IT.
WHAT?
HOW?

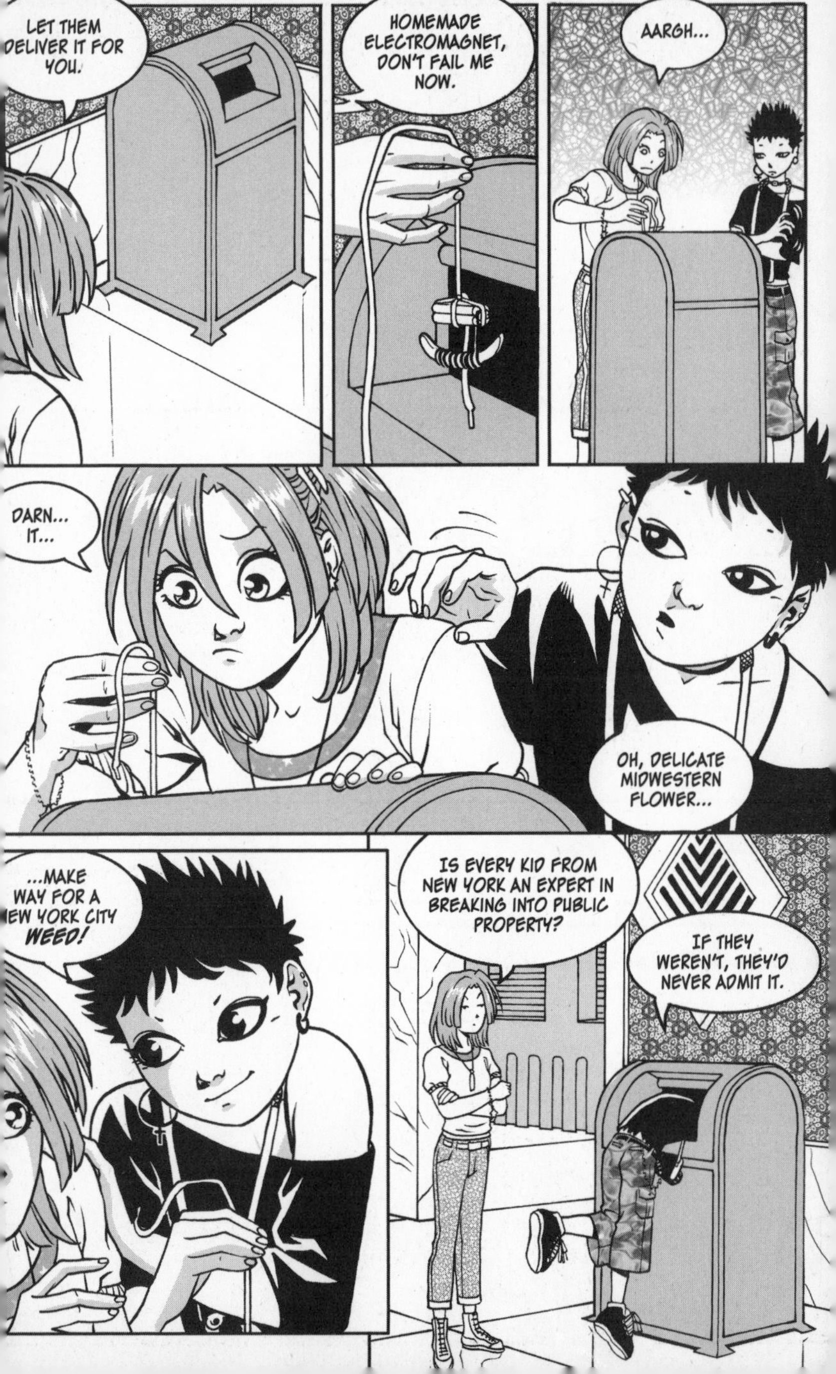
LET THEM DELIVER IT FOR YOU.
HOMEMADE ELECTROMAGNET, DON'T FAIL ME NOW.
AARGH...
DARN... IT...
OH, DELICATE MIDWESTERN FLOWER...
...MAKE WAY FOR A NEW YORK CITY WEED!
IS EVERY KID FROM NEW YORK AN EXPERT IN BREAKING INTO PUBLIC PROPERTY?
IF THEY WEREN'T, THEY'D NEVER ADMIT IT.

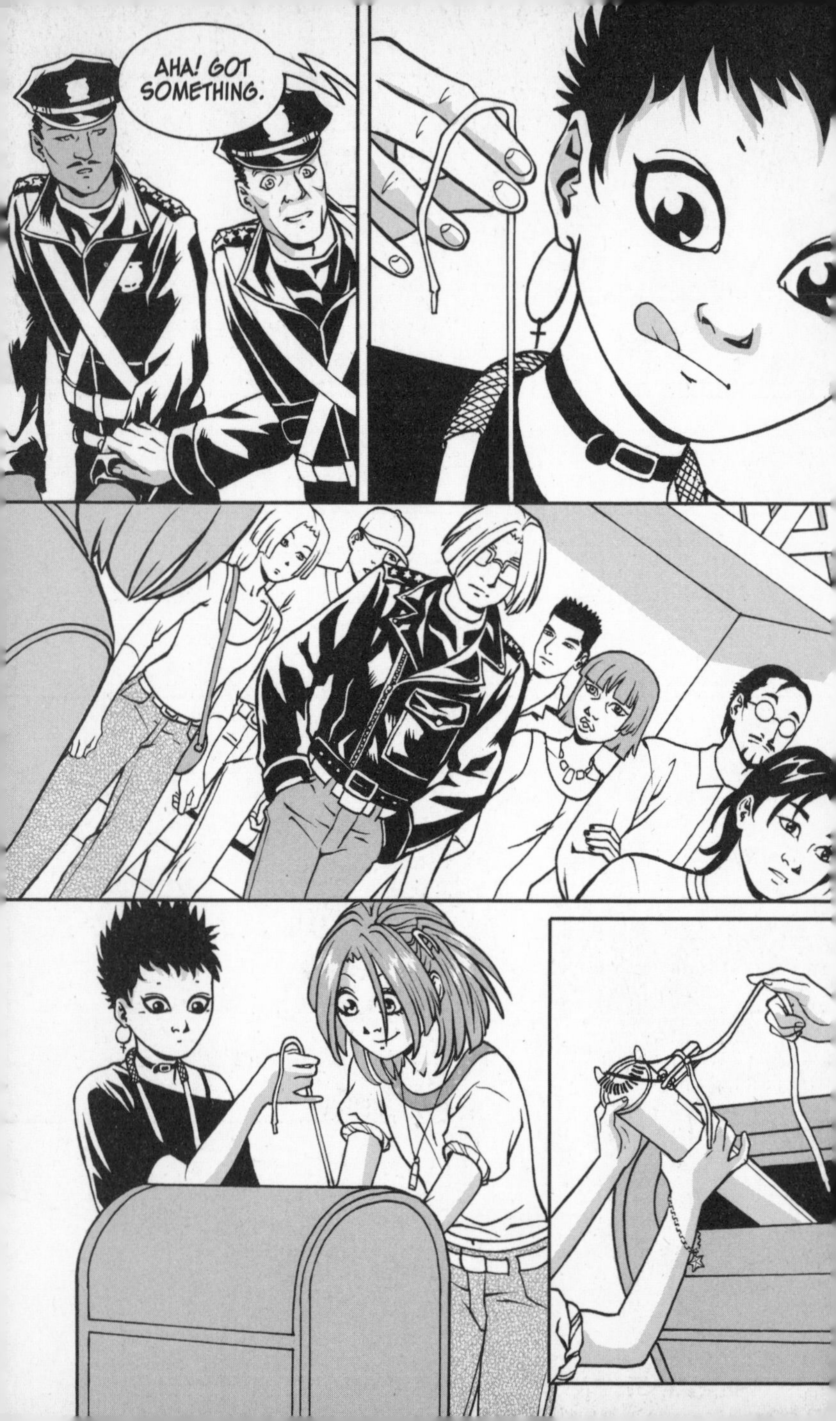
AHA! GOT SOMETHING.

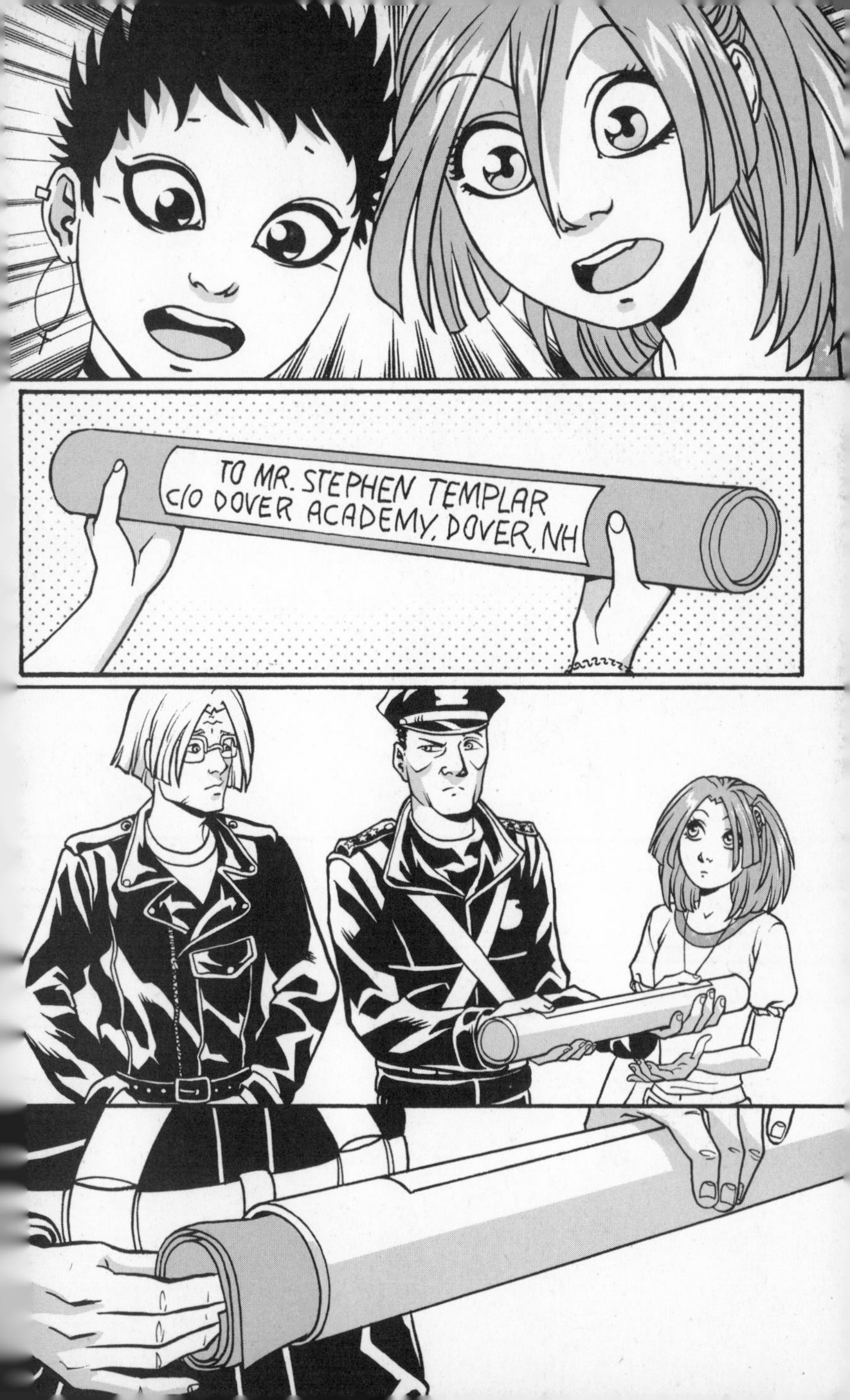
TO MR. STEPHEN TEMPLAR
C/O DOVER ACADEMY, DOVER, NH

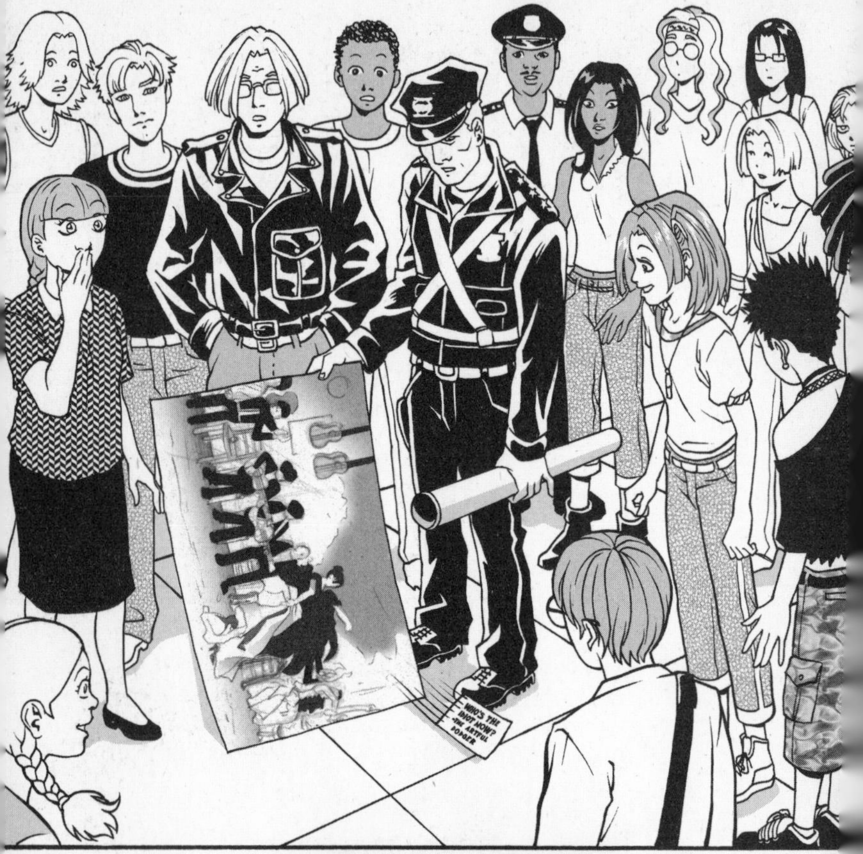
WHO'S THE IDIOT NOW? -THE ARTFUL DODGER

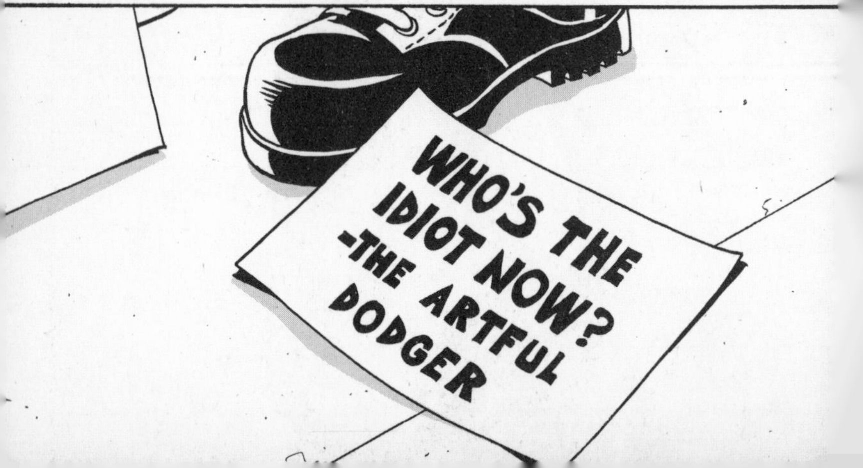
WHO'S THE IDIOT NOW? -THE ARTFUL DODGER

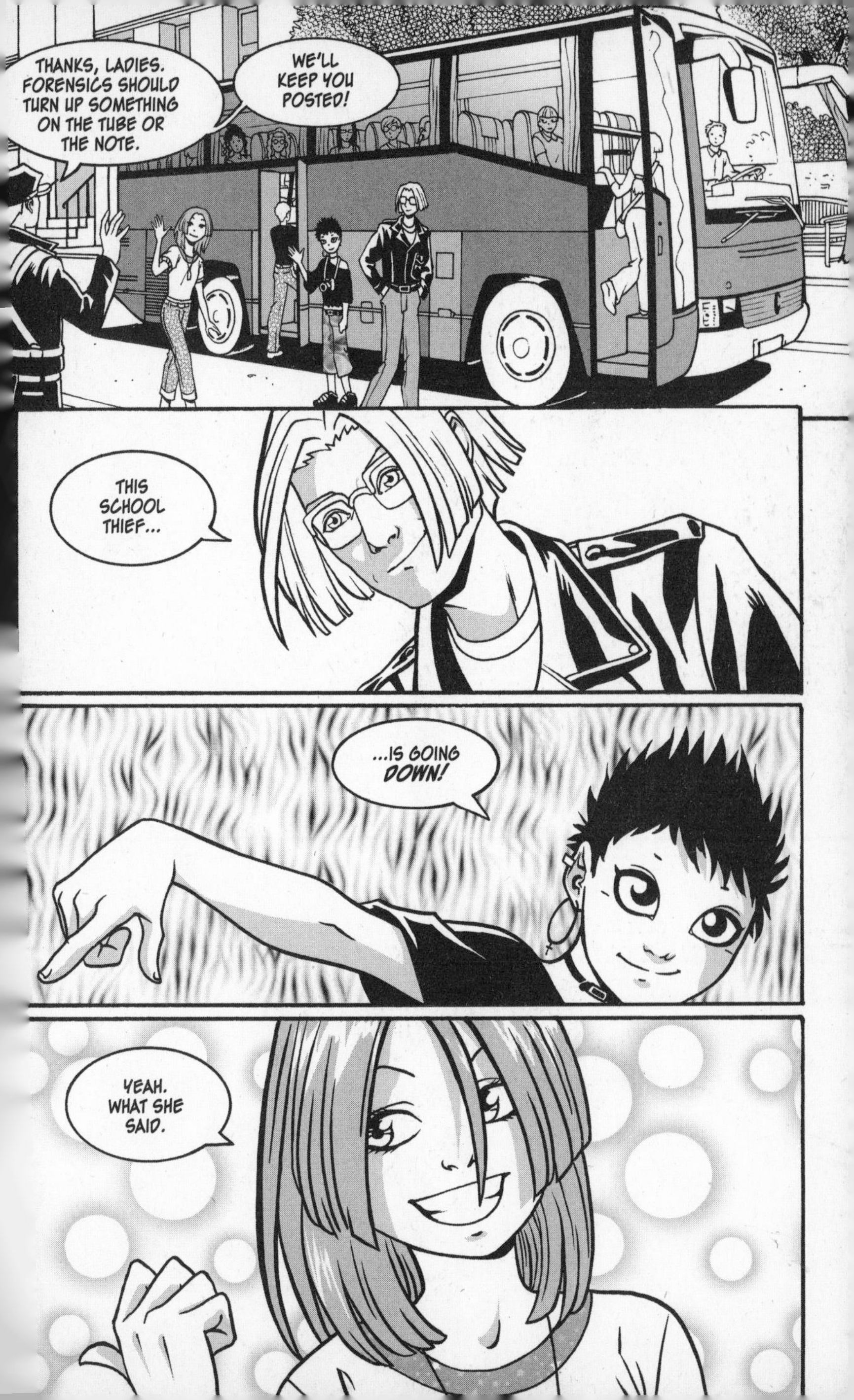
THANKS, LADIES. FORENSICS SHOULD TURN UP SOMETHING ON THE TUBE OR THE NOTE.
WE'LL KEEP YOU POSTED!
THIS SCHOOL THIEF...
...IS GOING DOWN!
YEAH. WHAT SHE SAID.

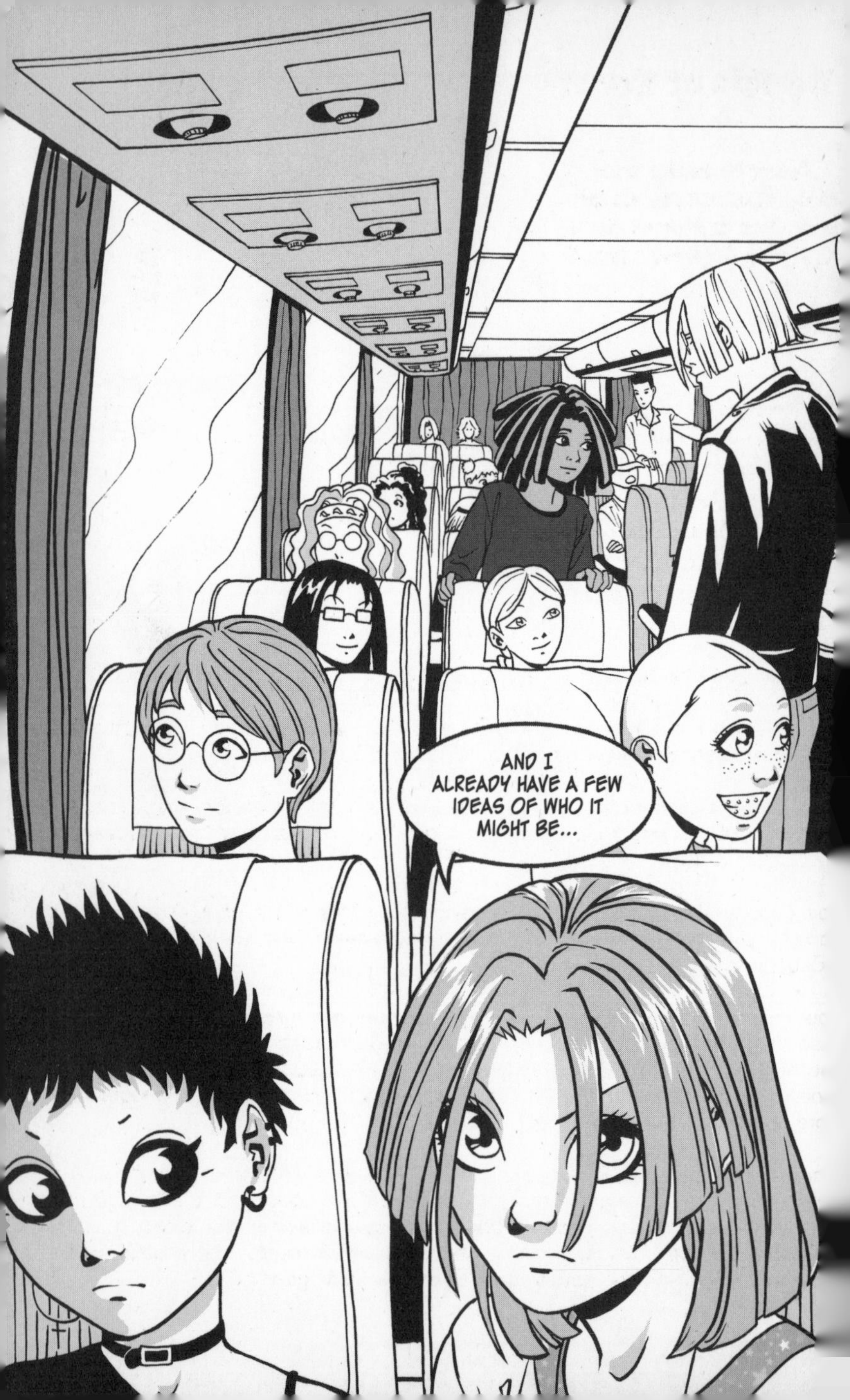
AND I ALREADY HAVE A FEW IDEAS OF WHO IT MIGHT BE...

Try This at Home!

Want to make your own electromagnet the way Kat & Mouse do in Chapter 4? Here's how!

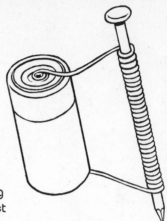

You'll need:

- A big iron nail, about six inches long
- Insulated copper wire, about 12 feet
- A D-cell battery
- A pair of wire strippers
- Some metal paperclips
- A little bit of duct tape
- A parent nearby

You should be able to find most of these things at your local hardware store.

Wrap the wire around the nail. The more (and the tighter) you wrap it, the stronger your electromagnet will be. Leave about a foot of wire at each end.

Strip off about an inch of the plastic insulation from each end of the wire. Tape one end of the bare copper wire to the top of the D-cell battery, and the other end to the bottom of the battery.

Now, empty the paperclips onto a smooth surface. Hold your nail near the paperclips. One end should push the paperclips away, and the other end should pick them up.

How does it work? Every electric current produces a magnetic field. Usually, this is so small that you can't feel it – that's why the paperclips won't move if you just put the wire near them. But by wrapping the wire in loops around the nail, you've concentrated the magnetic field so it becomes more powerful. The more loops, the more power in the magnetic field.

Where does the electric current come from? Well, when you attach one end of the wire to the positive terminal of the battery, and the other end to the negative terminal, the electrons go streaming from the negative side of the battery through the wire to the positive side. That's an electric current! As the iron nail is not naturally magnetic, if you take the current away, you have no magnet.

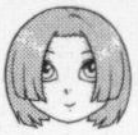

KAT'S HEROES 2: JOCELYN BELL BURNEL

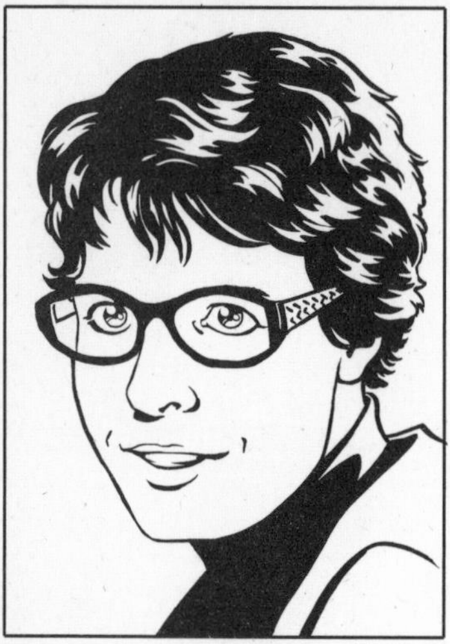

Northern Irish astrophysicist Jocelyn Bell Burnell flunked her hi school entrance exams when she was 11, making it difficult for h to get a coveted spot in Britain's school system. As a result, h parents sent her to a private boarding school in England, which, chance, had a fantastic physics teacher. Jocelyn was inspired, a went on to study physics at college, and eventually got accept into the world-famous Cambridge University to do graduate w in physics.

Jocelyn's PhD work was helping her professor, Anthony Hewi in building a gigantic radio telescope to study quasars: mass irregular sources of electromagnetic energy in space. As Joce was examining miles of printouts, she noticed some radio sign that were too fast and too regular for quasars. After analysis, determined that these signals must come from rapidly spinni super-dense, collapsed stars: pulsars. She and Anthony named first one "LGM-1", for "Little Green Men" (since they had first jo that the signals were aliens radioing them from space.)

Anthony got a Nobel Prize for the pulsar discovery, but Jocelyn famously, and controversially, left out. However, Jocelyn went o teach and hold research positions at many universities, includ Princeton and Oxford. She was also president of the R Astronomical Society.

Not bad for someone who was a "failure" at school!

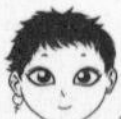

MOUSE'S HEROES 2: AMELIA EARHART

Amelia Earhart first decided she wanted to fly after attending a stunt-flying exhibition when she was 20. worked as a social worker to save up enough money to buy her first airplane: a second-hand two-seater bip that was painted bright yellow. Amelia named it "Canary", and set her first women's record with it: flying height of 14,000 feet.

Other records soon followed. She achieved the first women's transatlantic flight, then the first solo women's transatlantic flight. Amelia soon became a national celebrity, but what really made her happy was proving that men and women were equal in "jobs requiring intelligence, coordination, speed, coolness and willpower."

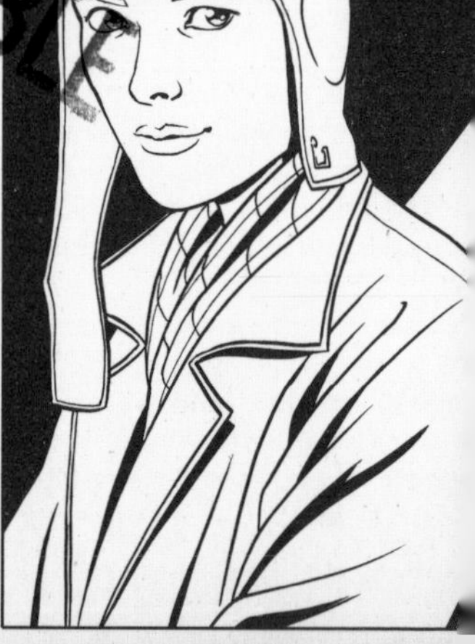

Amelia kept racking up records, including the first solo flight across the Pacific from Hawaii to California. As she approached her 40th birthday in 1937, Amelia planned one last great challenge: to be the first woman to fly around the world, a distance of 29,000 miles. She departed on June 1st, and on June 29th, Amelia landed in New Guinea with only 7,000 miles to go.

Overcast skies made navigation difficult, and Amelia's radio broadcasts were often drowned out by static. At 8:45 a.m. on July 3rd, after a final radio broadcast announced that she was "running north and south", nothing was ever heard from Amelia Earhart again. In a letter she left for her husband in case anything happened on the flight, she wrote, "Please know I am quite aware of the hazards. I want to do it because I want to do it. Women must try to do things as men have tried. When they fail, their failure must be but a challenge to others."